ALGOMA

FIC Coutu

Couture, D.
Algoma.
Cambridge Libraries
MAR 2012

PRICE: $12.17 (3556/qs   )

CAMBRIDGE PUBLIC LIBRARY
QUEENS SQUARE

WITHDRAWN
from the
CAMBRIDGE LIBRARIES

ALGOMA

BY DANI COUTURE

Invisible Publishing
Halifax & Toronto

Text copyright © Dani Couture, 2011

All rights reserved. No part of this publication may
be reproduced or transmitted in any form, by any method,
without the prior written consent of the publisher.

This is a work of fiction. The narrative in no way reflects an opinion, positive or
negative, about the Algoma Central Corporation, its products or employees.

Library and Archives Canada Cataloguing in Publication

Couture, Dani, 1978-
  Algoma / Dani Couture.

Issued also in electronic format.
ISBN 978-1-926743-14-1

  I. Title.

PS8605.O92A64 2011   C813'.6   C2011-905769-7

Cover & Interior design by Megan Fildes

Typeset in Laurentian & Gibson
Special thanks to type designer Rod McDonald

Printed and bound in Canada

Invisible Publishing
Halifax & Toronto
www.invisiblepublishing.com

We acknowledge the support of the Canada Council for the Arts which last
year invested $20.1 million in writing and publishing throughout Canada.

Invisible Publishing recognizes the support of the Province of Nova Scotia
through the Department of Communities, Culture & Heritage. We are
pleased to work in partnership with the Culture Division to develop and
promote our cultural resources for all Nova Scotians.

Canada Council   Conseil des Arts
for the Arts   du Canada

*For Carolyn Black, Stacey May Fowles,
& Natalie Zina Walschots*

"We all have reasons for moving.
I move to keep things whole."

–Mark Strand

"To have joy, one must share it.
Happiness was born a twin."

–Lord Byron

*5:14 p.m. -12°C. Wind NW, strong.
Snow drifting in waves across river.*

New ice groaned beneath the hard plastic soles of Leo's winter boots. The temperature had dropped dramatically two days earlier and sealed the river, however thinly. Small pressure cracks exploded beneath his feet as he leaped to each new stretch of ice. Although the bear was emaciated—fur and skin hanging off its frame like grotesque drapery—it moved quickly.

If Leo kept a quick pace, didn't stay on the same fragile stretch of ice too long, he wouldn't fall through. He was sure the river teemed with a thousand toothy pike looking to exact revenge on his summer limits.

When he'd encountered the bear on the south shore, he'd immediately forgotten about his network of snares in the woods behind him. The thin coil of wire and wire cutters attached to his belt bounced against his hip like a heartbeat as he ran. Although he didn't know how, he thought he could help the animal. And even more than that, he wanted to touch it, feel its rough fur in his hands, the sharp contours of its shoulder blades that pumped up and down like a locomotive. He'd never seen anything like it before, and he was glad his brother was not there, that he'd managed to slip away from him after school. Ferd would have only wanted to find a way to get its hide, teeth, and claws. Leo wanted it all, and alive.

Fifty feet ahead of him, the bear stopped, stumbled,

then quickly regained its footing. The animal did not turn around to acknowledge its stalker, a boy dressed in a dark blue parka with white fur trim around the hood, black tuque, and a thin red scarf at his throat.

Leo took the bear's missteps as a chance to catch up and picked up his pace. The tree line on the north shore of the river had lost definition in the last minutes of daylight and was now only a fence of black wood capped by a darkening blue sky. The bright white ice that stretched from shore to shore held the remaining light of the day and every ounce of the cold.

The bear stopped again.

The crunch of snow and ice beneath Leo's feet was deafening. He stopped, held his breath, worried that at any moment the bear would hear him, smell him, turn on him, and it would be over. Whatever this was. He was so close, he could almost touch it if he reached out his hand.

The bear—diseased, starving, or both—struggled to release one of its front paws from the hole it had created. The animal bared its large yellow teeth at the ice, growled, and tried to gnaw its trapped limb free.

Under the weight of the boy and the animal's struggle, the ice started to cave.

As he fell into the water, Leo reached for the bear, desperate for something to hold onto. Its fur was softer than he could have ever imagined.

From the train bridge, Ferd stood on the slippery railway ties and watched Leo chase the bear across the ice as darkness fell. Frightened for his brother, but more afraid that Leo would find out he'd tailed him after school, he remained quiet. He watched the gap between brother and bear grow smaller and smaller until it was difficult to make out two distinct shapes. They appeared as one mass until they disappeared into the river leaving Ferd to stand on the bridge. Alone, it felt, for the first time.

DECEMBER – JANUARY

*7:04 p.m. -14°C. Light, crisp N wind.
Salt glittering on the sidewalk like costume jewellery.*

Inside the darkened lobby, Lake used both hands to flip on all the light switches at once. Outside, the marquee bulbs flickered and popped on to reveal her six sisters shivering on the cold sidewalk, a mix of steam and cigarette smoke rising from their mouths as they waited for her to open the doors. She took a rare moment to watch them all without being noticed. They were never together like this—alone—without partners, children, or friends. She wished times like these happened more often and not just on the anniversary of their parents' deaths.

"Unlock the goddamned door," Bay yelled. "It's fucking freezing."

Everyone always did what Bay said, mostly because she was the loudest.

"Your mouth," Port said. "Watch it."

Bay flicked her cigarette into the street and sulked. "It's cold is all." It was as close as she could come to an apology.

Cen and Steel rolled their eyes. The eldest of the seven, they had gone from trying to manage their siblings to being resigned to the realities of their personalities. Easier to go with the river than against it. Algoma and Soo huddled together to stay warm, their arms wrapped around one another's waists. They rarely got into the middle of any argument, preferring to let things resolve on their own.

Lake opened the door to the ticket booth and stepped in.

She leaned down to the hole in the glass: "Did you see the marquee? Go look."

The women looked at one another and stepped back.

"3rd Annual Mom and Dad Film Festival," Cen read aloud. Steel looped her arm with Cen's and put her head on her sister's shoulder.

Lake exited the booth and propped open one of the four main doors. "Come on in. Have your tickets ready and grab a glass of wine. Show starts in twenty."

The theatre was the only one in town. Built in the sixties, it was abandoned by the early nineties, until a local man had renovated and reopened it under the name Fox Theatre after a theatre he'd visited in Detroit in his youth. Thomas Deneau had spent his early twenties thinking he'd make films; thirty years later, he had several uncut reels in his basement that he tried not to think about. Buying the theatre seemed like a good compromise. Instead of making films, he'd show them.

After five years of running the theatre by himself with the help of an ever-changing roster of teenagers to run the ticket booth and concession stand and clean up after each showing, he decided he needed a business partner. Someone to help run the place so he could have a few days off every week. Maybe finish one of his films, even though the actors were likely too aged, missing, or dead.

Lake had just graduated from the University of Montreal with a degree in demography and geography, but she didn't want to work in her field because it would take her away from home. She'd applied for the job and was immediately hired. "If someone ever needs a map so they can find their seat, we're set," Thomas joked during her interview.

He treated Lake like a daughter, giving her free rein of the theatre when she wanted it; and for the past three years, she'd hosted an evening of home movies for her sisters on the anniversary of their parents' deaths. The first year, Lake had had to explain to an angry would-be patron that the theatre was closed for a private event. The man had pounded on the ticket booth glass until she'd appeared.

"One ticket for the eight o'clock," he'd said. In the end, she'd let him sit in the back like an extended family member no one could remember.

Lake brushed her bangs out of her eyes and ducked behind the concession stand. She pulled out a half dozen bottles of red and white wine and placed them beside the boxes of Whoppers and bags of Swedish Berries and Sour Patch Kids. "Small, medium, or large?" she asked.

Bay pushed passed her sisters to the front. "Large," she said, pointing to a jumbo soda cup.

"I have to set up the movie," Lake said. "Pour some for everyone else first." She never gave into Bay's demands.

"But..." Bay started. Undeterred, she emptied the better part of one of the bottles of red into a cup. She took a sip and nodded. "All right, who's next? We're almost out of red though."

When Lake turned to go to the projector room, she felt a hesitant tap on her shoulder.

"Can I put it on this year?"

It was Algoma, the youngest of all of them. Someone who was closer to being a family mascot than a sister. She also carried the notable distinction of being the only non-twin of her siblings. "My only mistake," Ann often said when referring to her youngest. She'd said she was joking, but everyone knew otherwise, especially Algoma. Like the Dionne Quints in Ontario, Ann had hoped to achieve reproductive fame, but it never came. She blamed it on two factors: that one set of siblings was not identical and that Algoma had come out alone. "Wanted the womb all for yourself, didn't you," she'd said when her newborn daughter was brought to her for the first time.

Few could refuse Algoma anything. Last year, Lake had showed her how the projector worked.

"Here you go," Lake said, handing over the disc. "The office is unlocked. You know the rest."

Algoma smiled and ran into the office like she was a teenager and not the mother and wife she was.

The projector room was only accessible from the office. Lake's and Thomas's desks were pushed up against one another in the centre of the room with two sticky notes on either side of the border between them. One read "Haiti" and the other "Dominican Republic." Apparently Lake hadn't completely left her studies behind. Behind Lake's desk was the steep metal staircase that led to the projector room.

Upstairs, a narrow doorway opened up into a long room with a high ceiling that held three large silver projectors—two for 35-inch film and one for 16-inch. And in the corner, what Algoma was looking for, the DVD player. She turned on the machine and placed the disc on the tray.

Through the window, she watched her sisters mingle and talk below. They stood on the casino-style carpeting behind the last row of theatre seats, not ready to sit down yet. Lake circled around, refilling glasses with wine. Algoma pressed her forehead onto the glass. The sight of them should have made her happy: it didn't. Despite the identical parentage, she always felt foreign, extraneous in their presence. Unnecessary.

Her entire life, she'd been looking for someone with the same dull green eyes, blonde hair, and pale skin. She was the extra card in a game of memory.

Growing up, she'd always felt like she was missing something. The required companion her mother had created in utero for every girl born into the Belanger family. Every girl except her. Day after day her sisters paired off after breakfast, not separating until bedtime, and even then they stole into one another's beds. Twin-speak was the official language of the house, a handful of dialects lilting, giggling, and whispering into the night.

As years passed, Algoma gave up a number of comforts: the tooth fairy, Santa Claus, the Easter Bunny, and, finally, the most difficult, her twin. She vowed to make do with only herself, her own two hands, two feet, two eyes. Her life, she believed, was inferior to those of her sisters, who seemed like many-armed gods radiating light and ability.

She'd found it ironic, almost cruel, when she'd given birth to twin boys: Ferdinand and Leopold. She felt betrayed at a cellular level. When she'd first found out she was pregnant, she'd confessed to Gaetan that she was looking forward to raising someone like her. An only. After Leo's death, she'd blamed those early thoughts for his loss, as if the world had conspired to give her exactly what she'd asked for.

Lake looked up at the projector room. Everything okay? she mouthed.

Algoma nodded quickly and stepped back from the window. She flipped all the necessary switches for lights and sound and hit play. For the past several years, Lake had worked with their father's collection of home movies, editing a new family movie each year. The movies always followed a theme, which Lake kept secret until the night of the viewing. For once, Algoma had a head start on her sisters. Written on the disc in permanent marker was one word: "Water."

The lights dimmed and the aging red curtains yawned open. The sisters moved to take their seats. Algoma watched as the six women turned into three packs of pairs. Her father, Richard, had joked that lightning had struck Ann's womb three times and they'd won the jackpot—six girls in half the time. He'd held efficiency above most things, and the thought that he'd had something to do with it had only made him prouder.

Algoma went down into the theatre. On the screen, she saw her father teaching a lanky teenage Cen how to fish in the Charles River. The scene cut away to three-month-old Soo being bathed in the kitchen sink in the old house. Teenage Lake and Port running around in the rain in the backyard, mud streaked across their faces, her parents sitting under the cover of the back porch.

She took a seat in the back row, the same she took every year, able to see everything and everyone all at once, no one able to see her.

7:42 a.m. -10°C. Wind NW, calm.
Top of cedar hedge covered in crown of new snow.

Whatever Algoma brought into the house began its long journey at the side door, a slow migration that would sometimes take months before the item would arrive at its final destination.

A shower curtain she'd purchased last February, still in its original plastic packaging, had spent weeks on the small wooden table by the front door until it had blended in with the keys and half-empty packs of gum. By April, the curtain had made it across the kitchen and sat beside the phone until June.

By the time the curtain had made it into the bathroom in October—packaging covered in ink doodles, to-do lists, and phone numbers—the old curtain was in terrible condition, discoloured at the edges as if ravaged by tropical disease.

In November, the curtain had rested on the edge of the tub for weeks, sometimes falling in when someone showered, only to be picked up and placed back on the ledge until one morning the new curtain, free of water stain and hard, curled edges, had been put up.

Algoma pulled the slick green curtain back without a thought of regret or longing for the old curtain that had served her family for the past year and was now nailed to the unfinished shower wall in the basement washroom to stop a leak. Naked, she stepped into the tub and frowned at the dark footprints she could never scrub clean. The enamel no longer thick enough to repel the outside world. The footprints all faced the same way—toward the drain. It looked like a trail that ended at the bullseye of metal that was meant to keep things from slipping away.

She leaned forward to turn on the water taps and mouthed a small prayer that her husband and son would remain asleep and stay away from the other faucets in the house for at least ten minutes. Long enough for her to rinse the conditioner from her hair. The shower head choked to life and hot water rained down on her shoulders, her aching muscles. She tilted her head back and wet her hair, running her fingers through tangle and curl.

As she massaged shampoo into her scalp, Algoma felt the waterline rise over the tops of her feet. The drain was plugged. She crouched down to take a look. Slippery clouds of lather slid down her back and landed in the tub. All she could see was water and the rust-pocked silver rim. She pushed a strand of sopping hair away from her eyes and stuck her long thin fingers into the drain. Her stomach tightened with disgust as she fingered the rough sides— gummy slivers of soap and knotted hair. She dug deeper, her fingers now knuckle-deep, until she felt something unfamiliar. Something with a soft edge. With two fingers, she fished the thin fold up toward the mouth of the drain. A sodden wad of paper.

She turned her back to the shower spray and held up the note. Blue ink bled through the lined paper, but she could not make out the words. She tried to open it, but the note began to come apart in her hands. She pieced it back together as best she could and stuck her hand out of the shower, placing the note on the edge of the sink. Later, she thought, when it was dry. She was a nervous woman by nature; having to wait for what she thought could only be bad news just made it worse.

She thought about all the things it could be and none made sense. But then, not much did anymore.

Warm and scrubbed clean, Algoma turned off the cold water first and then the hot. As the last of the water slipped down the drain, she pulled the shower curtain back and leaned forward to grab a thin white towel from the rack. Steam rolled out of the shower in thick waves. She worried the paint would start to bubble and peel soon. She worried the floor was wet and rotting beneath her and would send the tub crashing down into the basement one day. She worried there was too much snow piled on the roof. She worried about what she'd find when she peeled open the folds of the note.

While standing in the tub, as she did every morning, Algoma dried her forearms first, then her legs, leaving her stomach, chest, and back for last. After stretching around awkwardly to sop up the last drops from her shoulders, her eyes closed, she brought the towel to her face. When she pulled the towel away, her face tingling from her rough drying, she saw the note on the edge of the sink. She wondered how it had gotten into the tub. Why not just throw it away?

She spread the towel across the floor to avoid standing on the cold tiles and stepped onto it. She stood in front of the bathroom mirror and leaned in for her morning inspection, the edge of the note touching her bare hipbone.

Only a week ago, she had discovered a new freckle beneath her left eye. At first she'd tried to wipe the mark off, but soon realized it was skin deep. Today, at least, she was a carbon copy of the woman she had looked at in the mirror yesterday. Her inspection went as wide and low as the bathroom mirror allowed: shoulder to shoulder, head to navel. Her blonde hair was slicked back against her scalp and curled loosely at her shoulders, each end like a sharp, wet hook. Her eyes, the colour of warm lake water, stared back. The same tired gaze as yesterday, the day before, the year before. Her shoulders sagged more than she liked, but she still enjoyed her collarbone—sharp, ready to poke through her flesh. The bone looked like a weapon stashed beneath her skin, ready in case of emergency. Even her breasts seemed efficient, small, and compact, never in the way. She put a hand on her belly, the only place where her body defied its natural leanness. A modest pouch to remember her only pregnancy by.

Algoma grabbed another towel from the rack and wrapped it around her body. She picked up the note and walked into the kitchen, placing it next to the potted spider plant on the window sill. The coffee pot sputtered with the morning brew, the automatic timer having gone off while she was in the shower. She rinsed out her mug from yesterday—her favourite—and filled it with coffee. Arms tight at her sides to keep her towel from falling, Algoma carried her mug into the bathroom where she placed it precariously on the edge of the sink. She was sure that the mug would fall one day, shatter on the tiles, and cut her legs and feet, but still, every day, she completed this careful balancing act.

The note sat on the kitchen window sill all morning while she cleaned the house. She did not mention it to Gaetan when he kissed her goodbye in the afternoon. He and Ferd were leaving to visit his cousin's family. Algoma had asked to stay behind. "I just need a night to catch up," she'd lied.

During the day, the dry heat from the wood stove in

the basement rose up through the house, baking the note like a pulpy soufflé until Algoma picked it up and put it into her skirt pocket. She'd tried to put the note out of her mind all day, but her thoughts kept drifting back to the carefully folded message. Whose was it? She cleaned until there was nothing left to be scrubbed or bleached and the sun had gone down.

Early evening. Algoma walked about the main floor of the house. She switched on light after light until the house was lit with a warm yellow glow. She stood in front of a bare-bulbed lamp in the living room, the lamp shade having been destroyed the week before during one of Gaetan and Ferd's wrestling matches, and warmed her hands. They hadn't returned home from their day out. She forgave Gaetan's keeping Ferd out late when it was at Michel's house. Michel was one of the only family members Gaetan remained in contact with, and he needed family. They were likely on their tenth game of cards—the adults and children all playing at the same table for the same pot of quarters. By the end of the night, the adults' ability to strategize would be blunted by bottles of red wine and beer and the children's pockets would be heavy with silver. The adults would mask their bruised egos with parental pride and overly zealous back-slapping.

Crouched down in front of the large wood hutch in the living room, Algoma pulled a bottle of wine out from the bottom cupboard. An inexpensive yet functional Shiraz she'd received as a birthday gift the month before. She was surprised to see that the bottle had lasted that long in her house. Gaetan must be on a white kick, she thought. Or maybe he was giving her the chance to enjoy her present in her own time. She allowed herself the opportunity to be surprised.

The weight of the bottle felt good in her hands. Solid and present. She pulled the cork and poured herself a generous glass. Guiltily, she sat down in her husband's favourite chair—a well worn oatmeal-coloured recliner that no longer reclined—and propped her feet up onto the coffee table, something she would not let anyone else do. She took a long drink of her wine and pulled the shower note from her pocket. She carefully unfolded the paper, hoping the water hadn't ruined the message. The ink was blurred and barely readable. It looked like it had been written in marker.

Leo...

Saved... for...

She carefully folded the note back the way she had found it and tucked it back into her pocket. She swirled the wine around in her glass, a small red tornado. The television was on, but muted. The actors slid back and forth across the screen, fluid and seamless. Silent. She poured herself another glass. No, the note wasn't good at all.

"Algoma. Algoma," Gaetan whispered, his hands on her shoulders, "go to bed." His breath was hot on her cheek.

Algoma woke with a start and knocked over a stack of magazines on the coffee table. "What?" she asked. She was agitated, still half asleep. "What's going on? Is something wrong?"

"No. You just need to go to bed, Allie." Gaetan replied. His eyes were bloodshot. His shirt half unbuttoned.

Algoma bent down to pick up the magazines. When Gaetan tried to help, she waved him away. "Go. I've got it. Where's Ferd?"

"I don't know why you read these things anyway," he said as he picked up one of the magazines. He flipped through the pages. "You could teach them a thing or two. Look at this here." He tapped at a recipe for a meat pie. "You make something like this and yours is probably better. Hell, I know it's better."

Algoma turned away and busied herself folding a throw blanket. Gaetan's breath smelled like beer and his hair of the American cigarettes his cousin bought. She would have to make space in the freezer for the carton she knew was sitting in the backseat of the car. Gaetan's attempts to hide his bad habits were lazy at best.

The basement stairs creaked. Ferd. Algoma turned around but he was already at the bottom.

"Goodnight," she called out.

"G'night," he replied flatly. He shut the door behind him. A soft click.

Ferd had moved into the basement last summer. Algoma had watched their then eleven-year-old son haul his blankets and pillow down to the pull-out couch downstairs. He lived below them like a rabbit under the porch. If she stood still, she could hear him moving around below, getting ready for bed, brushing his teeth in the laundry basin. She was grateful the house was old, that the stairs creaked, otherwise she might never hear him coming and going. The stairs that led down to the basement were right beside the side door. Three steps up to the kitchen, or ten down to the basement. Always a choice, or an easy escape. At least he wasn't having nightmares anymore.

"A nightcap before my nightcap." Gaetan ran a hand through his black hair, pushing it out of his face. He opened the fridge and pulled out a bottle of beer. "Can I interest you in one, missus? Like old times?" He flicked the beer cap into the sink.

"You can't be driving like that. Not with Ferd in the car. I'd never forgive you."

"The kid won ten bucks tonight playing thirty-one," he said proudly. "I gave him a few tips on the way over. He's good, like me."

Algoma sat on the couch and focused on the television, a late-night talk show. Gaetan joined her, tucking his beer between his legs. They rarely watched any show with the sound on since Algoma found the noise irritating. The actress who was being interviewed flashed her bright white canines, arched a perfectly shaped black brow, and flirtatiously placed her hand on the talk show host's forearm. The host beamed at the camera and straightened his tie, shook his head, and smiled. He said something and pointed to someone in the audience outside the camera frame. The actress laughed and her face faded to commercial.

"I'm going to go say goodnight to the kid," Gaetan said. He stood up and stretched.

Algoma didn't take her eyes off the television. "He's probably already asleep. Let him be."

Gaetan ignored her and walked toward the basement stairs.

Algoma turned and frowned at his back. "Where are you going? I told you he's probably sleeping."

Gaetan looked back over his shoulder at his wife. In the dim light of the living room, she looked softer. Younger. Like the person she'd been before the accident. Now, she looked older than her twenty-nine years. Harder. "I'm going to throw a log on the fire. So he'll be warm."

"Oh." Algoma sucked her teeth and turned back to her show.

He knew she would never argue with something that

saved them money since they needed it so badly, and using the wood stove saved them a few dollars on their heating bill each month.

Gaetan thumped down the stairs and opened the door. The basement was dark except for the dancing orange light in front of the wood stove. He could make out Ferd's shape on the pull-out couch in the middle of the room.

"You sleeping, buddy?" he whispered loudly, his voice lilting at the end. Hopeful.

No response.

Gaetan walked to the wood stove, bent down, and opened the door, a gust of heat burning his face. He stumbled back and pawed at his eyes, thinking that last beer hadn't been such a good idea. Ferd must have tossed a log on before he'd gone to bed. Once Gaetan realized he was fine, that his eyelashes were intact, he threw another log onto the fire to feel useful. The birch bark crackled and popped as he shut the heavy glass-and-iron door. He looked at the wood bin: close to empty. He'd pick up more wood on the weekend.

The basement was dark, but not so dark that he couldn't make out the things closest to him. Gaetan stood still and allowed his eyes to further adjust to the semi-darkness, his head almost touching the low ceiling. The edges of the furniture on the far side of the room slowly revealed themselves to him. He'd finished the basement several years ago—a summer project—all wood panelling, sturdy brown carpet, and a new wood stove.

Gaetan walked over to the pull-out couch and sat on the edge, the thin mattress bowing beneath him. He placed a hand on his son's sleeping body. Warm. Ferd's face was barely visible under his covers, only part of his forehead and a closed eye peeking out from beneath the comforter. If

Gaetan allowed his eyes to go out of focus, he could almost pretend that Ferd was Leo. He imagined that Ferd was upstairs getting a snack, or a glass of water. That his wife was getting ready for bed and waiting for him, not sleeping in the boys' empty room another night. She only came to him on good nights, and he couldn't remember when the last one had been.

He blinked. Everything clear again. Sharp.

He stood up. Tomorrow he'd get a piece of plywood to put under Ferd's mattress to make it firmer, more stable. Gaetan bent down and kissed the top of Ferd's head and went back upstairs, closing the door softly behind him.

Once he was sure the door was shut and his father was upstairs, Ferd sat up in bed and threw off his blanket. The basement was blazing hot. He peeled off his pyjama shirt, wiped his sweaty chest clean with it, and tossed it on the floor. Sure that his breathing had given him away, Ferd wondered if his father had caught on that he hadn't been sleeping. How did people breathe when they slept? He'd kept his eyes tightly shut and his breathing so deep and slow it felt like he was suffocating. At least his father hadn't stayed long.

Ferd was tired of enduring his parents' sad looks. The longing in their faces that asked him to multiply. Duplicate. Every time his mother or his father didn't say his name for a few hours, he knew what they were doing, what they were pretending. He wished they believed him. They didn't need a substitute.

Leo was coming back.

When people spoke about missing someone, they often said they felt hollow. Ferd was the opposite: he felt full. And this is how he knew his brother was still alive. He could feel Leo's presence as much as he ever could, as if he'd arrive at any moment. All he had to do was wait. If he grieved, it was because he missed his brother's company. Despite the almost constant fighting between the two in the months prior to his disappearance—the push-pull of Leo's mostly failed attempts to do things separately from his twin—there was no one Ferd needed more. If Leo was gone, Ferd had no mirror. He did not exist.

5:38 a.m. -21°C. No wind.
Furnace choking out the occasional breath of
warm air, wood stove gone cold.

Awake, but unwilling to commit to another day just yet, Algoma remained in bed. Ferd's old bed. Her bare feet dangled off the end of the short mattress. Even if Ferd hadn't already moved into the basement, he would have needed a new bed soon. He was getting taller every day, outgrowing most of his clothes. Even the planes of his face were different now. The changes were subtle, like tectonic plates shifting beneath his skin, the transition so gradual she had to remember to notice it.

Algoma turned onto her side and looked at the digital clock. The glowing green numbers read 5:42 a.m. She turned back over, managing to avoid looking at Leo's empty bed on the other side of the room, stripped of sheets. Empty. She pulled her feet back under the covers and listened to the sound of her neighbour's car radio blare as he turned on the ignition, the crunch of snow under his tires as he backed out of the driveway. In the next room, she could hear Gaetan tossing and turning, the rustling of his sheets, his grunts. He'd never been a good sleeper, but had become worse lately and nothing seemed to help.

She closed her eyes, but could not fall back to sleep. Night-spell broken, she threw back the blankets and put her feet on the cold floor. Her eyes adjusted to the low light of the room. The light from the streetlight outside illuminated the crack in the window pane she'd been meaning to fix once there was extra money. There was a film of dirt on the glass and the curtains needed to be replaced from where Leo had accidentally torn the checkered fabric. Algoma's chest heaved. She cried into her hands until there was nothing left.

"Did you remember the tinfoil?" Ferd asked.
Algoma nodded. "Like I always do."
"Like you always do now."
Algoma grabbed Ferd's lunch from the fridge and put it on the counter: one chicken sandwich with a thin spread of mustard (only on the top slice) on brown bread, a cup of coleslaw, one Macintosh apple with the sticker already peeled off, six Saltines, and six pieces of marble cheese coated in a crust of salt and pepper. Everything, except for the apple and the coleslaw, was wrapped in tinfoil.

After the first day of school last year, Ferd had presented her with the sandwich she'd made for him earlier that morning. It was soggy, the edges mashed into a yeasty pulp, watery mustard oozed from the edges.

"Tinfoil won't make it sweat," he said, tossing the sandwich into the garbage pail and knocking over the plastic bin.

Now his lunch crinkled when he grabbed it. Algoma worried about lightning.

"Please remember to bring your Tupperware home today." She pictured a half dozen dirty plastic containers stacked under Ferd's desk, the leftover food rotting. "Promise?"

Ferd nodded, dodged her kiss, and ran out the door.

Algoma went downstairs to get a load of laundry from the dryer. When she returned upstairs, arms full of warm bedsheets, she saw Ferd's lunch bag sitting on the counter.

"Shit."

She dropped the bedsheets onto the kitchen table, where they soaked up the spilled orange juice from breakfast, and ran to the closet for her coat. Wearing a parka and her blue flannel pyjama pants, her scratchy wool hat still in her hand, Algoma ran outside to see if she could catch up. She got as far as the end of the driveway before she realized she'd forgotten his lunch inside. She stomped her foot and ran back into the house. The day was not off to a good start.

Canvas lunch bag firmly tucked under her arm, Algoma walked down the street. She would have to walk all the way to the school to give Ferd his lunch, making her late for work. Josie was opening. It wouldn't matter too much. She relaxed and slowed her pace. She could take her time.

The day was bright and sharp, the air so cold it was like a void stealing her breath. A sucker punch. If Algoma was going to walk outside in freezing temperatures, she preferred to walk in the early evening when she could look into her neighbours' windows. The blue glow of the televisions, a dining-room light left on, dishes still on the table. Each window a different story. During the day, the windows were black. Uniformly uneventful. At least there was no one to see her in her pyjamas, night-knotted hair sticking out from beneath her hat.

The end of the street opened up into a football field, half of which was converted into two ice rinks during winter—one for children, and the other, the one with the white boards, for hockey. On weekends and holidays, the unwritten rule was that informal hockey games started at 1:00 p.m. Around 2:00 p.m., the less-skilled players were kicked off to the kids' rink. Everyone wore different jerseys, so onlookers had trouble identifying the teams, even if the players never did.

Ferd's school lay past the rinks and across the road. A one-storey red brick building, the windows adorned with symmetrical paper cut-outs of white and blue snowflakes and multicoloured paper chains. And behind it, forest. Everything in town was book-ended by woods.

The wind picked up and bit at the part of Algoma's throat that was exposed. With one hand she held the top of her jacket shut, with the other, Ferd's lunch.

The school bell rang. From across the snow-covered field, Algoma watched the last students round the corner of the building and disappear inside. She could almost hear the swishing of their snow pants as they ran. She continued along the well-trampled path the kids had created from their daily trips to school and back. The path stretched diagonally across the field, wove in between the two open-sided rinks, until it ended at the crosswalk.

As Algoma neared the rinks, she saw they were wet and glossy. A new coat of water hardening over old layers. Another gust of bitterly cold wind blasted her face. Head down, eyes up, she admired the perfect rinks, the old skate marks made smooth with water and constant care. There was a craft to maintaining ice. To enjoy it, to be on it, was to ruin it. It was only ever this perfect in the morning. Two sightless scleras of ice.

Algoma approached the hockey rink where the boys and Gaetan used to play. The white boards were topped with a chain-link fence that kept pucks from hitting passers-by. She looked in, half expecting to see Ferd and Leo skating in circles around the rink, shooting pucks into the boards.

While there was no one on the ice, there was something on it. A small, white square marred the surface. Before she even realized what she was doing, Algoma walked along the outside of the boards until she reached the opening. She carefully stepped onto the rink. Smaller boot prints had congealed into the ice. Ridges that would trip up players later on. In the middle of the rink, she squatted down, careful not to slip, and peeled the glazed paper from the ice. A piece of dry skin on an otherwise perfect face. She took off her mitts and unfolded the half wet, half frozen paper.

Dear Leo...

A month of lunches came and went. At every turn, Algoma found notes in the house, anywhere there was or had been water. Soon, the notes exceeded the stitched limits of her pockets, and nearly her sanity. With every note she retrieved, the word count increased. Soon, she could not find a single piece of paper on which to write her grocery list, nor could she take a shower without leaving with a wad of wet paper moulded into her palm. A one-sided conversation drying on the window sill.

Desperate to keep them from Gaetan, she had taken to storing the blurry notes in a shoebox behind a bucket of old rags under the kitchen sink. Each note looked similar to the last, different only in the way the water had blurred the ink. A homemade Rorschach test. She wrote down every word she could make out in a small journal she also kept in the shoebox. Within the first two weeks, she'd collected two hundred words, all strung together like a strand of mini-lights constantly blinking off and on in her mind, exhausting her.

Gaetan moved through the motions of his job and home life with little deviation from one day to the next. A bartender, he typically worked nights and slept through most of the day, seeing little of his family. He woke up to eat his breakfast in the early afternoon when the house was empty and came home from work when everyone was asleep. The tide of beer in the fridge rose and fell with the weeks.

"I don't have a problem," he said when Algoma had asked him if he thought he drank too much. "It's part of my job," he said. "It's research. Technically, a write-off."

The empties were piled high in the shed, boozy chimes that crashed together whenever Ferd tried to pull his bike out from the teetering stacks.

If Algoma pieced together her family member's lives—her son's early mornings, her husband's late nights, and her middling days—it was endless, breathless. Each time of the day belonged to someone in the house, one person owning it as they would a room, arranging it to suit them and leaving everyone else to adjust.

Algoma owned the day, all overhead sun and shadowless.

*7:17 p.m. -17°C. Wind from everywhere, blustery.
Electric kettle at full boil.*

Gaetan blew into the house after an unusually scheduled day shift at Club Rebar, a small bar a bottle's throw away from the town's pulp mill. He was in a good mood and sober, two things that rarely coincided.

"I brought home steaks!" he said. His dark brown eyes sparkled with pride.

Algoma poured water for her tea and tried to not think about what kind of groceries she could have bought with the money he'd spent on steaks. It was payday and he was king for a day.

As soon as she set the kettle down, Gaetan grabbed her by her waist and spun her around in the air, narrowly missing hitting her head on the doily-covered swing lamp.

While mid-air, she decided to tell him about the notes. He was her husband; he should know. When he set her down, she turned to him. "I have something to tell you."

"I was thinking we could fry them up with butter like my mom used to do," Gaetan said. He tossed the package of steaks onto the counter. "Do we still have that cast iron pan? The big one?"

"Uh, sure," Algoma said. "I mean, yes." She wasn't sure if he'd heard her or if he was trying to avoid any conversation that might bring down his mood. She looked at her husband. For the first time in a year, she felt comforted by his presence. Maybe she would wait until after dinner to tell him about the notes, about the crack opening around their remaining son. A few hours wouldn't matter.

Algoma set the table for two while Gaetan pan-fried the T-bones with a heaping mix of onions and mushrooms. Ferd was watching a movie with Lake at the Fox, a monthly ritual his aunt had instituted after Leo's accident. After the movie, they always went back to her house, ate plain cheese pizza, and fell asleep in front of the television like teenagers.

"You smell like the bar," Algoma said.

"You're right. Watch this," Gaetan said, turning down the stove. "I'll take a shower. I'll be quick. Five minutes."

A half hour later, they sat down to a meal of steaks, frozen French fries, canned peas, and sautéed onions and mushrooms. Algoma looked expectantly at Gaetan who was shoveling forkfuls of over-salted peas into his mouth. He was smiling. The words did not come to her; they remained lodged in her throat like a dry piece of bread.

As soon as she was done eating what she could force down, she scraped the rest of her food onto Gaetan's plate and stood up to put her dishes in the sink. She couldn't tell him. It was only fair to Ferd that he had one parent who was keeping it together, even if only by a little. She resolved to keep each word she'd fished out of tub and drain to herself. The house was speaking to her one sopping, stuttering word at a time.

Gaetan ate quickly and in silence.

"Good?" she asked.

He nodded furiously, his fork and knife hacking apart the meat, drops of blood and grease spilling onto the table.

"Good," she said, and sat down at the table.

As he ate, she drifted into worry about Ferd. Last winter, he'd been the only one to see Leo slip through the ice. The emergency workers who'd dredged the river never found Leo's body, nor had the fishermen who lined the shore the following spring. Even the bear Ferd had reported seeing never turned up by hook or oar. Most people in town believed he'd made the animal up as a coping mechanism. An excuse. Something to take the blame away from his brother. While his parents openly grieved the loss, it was obvious Ferd did not believe his brother was gone.

Lost, said one of the notes. Come back when you're ready, read another.

"You make good dinner," Gaetan said to Algoma.

"You bought it," she replied.

They sat together in a moment of comfortable silence.

Gaetan popped the last piece of meat into his mouth and smiled. "Let's watch a movie after this, okay?"

Algoma nodded and stood up. As she reached over to pick up his dishes, Gaetan, feeling the water from Ferd's latest note bleed through the back pocket of his jeans, inched his chair away from her. It was the third note he'd found in the shower drain that month. He was surprised the pipes in the house still worked at this point.

"Everything will be fine," he said, as she walked away.

Algoma looked over her shoulder. "What did you say?"

"Nothing," he said. He couldn't say it twice because he didn't believe it.

Ferd woke up from a dead sleep, jarred awake from a terrible dream. Feeling the hard ground beneath him, he panicked. He couldn't remember where he was. As his eyes adjusted to the light, he remembered he was at his Aunt Lake's.

In the past year, he'd felt adrift on a series of different beds in different houses, mostly those of his aunts who felt it their duty to care for him, feed him, have him sleep in their spare beds, on couches, and at Lake's, mostly on the floor. He'd become a talisman. If they held him close, did well by him, nothing would happen to their loved ones.

He stood up and went into the bathroom to pee. After washing his hands and drinking from the tap, he eyed the bathtub. The clean, white enamel and round edges looked inviting. He climbed into the tub, curled up, and fell back asleep. With his head next to the drain, it was the closest he'd felt to Leo in months.

4:00 p.m. 22°C. Wind S, light.
Birds bathing in the Coca-Cola-spiked birdbath.

From the backyard where they were lying in wait behind the shed, Ferd and Leo could hear their mother cry out from the guest room and the sound of her pumps hitting the pale green linoleum. The side door opened.

"The chocolates! You ate all of the chocolates and wrapped the box back up again!" Algoma said, her voice high and shrill. While the backyard appeared empty, she knew her boys were hiding there. She shook the empty box in the air. "I can't believe you two! What am I going to do now? They were special."

The boys tried to muffle their laughter, hands over their mouths.

Algoma was going out with an old friend to celebrate her birthday. She'd bought the chocolates as a gift, an annual tradition that had started before the boys were even born. They would never understand, and there was no time or money to replace the gift. The Beaudoins lived pay cheque to pay cheque with Gaetan's drinking soaking up any extra they had each month, and then some.

"Ferdinand!" Algoma stamped her foot in frustration, tight fists at her sides. The point of her heel slid neatly into the sprinkler-softened lawn.

"Leopold!" She struggled to release her pump from the ground and almost fell over.

The boys peeked around the corner of the shed just in

time to see their mother turn around and storm back into the house. The door slammed behind her, the brass Virgin Mary rattling against the wood.

Ferd turned to Leo. "Guess she hasn't seen the fridge yet."

A howl erupted from the house.

Leo put his face in his hands. "Maybe we shouldn't have done that," he said through his fingers.

Like he'd seen his father do with friends, Ferd threw his arm around his brother's shoulders. "It was fun, right? And you're full? Don't worry, everything will be okay. I promise."

Leo pulled his hands away from his face and nodded. He wanted to believe his brother, but didn't. He'd gone along with it because he wanted to see if it was easier to just do whatever Ferd wanted. Yet he had known he would regret it and already did.

Waiting for their father to return home from work, Ferd and Leo sat at the kitchen table, their legs too short to hit the floor. Down the hall, Algoma sat on the closed lid of the toilet seat in the washroom and sobbed into her hands. A narrow woman, she was folded over herself like a switchblade, her power, her edge, for the moment at least, weakened. She'd cancelled dinner with Audrey by feigning sudden illness—something "food related"—and told Soo she wouldn't need a sitter. Algoma had telephoned Gaetan at the Club and had told him what had happened. He'd left right away citing a family emergency.

In the kitchen, the fridge door was open to reveal the thin ribs of two wire shelves and the empty plastic belly of the crisper. The boys had eaten everything to be had. All of it eaten in the short amount of time between the beginning of Gaetan's shift and the end of Algoma's. A small window of time where the boys were trusted to not burn down the house. Instead, they'd eaten it.

What had been consumed: two pounds of potatoes, a loaf of brown bread, a jar of Cheez Whiz, a package of cretons, three apples, a pot of leftover cabbage soup, one roasted chicken, two chunks of venison sausage, a bag of carrots, a brick of marble cheese, a tin of cookies, and a bowl of strawberries. The only evidence of the missing food was the boys' uncomfortably distended bellies.

The potatoes had been sliced into silver dollars and fried, batch after batch, until the saltshaker had run dry. The chicken had been eaten down to the gummy bones and then the boys, like animals, had cracked the bones open for what marrow they could find. At least they had been considerate enough to set the wishbone out to dry on the counter as a gift to their mother. Stringy bits of meat hardening as the hours passed.

When Gaetan arrived home, Leo grinned in a feeble attempt to disarm him.

"Hi Dad," he said. His eyebrows were raised high and his eyes wide as he tried to gauge the severity of their offense.

Ferd elbowed him in the ribs. "Shut up."

Gaetan stood silently at the door for what seemed, to the boys, like hours. He stared at them until they began to shift uncomfortably in their seats. Leo nervously picked at a small gouge in the table. A curl of Gaetan's shiny black hair slipped free of its heavily gelled design and fell onto his forehead. The loose curl defied the sternness of his deep-set brown eyes. Gaetan knew his face from every angle, that all he wanted to say could be said with a look, and he was blessed with the sharp features to deliver it.

In his arms, Gaetan held offerings from the bar to help get his family through the rest of the week, until his next cheque: two jars of pickled onions, a tin of peanuts, a large bag of barbecue chips, a package of beef jerky, and a jar of green olives. He dumped the goods onto the table, the tin of peanuts almost rolling away.

"I'll give you some money for eggs," he said to Algoma. She could do a lot with eggs.

Algoma was now standing in the kitchen. She wiped the black smudges of mascara from beneath her eyes and wiped her hands on her sleeves.

"They ate everything," she said. She stared blankly at the wallpaper's beige and green floral print, traced the smooth flat petals with her finger. The wallpaper that had been there when she and Gaetan had moved in, before the boys were born. She tried to remember a time before them, the empty space they now occupied.

Gaetan looked at his wife and then turned to his sons. He leaned down low, menacingly, and put his hands flat on the table.

"You took food from our table. Now, you put it back."

Ferd punched his brother in the shoulder. "Hold the goddamned thing straight up," he said, "not sideways. I don't want a hole in my stomach."

"You must have a hole in your stomach," Leo said, rubbing his shoulder, "you ate most of the potatoes."

"Whatever. You ate the chocolates and those were important."

"It was all important according to Dad."

"You should get that removed."

"What removed?"

"That," Ferd said, pointing at his brother's birthmark, the sprawling deep red port wine stain on his neck. The birthmark covered the right side of his neck and reached as high as his right earlobe and as low as his collarbone. It was the only visible difference between the two boys and Ferd resented it, the separation it created between them.

Leo touched his birthmark. It was smooth like the skin around it.

"I like it."

"If you were an animal, the other animals would kill you because of it. Because it's different."

Both boys went quiet when they spotted a partridge pecking at small stones on the side of the gravel road. Leo raised the barrel of his .22 in one smooth motion and pulled the cool metal tongue of the trigger. The bird slumped forward.

"I wanted to see what it looked like," he'd said to his mother after he'd shot a mourning dove in their backyard several months earlier. Algoma had turned the limp bird over and over again in her hands, as if, wound up like a watch, its thumbnail-sized heart would beat again.

At eleven years old, Leo could take his pick of the sky. Despite being twins, the boys were both taller and broader than most children their age. There was no time to be a child in the Beaudoin family. They'd hit the ground running.

Gaetan had introduced the boys to the clearings, stretches of forest, and creeks where they were allowed to hunt and fish on their own, places where they would not likely become lost or be bothered by other hunters or Ministry officials who would take issue with their age or what they were hunting. He wanted them to grow up as he had and no one could tell him different. It was like they were living in a time warp, living as if it were twenty or thirty years ago. That they were little more than children didn't bother him. "If it was good for me, it's good for them," he'd said to Algoma when she expressed concern. Eventually, she knew it wasn't a subject to be debated if she wanted to be considered a good wife.

Even though Gaetan encouraged their hunting and fishing, shunning activities other boys their age did like playing video games or making skateboarding videos, the boys knew enough to keep it to themselves, and did not tell the few friends they had. Every weekend, Ferd and Leo disappeared into the woods behind their home. The entire town was surrounded by forest dense with spruce. It was like living on an island and just as hard to leave. Little of the outside world made it through.

Once the boys were close enough to home that they could see their house through the branches, Ferd grabbed the partridge and two hares from Leo's hands and walked the rest of the way. His pockets were stuffed with four mealy apples he'd poached from a hunter's bait pile. "Finders keepers," he said.

Leo let his brother carry the animals. He knew better than to argue with Ferd. It would feed them all the same. "Ever wonder why Mom and Dad aren't like other parents?" he asked warily, a rare attempt to connect with his brother.

"What are you talking about?" Ferd snorted.

"I mean other parents would just buy more food, like at the grocery store."

Ferd laughed. "Why, when we can feed ourselves? Are you stupid?"

"Yeah," Leo said, and kicked at the ground. "Stupid."

If Leo was like his mother, Ferd took after his father in most ways. Stubborn and deeply entrenched in his opinions even if he didn't know why.

Once the boys passed through the opening they'd made

in the cedar hedge that surrounded their backyard, they found their mother on her hands and knees in the garden. Her hands darted frantically through the leaves, searching for anything she might have missed. She dug through the dirt as if she were looking for coins in the sofa the last day before payday.

7:00 p.m. -11°C. Gusting winds.
Blasts of cold air every time the door is opened.

A beer bottle exploded against the wall behind the bar and rained down brown glass onto the counter and floor. The noise was deafening.

"What the fuck!" Gaetan yelled, hands still protecting his head in case there was a second bottle. "What's wrong with you?"

His younger brother had shown up unannounced at the bar. It was the first time Gaetan had seen him in over four years, and the last time had been for mere seconds. A familiar face in a passing car. Since then, he'd heard that his brother had picked up work in a town a couple hours south of Le Pin. He was shocked by how old his brother looked now, hard lines carved into his face and several scars that hadn't been there last time they spoke.

"Why haven't you returned Dad's calls? Are you coming to Mom's 60th birthday?" Simon asked.

"Will you be there?"

"Yes. That's why I'm in town."

"Then I won't be. Nothing's changed unless you've changed."

Simon turned his back to his only brother and stared at the regulars who were trying to pretend they weren't watching the fight between the bartender and the guy with the badly hooked nose.

Simon eyed down the man in the leather vest who was

sitting alone in the corner. The man was nearly twice his size. "What the fuck are you looking at, buddy?"

Gaetan had severed ties with his family the same year he and Algoma married, and he had not set foot in his parents' home since.

"It's political," he'd told Algoma when she pleaded with him to invite his family over for Christmas dinner one year.

"You don't even read the paper or watch the news. How do you have politics?" she shot back.

The two brothers sat on opposing sides of the sovereignty debate. After a physical confrontation on the front lawn that had resulted in Simon's broken nose, their mother had banned all talk of politics in the house. Instead of resolving or avoiding the subject, Gaetan ignored everyone involved and even those on the peripheries, like his sister.

"And what about Mary?" Simon asked.

Gaetan visibly winced as he took a sip of the gin buck he was nursing behind the bar.

Simon grinned knowing he'd hit a nerve. "She still thinks you're going to call or come home one day." He wiped some glass shards off the bar onto the floor. Emboldened by his brother's silence, he carried on. "You need me more than you think you do. And if you really didn't want to know us anymore, you could have moved away. It's up to you to leave, not us."

"Out now," Gaetan said.

Simon smiled and waited another full minute before standing up.

The man in the corner half stood up, but Gaetan waved him down. He turned back to his brother. "Leave," he said.

Simon stood up and headed toward the exit. As he put

his hand on the door, he looked back at Gaetan. "I'll tell Mary you said hi," he said, and ducked to avoid the highball glass his brother launched at him. Simon laughed. "Same delayed fuse you've always had. You've never had good timing." And with that, he was gone.

Shaking, Gaetan walked over to the jukebox and dropped in several coins. He punched in a series of numbers from memory; however the music did little to drown out the sound of his brother's voice still ringing in his ears.

If he could have done it differently, he would have.

Ferd snapped another cedar twig and tossed it onto the snow to join the others he'd already thrown there. It was Sunday and he'd been outside since the early afternoon, holed up inside an opening in the cedar hedge. It was dark now, almost time for bed. He ignored that he couldn't feel the tips of his toes and fingers anymore. He'd been sitting on a piece of cardboard on top of the snow for hours. He wiped his dripping nose with his snow-crusted mitt and tossed another twig onto the pile. Under the weak light from the back porch light, he stared at the unfinished note in his lap. He didn't know how to say he was sorry for all he'd done.

Ferd looked up: a constellation of blank notes suspended in the branches around him. Each folded into a fortune teller with no fortune in it. No message.

For the most part, Ferd tried to tow the line when people, even his family, talked about his brother in the past tense. He never told anyone about the notes he sent to Leo. They would never understand. Instead, he quietly slipped his messages down drains, folded them into small paper boats and left them in the washing machine, tied them to rocks and dropped them to the bottom of the river, flushed them down toilets at school.

What he couldn't tell anyone was that a part of him worried that his brother stayed away because he was mad at him. He thought of the ways he'd hurt his brother in the past, how he'd undermined everything Leo had wanted for himself. There was the incident with the killdeer egg, and how it had changed everything between them. Ferd didn't know why he'd done what he had, his actions had come faster than the thoughts behind them. He only knew that he'd wanted to hurt his brother, and he had. Where he was hard and loud, Leo was soft and quiet. Incapable of dealing with a force like his brother. That everyone took to Leo only made it worse. No one looked at him the way they looked at his brother even though they had the same face. A wash of shame coloured his neck and cheeks, and then finally he wrote: It will be different this time. Come home.

Gaetan arrived home while the sun was still down, the darkest blue lightening the eastern sky. Still upset by his brother's appearance, and fuzzy from the whiskey shots he and the vested man had downed at closing, he fumbled with his keys at the door, scraping paint off the wood as he tried to get his key in the lock.

Once finally inside, he leaned against the closed door and shut his eyes. After kicking off his boots, he walked down to the basement where he lay down on the hard carpet beside Ferd's bed. He was drunk enough, tired enough, that if he tried to imagine that his remaining son was twelve-year-old Simon, he could. It was the last time he could recall things being good, that he had someone he thought he would be close to forever.

10:47 a.m. -19°C. Wind N, light.
Car frozen shut. An iceberg in the driveway.

Le Pin was located two hundred and forty kilometres northwest of Quebec City and was linked to the south end of the province by a single aging highway. A thin ribbon of crumbling asphalt that regularly failed those looking to leave town after heavy rains or snow. The town itself was roughly the shape of a pentagon. A fortress of stacked duplexes, small brick bungalows, a hospital, a mall, and a pulp and paper mill to keep the wilderness back. Thick boughs pressed against hard wood fences. If only so there was a place with an unobstructed view, the town had been built alongside the Charles River. The Charles was a steeply banked and deep river that, after being sieved by two generating stations, emptied into the St. Lawrence.

Just north of Le Pin, four smaller rivers fed into the Charles; south of town, another river joined the spill from the rest. Seen from air, the network of rivers looked like a hawk's claw clutching a treed mass of earth, threads of logging roads trailing behind it.

While provincial signs were staked at the town's north and south borders, it was the wet egg smell from the pulp mill that greeted visitors first, that seeped into lungs and clothes. Set at the north edge of town, the pulp mill rose like a silver smoking castle. A quarter of the town—roughly twenty-five hundred people—worked in forestry. It was a town of injury lore. Splinters and stitches. Falling trees and head injuries. Slips and chainsaws.

The pulp mill was the tallest structure in town, its jagged profile visible from the Beaudoins' front yard. Their one-storey brick home had been cheaper because it stood so close to the mill. Algoma and Gaetan had bought the house thinking they'd move to the south end of town one day. The nice part of town. Until then, along with the mill, they lived on Le Pin's unofficial northern border. Only several houses and a gas station beyond their house, civilization wound down to two hundred kilometers of forest until the last clutch of villages rose up. Industry's last gasp. Communities living on the edge of the map.

"We should go up north this summer," Ferd said. He kicked the back of the driver's seat.

"Would you stop it," Gaetan said, palm flat on the top of the steering wheel. "We *are* up north. How much further you want to go?"

Ferd rattled off the names of several villages north of Le Pin.

Algoma looked over her shoulder. "You forgot Pike Falls."

Gaetan laughed. "Does that even count as a village? Twenty people live there. Compared to them, we're big time. Hell, we even have a hospital. This is big city living."

"Watch the road," Algoma said. She twisted her gloved hands nervously in her lap, the green leather worn down to the beige lining at her fingertips from her constant fidgeting. It had snowed the night before, the silvery powder kind that left the roads slippery even after they'd been plowed. New snow crunched beneath the tires.

"The snow's talking," Ferd said, pressing his ear to the cold window.

Algoma asked him what it was saying. Call and response.

The same routine they'd been doing since Ferd had been old enough to talk. Only the answer ever changed.

Ferd paused. "It's saying it wants a doughnut."

"Well, tell it that it can have a doughnut if it stays with us at the market," Algoma said.

Ferd kicked the back of the driver's seat again. "Fine."

Gaetan looked at his son in the rear-view mirror, his eyes thin black slits. "Or not."

Ferd turned away and looked out the window. Row upon row of stacked duplexes that varied little from street to street. It looked like every building in town had been built in the same year, each tired in the same way: sagging porches and rusting metal staircases that led to the upper units. When they passed a mint green duplex with two empty urns on either side of the ground floor unit's front door, Ferd pounded the window with his mitt. "Can Aunt Soo come, too?"

"Maybe next time," Algoma said. She glanced at her sister's house as the car slid by. She could picture Soo's yarn-strewn couch. Several afghans in progress. It was nearly impossible to extract Soo from her house in the winter, the clicking of her knitting needles counting down the seconds until spring.

"Whoa, whoa, whoa, girl," Gaetan yelled. He commanded the car to stop as it slid into the middle of the intersection.

"Gae—" Algoma choked, her hands on the dashboard.

"We're good, no cars. No cars." Gaetan smiled. Algoma did not. "I'm doing the best I can," he said, putting a hand on her thigh. She stiffened under his touch.

Ferd yelled, "Look, look!"

Gaetan and Algoma turned their heads to the right. A bride, groom, and seven wedding party members stood on the steps of St. Alphonse church while a photographer in a massive parka snapped photos. Iced taffeta and crinoline. The church was one of a half dozen in town in competition with one another, each steeple reaching higher than the last, like children raising their hands in a classroom where there was only one right answer.

"We should go more often," Algoma said, but she didn't mean it. It was a resolution she made every year, but never kept with the exception of midnight mass and maybe Easter if she felt guilty enough.

Gaetan pulled the car into the market's parking lot and parked in one of the only empty spaces left. He undid his seat belt and took the keys out of the ignition. "Now how about some doughnuts, then?"

The market was only open one day a week: Saturday. Vendors from the area and even a couple hours away ritually converged upon the building to staff the same booths they had for years. Glowing towers of jarred honey. Fat-speckled sausage links hanging from large silver nails. Frosted baked goods carefully arranged under glass. An easy-listening radio station playing over the loud speakers.

"Don't mind if I do," Gaetan said, pouring himself a small paper cup of rum punch. A table with two huge punch bowls was set up at the entrance to the market. Every year, early in the New Year, the market offered complimentary rum punch and a second bowl of fruit punch for the kids. From our families to yours. Health and happiness in the New Year.

Algoma crossed her arms. "It's only eleven in the morning."

"They wouldn't put it out if they didn't want us to enjoy it," he said, and poured a second cup. "C'mon and have some with me." He handed her the cup.

Algoma softened and accepted the punch. She brought the cup to her mouth and sipped, almost choking from the sting of cheap rum against her throat.

"Can I have one, too?" Ferd placed his hands in front of his chest like a begging dog. "The good one?"

"I don't think so." Algoma drained her cup and tossed it into the garbage can beside the table.

"Three points," Gaetan cheered. "The lady is a champ."

"Stop it," she said, but she was smiling again.

Gaetan saw the opportunity and slipped his arm around her waist and kissed her. It had been so long since they'd kissed that her lips felt foreign to him, but good. Encouraged, he pulled her closer.

Self-conscious, Algoma laughed and pushed him away and slapped his chest. "Enough!"

Ferd tugged on his mother's jacket. "Doughnuts?"

Gaetan poured himself another cup of punch and raised it in the air. "One for the road!"

Arms laden down with bags of bread, cheese, meat, and winter squash, Ferd, Gaetan, and Algoma stood in front of their favourite bakery stand, the highlight of every visit. Under the home-made Plexiglass cover were an assortment of cakes, pies, and pastries. The doughnuts were kept on a painted wood shelf behind Mrs. Walschots. She was a Dutch immigrant who'd married a local man and moved to town thirty years ago. People in town still referred to her as "new."

"Three dozen doughnuts," Ferd said, as politely as he could muster. "Please."

"He means we'll take a dozen," Algoma corrected, and handed over a five-dollar bill.

Mrs. Walschots took the money and tucked it into her

apron. "What kind, Leo? Sugar or maple?"

"Ferd. It's Ferd," Algoma said, too quickly.

Gaetan looked at the floor.

"Oh, yes, yes," Mrs. Walschots said, her face reddening. "I'm so sorry. Here, let me add an extra maple one. For Ferd."

By the time Gaetan pulled the car into the driveway, the plastic bag the doughnuts had come in was empty. Ferd's hand prints were fossilized onto the back window, ice-hard syrupy prints that Gaetan would promise to wash off for weeks.

Algoma threaded the grocery bags onto her arms and walked toward the house, the bags scraping against the bricks. She thought about the market. It was the most time the three of them had spent together in months. Gaetan ran up from behind her and opened the door. "Madam," he said, and gave her a dramatic bow.

Algoma nodded and walked inside, not stopping to take off her boots before putting the groceries in the kitchen. Ferd ran inside after her, and, to Algoma's surprise, he started to put the groceries away, a job he normally shirked. He avoided housework whenever he could, so when he put the squash in the fridge, she did not correct him.

After a dinner of roasted chicken, potatoes, and salad, Gaetan sat down on the couch and wrote in his weather journal, the television on in the background. Algoma cleared the rest of the plates and wiped down the table. Instead of doing the dishes, she sat down beside her husband and put her head on his shoulder. Gaetan switched the channel to her favourite show.

"Going downstairs," Ferd said, stomping down the stairs to his black-and-white twelve-inch television. A find from The Shop, the second-hand store where Algoma worked.

"Goodnight."

Algoma and Gaetan said goodnight back.

Gaetan muted the television.

Algoma stretched her legs out on the coffee table, her hand now resting on his thigh.

Gaetan switched off the television, looked at Algoma, got up, and went into his bedroom.

Algoma followed.

6:58 p.m. -17°C. Wind NW, strong.
Frost spreading like road maps across the window.

The cement floor in the back room of The Shop where Algoma sat was cold and uncomfortable. She was surrounded by a circle of plastic laundry baskets that were bowed with age and use, clothes spilling out where the faux weave was broken in places. The five baskets behind her were full of unsorted newly donated clothing; the five baskets in front of her empty and neatly labelled: women's pants, men's pants, women's tops, men's tops, and children's clothes. Her lap held a treasure trove of assorted accessories. A long, braided, gold metallic belt with an oversized black patent leather buckle, a silver cross pendant with a large rhinestone in the middle of it, a neon blue umbrella with bright yellow plastic handle in the shape of a duck's head, and a white balaclava with a small cigarette burn below the left eye. A crisp black hole with a dirty yellow halo.

The balaclava was the kind the snowmobile drivers around Le Pin used to wear as soon as there was enough snow to ride; however, since most drivers had switched to Neoprene masks, The Shop's collection of acrylic balaclavas grew unchecked like mice. The store's owner, Josie, was sure this was going to be a banner year for snow and The Shop would "clean up" in the balaclava department. "Everyone needs a spare. Neoprene rips."

"Hoarder," Algoma said.

"Hoarder who owns the store you work for," Josie replied.

Algoma had worked at The Shop, a second-hand store in the middle of town, for almost a decade. It was time enough to see some of the same items make second and third rounds on the floor. She sorted the incoming clothes during the week and sometimes tended the till on weekends when Josie took some needed time off. The pay was modest, but it was enough to furnish Algoma's refrigerator with food and her family with clothes.

While The Shop was the most popular of all the second-hand stores in town, there were a dozen others like it. Each store owner was a curator, how they saw the town and the people in it evident in what they offered for sale and for how much. The store was a time capsule that was opened every time someone walked through the front door, nothing stayed buried for long. Looking for what treasures countless others had missed, shoppers rooted elbow-deep through the sale racks and bins. An Italian silk scarf in a sea of rayon eels.

New clothing and furniture could be had at the town's only mall—a one-level affair with bad lighting and even worse food. However, while the second-hand stores thrived, the shops in the mall opened and closed in the same season. If someone really needed something that wasn't available in town—the latest video game or a new wedding dress—she could take a trip south to Quebec City or Montreal. Each city was roughly a three-hour drive away in good weather, four or five when the weather turned bad. For the most part, the town was a closed community, a throwback with its customs and rituals clearly defined. Few people left, and even fewer moved in.

While Le Pin was not a rich town, the people were proud. Each lawn was perfectly manicured, every sagging porch coated in fresh paint, and most people were content to live out their lives dressed in someone else's clothes—as long as those clothes were clean, pressed, and sold for a good price. Even Josie, a Manitoba transplant, had adopted the local custom and dressed in clothes she took from work. When she was done with a particular item, it went back into The Shop's rotation.

Josie lived by barter. She traded in the things people left at the curb in the morning for whatever she needed to flesh out her own comforts.

"Just doing my part," she told people.

A tall, sinewy woman in her late thirties with cropped brown hair and regrettable blue butterfly tattoos on each of her toned calves, Josie was perfectly built to harvest the outdated tables and bags of clothing others pitched. She also had the gift of being able to sweet talk people into giving her what she needed without making it seem like she was asking for anything at all. On a good day, her truck bed looked like a fully furnished living room.

Josie knew the intimate needs of everyone within her complex barter network: the butcher who always needed baby furniture for his constantly procreating daughters, the hairdresser who adored anything amber or suede, the unmarried plumber who collected end tables the way most people collected knick-knacks or spoons. Even her morning cup of coffee was an exchange. In return for allowing Café Drummond to extend its small patio (used for exactly three months every year) in front of her storefront window, she received bottomless cups of strong black coffee.

Josie kept a neatly printed list of everyone's needs tucked into her black leather wallet, which she kept in the back pocket of her jeans. She consulted it every time she ran into a potential barterer and updated it regularly with new items and information. The pen that sat behind her ear had replaced the cigarette that used to sit there. She'd traded one habit for another.

"Did Anna have her baby yet?" Josie had asked, the last time she was at the butcher's.

Theo nodded. "Another boy! And this one named after me." He thumped his wheelbarrow chest with his fist. "But now Susan is pregnant again." He sighed the heavy sigh of a man who was proud of his family, but also a man who wasn't looking forward to being a babysitter into his sixties. He shook his head and turned to finish butchering the meat he'd been working on. Josie tried to offer her congratulations over the sound of saw on bone. She underlined her previous entry for Theo: Crib.

Even Josie's rusty pickup truck had been a barter. One summer, she worked for a friend who owned several blueberry fields. She'd risen at 4:30 every morning to pick blueberries in the semi-dark before she had to work at The Shop. At the end of the season, her fingers were stained a deep blue, and she'd been given the keys to the truck.

In an attempt to avoid the insomnia that had plagued her from her teens, Josie spent most nights driving around town and the outlying regions in search of leftovers. She knew the secret dump sites on the outskirts of town and the streets where the credit cards had higher limits and the houses were more prone to renovation and discard. Homeowners would haul their furniture out to the curb, knowing that it would be gone by morning. They did not have to pay to have it removed or haul it to the dump themselves. Josie needed them and they needed her. Her heart was a twenty-five-cent cracked knick-knack salvaged from an estate sale.

Algoma

At the end of her shift, Algoma picked up a pencil from beside the register and wrote on the debit board. Each week, Josie checked the debit board for staff purchases, clothing and other items taken in lieu of pay, which was also the main reason the best offerings never made it to the sales floor. With a couple of quick strokes, Algoma marked down twenty dollars worth of purchases for two full-length fur coats. Two furs. Women's. Damaged. $10 each. AB.

Outside, she retrieved four bungee cords from the trunk of her car and lashed the two coats—fur facing out—to the front seats. Muskrat for the driver, fox for the passenger.

Comfortably seated on a soft bed of muskrat fur, Algoma drove home and felt warm for the first time in months. The fur cushioned her aching back from the jarring potholes that pocked the weather-ravaged streets. She drove fast and loose, one hand flat on the wheel, and the other fingering the wrist-worn hem of the coat sleeve like an amulet, like luck, like a lottery ticket before the numbers are called.

The youngest of seven children, Algoma had never worn a piece of new clothing in her life. It was a fact she was proud of. Even as a teenager, she had "shopped" for clothes in her friend's overstuffed closets. They had readily given her the things they'd confessed to no longer liking or wanting. An excuse to buy more.

Well into adulthood, she continued to accept the castoffs of her friends and siblings, however outdated and misshapen the pieces were. She could not bear the stiff seams of a new shirt, or the extra button sewed to the bottom hem that seemed to portend disaster. She preferred clothing that had already been vouched for, shoes that already knew the way home, a dress already comfortably stretched over the hips. Unconcerned with fit or style, only function, she had discovered that old silk scarves were the perfect way to cinch oversized shirts and dresses to her thin frame. If there was even a slight wind, Algoma was a tornado of fabric and scarves. Dogs barked, children cried.

Unlike her, Algoma's family had strict clothing requirements. While they would eat anything, and regularly did, they would not wear just anything. Even the boys wouldn't share the same clothes.

For Gaetan everything had to be one hundred percent cotton: "I need to breathe."

Leo had required all pants be long enough to roll: "I hate getting wet."

And now Ferd would only wear his brother's clothing: "Why shouldn't I?" His last teacher, the one who had also taught Leo, had been disturbed by the trend and prayed for the moment when he would outgrow the clothes. It'd been like teaching long division to a ghost.

It was dark by the time Algoma arrived home, a low moon visible through the picket fence of trees that lined the street. Looking through the windshield, she'd momentarily mistaken the moon for a streetlamp. She pulled into the driveway, careful to leave enough room between the car and the hedge so she could get out. The lights on the main floor were out, which meant that either no one was home, or someone wanted people to think there was no one home. She got out of the car and fumbled with her house key in the lock. She'd asked Gaetan two times in the last week to replace the burnt out light over the side door, but it remained dead in the socket.

"Use the front door," he'd said.

"It's taped up for winter."

"Oh, yeah."

Inside, Algoma let her purse slide from her shoulder down to the stiff bristles of the welcome mat. She kicked her boots off, draped her coat over the banister, and tossed her keys into the empty iron birdbath she'd put beside the door specifically for that purpose.

She heard a splash. What now, she thought, but already knew.

The birdbath was filled to its scalloped brim with water. A paper boat floated on the small tap-water lake. She plucked the pulpy ship and stuffed it, still wet, into her skirt pocket. At least he was getting creative.

Gaetan was at work and Ferd was likely writing more notes in the basement. She looked down the stairs at the basement door. It was shut, a thin strip of light at the bottom. She thought about confronting Ferd with the latest note, but didn't. He'd gone through enough in the past year. She hadn't seen his breaking point yet, and didn't want to. She walked upstairs to the kitchen.

"I'm home," she called out.

"Okay," Ferd yelled up from the basement. He sounded distracted.

The evening stretched out before Algoma. She willed herself to ignore the breakfast dishes stacked in the sink, the hardened gobs of jam and peanut butter. She made herself a toasted tomato sandwich for dinner and pulled out her favourite deck of cards. The cards were well used, the edge so frayed, they were as soft as thumb-worn cotton. One of her sisters had given her the pack after returning from a trip to Las Vegas five yeas ago. "For luck," Steel had said. Casino cast-offs with a hole in the middle of each card. She held up the ace of hearts and looked through the punched hole, her world further reduced.

Halfway into her game, the phone rang. Algoma ignored it and focused on her cards. The answering machine picked up and she could hear Cen's voice. She could wait, Algoma thought, and flipped over another card.

After Leo died, her sisters had called and dropped by unannounced with such regularity she'd wondered if they had created a schedule. It was a rare day that passed without a call or visit from two of her six sisters. They almost always arrived in pairs—twin with twin. To have one over was to have both over. While she longed for solitude, she was grateful for the heavy casseroles they stacked in her fridge and freezers. The casseroles—layered beds of re-purposed leftovers—allowed her to feel as if she was not taking from her sisters, or the world. She was simply living off the oven-hardened edges.

Algoma's father, Richard, had been a large man who towered over everyone he met. He had the broad shoulders of a boxer and the soft jowls and dark piercing eyes of an aging movie star. When the girls were little, they'd fought over who could sit in his lap and watch Westerns with him, which was all he ever watched.

Repairing refrigerators and air conditioners was Richard's life calling and it was the only job he'd ever had even though his wife hated air conditioning.

"It'll rot your lungs out," she said, when he brought a unit home during an unusually hot summer. She refused to let him install it. "It'll bring up the electric bill." The air conditioner sat in a corner in the basement until his eldest daughter took it with her when she moved out.

Richard could fix almost anything. His large hands had a strange grace. Anything could be repaired, he figured, as long as you had the right tools and some time. His wife, Ann, did not fix things as much as she manifested them. She had a way of making everything turn out the way she wanted it to. "If I'm happy, you're happy" was her favourite saying.

Ann was a plain woman who managed to convince everyone that she was an "unconventional beauty." Of average height, she had wispy brown hair that she styled strategically to hide her large forehead. It was almost impossible to find a photograph of her taken head on. Her face was always angled, her eyes looking somewhere else, possibly at the life she thought she should have had. The one she deserved.

Between children, Ann worked as a waitress at a restaurant in town that catered to the elderly—soft foods, stews, and soups—although she acted more like a therapist or doctor than a waitress. Over soup and sandwiches, customers told her about their problems and their pains. Ann gave out her advice and diagnoses freely, which the customers readily ate up. She left each shift with her pockets full of tips. There were few things that Ann wasn't a self-professed expert on, especially on the home front.

Ann let Richard have his way from time to time, allowing him a few big coups a year so she could hold domain the rest of the time over everything from dinner to how often the lawn was cut. There was only one instance in their marriage when Richard put his foot down. The names of their daughters.

While Richard had never been so much as the captain of a rowboat, he was obsessed with the freighters that navigated through the Great Lakes and across the Atlantic Ocean, the self-unloaders and gearless bulk carriers that transported everything from grain and ore to salt and gypsum from port to port. He was so taken by the ships that he named his daughters after freighters in his favourite fleet: Algoma Central Corporation. A photograph of the Algoma black bear on a stack or bow caused his heart to pump like a diesel engine and made his blood run hot.

In the final weeks of Ann's first pregnancy, when she looked ready to topple over from the sheer size of her belly, she'd begged Richard to consider more traditional names: Rebecca, Jane, or Julie. "Something normal," she said.

He refused.

"They'll be a team," he said. "And we'll be the captains."

Richard imagined his future children as empty ships he would send out into the world—across lakes, rivers, and oceans, and through all weather—children who would return to him with riches that would see him through the rest of his life, so that he could stop dreaming of the mille-feuille metal fins of the air conditioners he fixed. The ticking time bombs of failing motors.

And so he named his girls Algocen, Algosteel, Algolake, Algosoo, Algobay, and Algoport. Ann tried to tell people they were family names that had been passed down through the years, but no one believed her.

Richard favoured Algobay the most, likely because her namesake ship was also his favourite. He'd been heartbroken over the freighter's troubles in those first years after her launching: a collision that resulted in the loss of two lives, running aground the following year after the steering gear failed, and only a year after that a head-on collision with the *Montrealais* on the St. Clair River. He blamed the ship's bad luck on the wife of the bank chairman who'd christened the ship, and refused to deal with that bank his entire life. After each minor catastrophe in which the *Algobay* found itself, Richard would sit Algobay on his lap and ask her if she was okay, holding the confused child tight to his chest, tears in his eyes.

A fleet of girls was born, pair by pair, until the final installment: one singular baby girl, unlike the rest.

Ann's last pregnancy had surprised even her. When she discovered she was pregnant again, she was sure it was twins. Even when the doctor told her it wasn't, she left his office to buy two matching sleepers to celebrate. Months later, after the nurse put Algoma into Ann's arms, Ann asked the doctor for a second opinion. He'd laughed and walked out of the delivery room. "Enjoy your little girl, Mrs. Belanger." She'd left the hospital with one baby, almost convinced they had forgotten one inside her.

Algoma's birth had shattered Ann's theory about herself, and she went into a deep depression that lasted months. Privately, she'd considered herself a Noah-like figure, her destiny to guide pairs of God's creations into a world where she cut the sandwiches and poured the milk. She wore a pink plastic rosary around her left wrist, a gift from her younger sister who'd been to Jerusalem, and practiced her "Mary smile" in the bathroom mirror.

"God's willing vessel," she said to her reflection, and then said it again, trying to look humble.

Publicly, the town wondered what was in the water on the Belanger property. Twins had run in their family since the first Belanger ended up on the continent, but Ann's numbers were staggering. It was rumoured that women with fertility problems stole onto the property at night to drink water straight from their garden hose. When Ann went to church on Sundays, would-be mothers tried to brush up against her in the aisles. Ann recognized the "accidental" grazings and enjoyed them.

Richard let his seventh and final child go unnamed for an entire month before he settled on a suitable name for what he deemed a very special child, a child who had even defied her mother's command to be born as a pair.

Algoma.

Not the name of a ship, but the name of the entire fleet.

As the years passed, the girls' names were shortened to versions that were easier to yell, the unifying prefix dropped: Cen, Steel, Lake, Soo, Bay, and Port.

Algoma, however, remained Algoma.

At the age of sixty-one, Ann died of a heart attack. As she lay on the potato-strewn aisle of the produce section in the grocery store, she used her remaining strength to point at the cardboard bin of stacked grapefruits: "I'll take two."

Like a dead man's switch, the cessation of Ann's heart caused Richard's to stop. He fell at the plastic altar of a humidifier he was trying to repair for a neighbour. A thick fog of steam drifted over his body, filling the ravine between his spread legs.

Outside the Church of St. Joseph, the seven sisters escorted their intimate convoy of double-varnished mahogany toward its final harbour.

Years later, each one of Ann and Richard's girls would document—whether they admitted to it or not—news on their namesake ships. The details were prophecy on how their lives would turn out: which was built to Nova Scotia Class and could weather ice; which had been renamed and sold only to be bought back again; which was on long-term layup; which sold for scrap; which upgraded and lengthened; which could shoulder more and how much; which made it out to sea; which had taken on water, split in half, sunk. Algoma could only watch her sisters for signs of what was to come for herself.

She was still awake when Gaetan stumbled into the house at 4:00 a.m. Blurry with sleep, she was no longer sure of her cards, what needed to be placed where, yet she kept playing. She was sure she was winning. She had to be.

Gaetan placed a hand on the top of her head and kissed her cheek. He smelled of smoke and gin and moved around the room like he was underwater or on the moon. Slow and heavy steps.

He stood at the counter and made himself a cheese slice and butter sandwich, a sure sign he'd had one too many drinks after closing.

"I bought you something," he said. "I know what you're thinking. Don't worry, it's from a second-hand shop." He could feel Algoma bristle at the thought of "new." He cut his sandwich in four and shoved a piece into his mouth. Mid-chew, he placed a small silver flask on the kitchen table and stood back with his arms spread wide like a ring master's. "Ta da!"

Algoma picked up the vessel and turned it around in her hands. "Barry," she said, reading the name engraved into the flask.

"You're a bartender's wife," Gaetan said, as if it were a call to the priesthood or military. "You should never have to pay for your own drinks."

"I don't go to bars," Algoma said. "Just your bar." She ran her thumb over the engraving. Had Barry been someone's best man? Maybe he'd lost the position. Maybe he'd slept with the bride.

"Well, The Shop then," Gaetan said.

"I don't drink at work."

"Fine," he barked, annoyed by his ungrateful wife. "At home then."

Gaetan shoved another sandwich quarter into his mouth and leaned back against the counter. Algoma shook her head and went into the living room. She got down on her hands and knees in front of the liquor cabinet and searched through the bottles, quickly finding what she was looking for. She sat back and poured gin into Barry and took a drink.

Gaetan laughed appreciatively. "See, there you go. That's a good girl."

Obediently, Algoma took another drink, and sighed. She raised her flask. "Here's to Barry."

Like most things in her life, Algoma's husband was a hand-me-down, a cast-off from one of her sisters. One she'd happily taken.

Algoma was fifteen the first time she'd met Gaetan. Although money in a family of nine was tight, Richard and Ann scrimped and saved every year until they had enough to hire a landscaper to trim the trees. Landscaping and church were two of their priorities, and they preached both to their children. Every year, the trees were sculpted into two perfect orbs, as they had been for as long as anyone could remember. The annual pruning meant that despite their age, they were not very tall. The foliage, however, was incredibly dense, with near perfect coverage. At night, the trees looked like two planets caught in one another's gravitational pull. The style of pruning was not unique to the Belangers, so it was easy to spot which families in town were going through hard times. The branches of their trees grew unchecked.

Not a landscaper by trade, Gaetan was known to take odd jobs around town. He had no fear of heights and came with his own equipment. Most importantly to Richard, Gaetan charged less than anyone else. He was young—eighteen—and trying to make a few dollars to get him out of Le Pin; however, there were days when he'd accept a case of beer in return for an afternoon's work.

On his first day on the job, Gaetan arrived at the house and parked his red pick-up truck on the front lawn. Only equipped with a wooden ladder, a pair of pruning shears, and a small hatchet, he set about his work without letting anyone know he'd arrived. For three afternoons, he scrambled through the branches, which he pruned like a Lilliputian hairdresser, until the trees were perfectly shaped and Richard was happy.

During those three days, Bay had watched Gaetan from the living room window, her forehead pressed up against the glass, leaving behind a greasy oval smudge of make-up. She watched intently as newly cut branches fell to the lawn below. It was like he was taking apart a puzzle and littering the yard with its pieces. Bay begged her father to let her give Gaetan his pay at the end of the job. Richard saw the economic advantage of having an amateur landscaper in the family and obliged. He patted her on the back. "Wear something nice."

"Can I borrow the car for this weekend?" she asked.

"As long as you fill the gas tank back up."

Like her mother, Bay knew it was only a matter of time before she got what she wanted. She was already planning ahead for her first date with Gaetan. She'd seen his truck, and decided her father's would be better.

On the last day of the job, Bay, dressed in an ankle-length cotton skirt and white cotton blouse, breezed out onto the front lawn and smiled demurely in a way that she was not. When Gaetan noticed her, she lowered her eyes, laughed, and passed him the money. He stuffed the bills into the pocket of his jeans without looking to see how much was there.

"Tell your dad thanks," he said, his face flushed.

Bay beamed and neither one of them spoke or made motion to move.

Algoma watched the exchange from her bedroom window. A hand on her hip, she tried to cock her head the way her sister did. "Hi, I'm Algoma," she said. "Oh, my name? It's Algoma. Call me Al. No, Allie."

By the weekend, Gaetan was seated beside Bay at the Belanger dinner table, accepting helpings of Ann's scalloped potatoes and trying to remember everyone's names. By Christmas, his name was penciled onto a strip of masking tape in the coat closet. There was a strip of tape for each family member, lengths of heights and dates rising like cattails; however, by spring Bay had grown bored with her amateur landscaper. She sought the company of another semi-professional: the man her father had hired to fix the roof. She liked the way the word *shingle* rolled off her tongue. "It sounds like the name of a cocktail," she said to her twin, Port.

After Bay broke up with Gaetan, Algoma found him sitting on the front porch, an untouched beer tucked between his knees. Richard's attempt at an apology on behalf of his daughter.

"She broke up with me," he said. He was staring at the

trees he'd trimmed the year before. He could see where new growth had exploded from his rough cuts.

"She does that," Algoma said. She sat down beside him, so that their thighs touched. He was warmer than she had expected. A small furnace.

"The shed door broke off its hinges this morning. Could you take a look at it?" she asked.

By the weekend, Gaetan was back at the Belanger dinner table, this time sitting next to a different sister and he knew everyone's names. Within the year, Algoma—only seventeen years old—was pregnant with the boys, their future decided.

Algoma could hear Gaetan snoring in the bedroom. His shirt was abandoned on the floor in the hallway.

"Goddamn it," she whispered.

She picked up his shirt and emptied the rest of the gin in her flask down the sink. She turned off the lights, grabbed the blanket from the couch, and walked into the boys' old room to sleep.

1:01 p.m. 3°C. Wind S, calm.
Fist-punctured ice puddles.

For the moment winter had retreated. An unusual warm front. Heavy drifts of snow had shrunk back to reveal blankets of wet fall leaves and vast mud flats that made it nearly impossible to walk anywhere off the sidewalk or street. Once robust snowmen were now pitiful lumps of misshapen snow the kindergarteners kicked at with their bright neon boots. They ruthlessly stomped on the half-rotted carrots, tossed the charcoal eyes into the ditch. The rest of the kids had abandoned their thick winter coats and wandered around the schoolyard dressed only in long-sleeved shirts and snow pants. The school was surrounded by a pool of melted snow and ice. Icicles dropped from the edge of the roof and shattered on the asphalt. It was a season in between.

Ferd knew the weather wouldn't last. Nothing ever did. Winter would arrive again, and in full force this time. It would feel endless. For half of the school year the hallways were filled with the musty smell of damp wool, pools of melting slush, and wet socks. Come spring, when the students peeled their layers of sweaters and long johns, they'd hardly recognize one another. Pale versions of their fall selves.

Standing on the curved grassy hump of earth that flanked the east side of the school like a boomerang, Ferd watched his classmates from a safe distance. The bell rang. Lunch was over. He turned and walked in the opposite direction of the school. He wasn't going back, not today. Today was not a good day. Reminders of Leo faced him at every turn.

One of his brother's coloured pencil drawings was still stapled to the wall beside the gym, the edges curling inward, his name printed in dark block letters in the bottom right-hand corner. There was the framed photo of him the school had put next to the volleyball trophies in the school's trophy case. And the empty brass hook he'd left behind that no one would use because it was "bad luck."

Ferd stuffed his hands into the pockets of his jeans (Leo's jeans) and walked toward the woods. The school, like every other building on the east edge of town, was flanked by forest that was hundreds of kilometres deep, only stopping for the northward-swooping St. Lawrence River.

Several times a year, teachers and students were given a show: a rogue red fox, moose, or porcupine lumbering across the schoolyard. If a black bear was spotted in the area, the children were put under lockdown and forced to eat their sweaty sandwiches at their desks in silence until the threat had passed, although secretly they were always looking outside, trying to spot the animal that would allow them to go home early if it attacked student or teacher. They could only hope.

Once Ferd crossed the baseball diamond, he saw the familiar trailhead behind home plate. Large tree roots criss-crossed the path like varicose veins, worn smooth and silvery from decades of use, years of students skipping classes, their non-marking rubber-soled shoes wearing the bark smooth. He walked along the trail for a long time until the roots became ragged again and the path narrowed until it was little more than a suggestion. The crushed cigarette butts disappeared behind him.

After a half hour of walking through dense wood, breaking branches, clambering over fallen trees, and hopping muddy patches, Ferd arrived at his destination: a thin iron-stained creek that looked like a gash in the earth. Only the edges of the creek were still frozen. He admired the leaves that had been frozen into the ice and were now being slowly released. When he tried to pull one free, it ripped apart in his hand. He dropped the piece he held into the water and watched it slowly float away.

"Say hello for me."

The decomposing remains of a blue jay lay beside the creek. Ferd skirted the clutch of bones and feathers and pulled off his backpack. He was sweating and his shoulders ached. He unzipped his pack and dug past his textbooks, his uneaten lunch, until he found a small black canvas bag that held his tools: an assortment of pens, markers, paper, cards, twine, and tape. From his collection of cards, he chose a thick, creamy wedding invitation with gold lettering that he'd stolen from his teacher's desk. Her desk was such a mess she'd never notice, or at least not right away. The RSVP card was still lodged inside. Apparently, she hadn't made her decision yet. An old boyfriend maybe? Ferd tried to imagine the bride in her puffy white dress and the groom in his tuxedo standing side by side, both stiff as wedding cake toppers.

He used a red Sharpie to cross out the writing on the front of the card—Rebecca & Jean-Francois: Our Special Wedding—and flipped it over so he could write on the back.

Dear Leo...

Ferd's breath left him in small white puffs. He couldn't think of what to write next and his hand was beginning to cramp. In the short time he'd been at the creek, the temperature had dropped. The sky was moving fast, the clouds like icebergs being moved by an invisible current. The trees groaned with the effort to remain standing. He wished he'd brought his jacket.

If Ferd were to remove the salutations to Leo from his notes and replace them with dates, his notes could easily be mistaken for diary entries. In his notes to his brother, Ferd talked about this day, what he'd had for lunch, the homework he'd been assigned, the weather, or what he hoped their mother was making for dinner. He wanted Leo to know that he was waiting for him to come home. He wrote so Leo wouldn't miss a thing—not one thunderstorm or fried egg sandwich.

Ferd had been sent back to school two weeks after watching his brother go under the ice.

"It'll be good for you," Algoma said, but what she really wanted was the house to herself so she could cry without looking at the face of the boy she'd lost.

The first mistake the school made was to leave Leo's desk, which sat directly in front of Ferd's, empty in tribute. His unfinished science project and pastel-coloured notebooks still inside. Nobody would touch them.

Ferd kicked Leo's desk repeatedly, a persistent rattle that ended a lesson on multiplication tables. Instead of removing the desk, the teacher removed Ferd from class. He was sent home with a note that stated he was invited to move to the other grade seven class to help him adjust to his new circumstances, a note his parents never received.

Ferd's new teacher struggled with his mercurial moods, his sudden outbursts, fits of laughter, and breakdowns that, by the end of the day, left her hands shaking, her nails chewed down to the quick. Unsure what to do, she waited for Ferd's grief to slow from a waterfall to a trickle, but it remained constant. Thunderous. After March Break, she moved him to the back of class, close to the door, and counted down the days until the end of June.

In September, Ferd was introduced to his new teacher: Ms. Chantal Prevost. A recent university graduate, Chantal had blunt blonde Betty Page bangs that she cut herself and a predilection for Mary Janes, whatever the weather. She'd moved north from Montreal to put distance between herself and a failed relationship. A broken engagement. Now, she found herself living above a Chinese restaurant and sleeping on a single mattress the landlord had offered her. Chantal was often at school earlier than she needed to be and stayed longer than anyone else, often waving the janitor off.

From the first day of class, Chantal took to Ferd. His wet brown eyes. His tight suspicious mouth. She spoke in even tones around him, as she might to a strange dog. Firm, but not rude. She showed interest in his work, but did not praise him overly. Soon, he was calmer, but his lingering grief remained.

One day, several weeks into the school year, while the other kids ran off to recess, Chantal asked Ferd to stay behind. Ferd sat perfectly still and waited to be reprimanded for something he couldn't remember doing, but Ms. Prevost was smiling. A soft, sad smile. She set a pen and piece of paper on his desk and encouraged him to write a letter to his brother. "It will feel good to let him know how you feel." He looked up at her questioningly at first. Her bangs had grown out some and now partially shaded her eyes. He couldn't tell if they were blue or green. Ferd looked at the paper and then at her again. She nodded. He wrote.

After he finished writing his first letter to his brother,

Ferd thought of the perfect place to "mail" it. The ditch in front of the school. Somehow he knew it was not what Ms. Prevost had intended and did not tell her about his plans.

For years, parents had complained to the school administration that the ditch was dangerous. They'd argued about its depth, the culvert's ragged edge. Someone, maybe their child, could fall in and split their head open; however, nothing was ever done about it, and Ferd was glad for it. After school, as students left the building, he pretended he was waiting for someone. When the father of one of his friends asked if he was okay, Ferd said that he was waiting for his mom. "She's just going to be another minute. I swear."

Once the schoolyard was clear, he walked over to the ditch. He lay down on his stomach and punched a hole through the thin skin of ice. With a bare hand, he stuffed his letter into the cold water below. Ferd had no doubt the message would reach Leo. He imagined the submerged blades of grass standing upright like soldiers escorting his message along. A top priority mission. He left the ditch feeling calmer than he had in months.

The first major spring melt would reveal a dozen notes plastered to the yellow grass that lined the ditch. The messages pulped, unreadable, undelivered.

Newly inspired, Ferd filled the back of the wedding invitation with his hurried scrawl, the same electric red wire that linked each of his letters, like houses in the same village. He flipped the card open and made stick figures out of the letters, something he did to his textbooks to pass the time during class. He transformed the letters of the word "announcement" into eight boys and four girls. The pair of *N*s now fingerless twins holding hands. Beside his alphabet people he drew a crude interpretation of the school, the surrounding woods, the creek where he sat, and beyond that, the closest major cities, so that Leo would know where to find him when he was ready or able to come back.

Ferd walked out of the woods in time to hear the final bell and see a rush of students making a frenzied exodus from the front doors. He stood by and waited until the stream became a trickle of stragglers before he joined the slow procession home. Even then, he stopped at every interesting stone or malformed stick. He kicked at leftover clumps of snow, garbage, puddles. He wasn't ready to go home.

The sky was filled with ominous-looking clouds, peaked tufts of black and white meringue. Snow clouds. He wondered what the sky looked like from beneath water, if it distorted the images above, if the sun made it through at all. The last thing he wanted was for Leo to be cold. Ferd pictured his brother sitting cross-legged at the bottom of the river, his hair slick with algae and spiked with twigs. He saw his last note, the wedding invitation, floating closer and closer to his brother until, in slow motion, Leo plucked it from the current, like a chocolate bar wrapper caught in the wind.

But there was no current to buoy Ferd. He did not know how long he could live with his side of the conversation alone. The yards of the houses he passed were the colour of old teeth. Each step he took felt heavy and laboured, his body weighted down by his brother's decision to chase the bear. He was tired and he had math homework he already knew he wouldn't do. But it didn't matter. The teachers at school still looked at him with sad eyes. Ms. Prevost excused his poor assignments and forgotten homework. She didn't question him about the things that went missing from her desk.

A red-tailed hawk fell out of the sky like a meteor. Startled, Ferd stumbled backward, almost falling. With agile claws, the bird picked up something that had been hiding behind an overturned tricycle. The hawk swooped back and up and perched on the lowest bow of the tree closest to Ferd, who watched as it ripped apart a mouse with its sharp beak. The long, sinewy strips of the rodent snapped like rubber bands. Ferd rooted through his bag. He had to tell Leo about this.

5:47 p.m. -11°C. Wind N, calm.
Greasy thumb prints on the lower half of the window.

Gaetan was uneasy serving only himself. He appreciated the direction and structure that other people's drink orders gave him. Time parcelled out in highball glasses.

A drink in one hand—two fingers of rye with three ice cubes—he stared out the window into the already dark early evening. Cold radiated from the glass. Only two months ago, he would have been able to see past the football field at the end of the street, but now it was a black void with a twinkling of house lights on the other side.

Every June, the town held a massive bonfire in the centre of the field to commemorate Saint-Jean-Baptiste Day. In the fall, football teams from other towns shared locker room theories about the burned patch, the ritual sacrifices of the hometown team. What they would do to win.

Gaetan wiped his forehead. He was sweating and the window was beginning to fog up. In the kitchen, the vegetables and bones of dinner jumped and rattled in a steady roll of boiling water, the element red hot. Judging by the size of the pot, he guessed he'd be eating the same dinner for days. He'd complained about boiled dinners for his entire married life, but Algoma ignored him. She was convinced his taste buds would alter, become more sophisticated with age. He just thought that it was her way of nicely telling him to go to hell.

"It's healthy," she called out from the kitchen as if she'd

read his mind. "Full of vitamins for what ails you and you've been looking grey." She stirred the bubbling pot of fat and cellulose with such vigor he thought she'd knock it over.

Gaetan turned back to his window.

"Five more minutes," she said. Water splashed and sizzled on the burner.

Defeated, he picked up his weather journal from the window ledge and ran his fingers along the smooth leather.

He fisted away a circle of condensation from the window, so he could see outside. His thermometer was nailed to the middle porch beam. It was cheap and simple, but accurate, and the numbers were large enough that he could read them without going outside.

-11°C.

The forever-green AstroTurf that lined the porch mocked the cold. It looked like a putting green.

"Minus twelve," he said, and shook his head.

If it had been him, a man weighing 180 pounds, he would have lived. He would have survived the plunge into cold water. He would have found a way to get out. He was sure of it. Maybe he would have lost some fingers, or a toe, but he would have survived. A boy like Leo—thin and hairless as a skinned hare—would have never stood a chance. He shook his head and tried to focus on his weather journal, its familiar weight in his hands. Its religion of wind, sun, and precipitation.

Gaetan had recorded the weather every day since his thirteenth birthday when Simon had given him the red leather journal, which Gaetan assumed he'd shoplifted. Simon likely thought his brother would keep a diary that he could read; instead, Gaetan recorded the weather. By fifteen, he was able to match his best hunts and fishing outings with certain weather patterns. And by twenty he could track his life, how he was feeling, through the way he wrote down the details of the rain or snow, his own secret code. The habit had formed as easily and seamlessly as drink would later on.

The formula was simple: time, temperature, wind, and a short note. His formula, from which he allowed himself no deviations, meant that he'd never had to purchase a new journal, even though friends and family bought him new ones every birthday and Christmas. They always hoped theirs would be the next one he'd cling to. One line a day for over two decades and he'd still only used half the pages. He noted with some satisfaction that his penmanship had changed and improved over the years. It had become neater, more precise. At least something had changed.

"Dinner," Algoma said, the white sleeves of an oversized men's dress shirt rolled up sloppily to reveal her knobby elbows. Gaetan turned around to see his wife holding up a BBQ fork with a sopping ham on the end, fat gobs of oily water dripping onto the floor.

She smiled. "Protein. You like protein, right?" It wasn't a question.

And you like to save a buck or ten, he thought, and took his seat.

"What did you say?" Algoma asked.

"I said great."

On cue, Ferd walked through the side door, took off his boots, and sat down at the table with his coat still on. His cheeks were bright red and a clear stream of snot dripped from nose to lip.

"Where've you been?" Algoma asked. "Take off your coat and wipe your nose."

"I'm cold," he said. Ferd wiped his nose with his coat sleeve.

Gaetan turned to his son. "Listen to your mother. Take off your coat." The one area where he and Algoma were a united front was in parenting their remaining child. He was all they had. A thin blood tether.

Ferd ignored them both and pushed the salt and pepper shakers in front of the empty seat at the table, so it looked purposeful. Occupied.

Seated with his back to the living room, Gaetan was convinced he could feel the weather changing behind him, the barometer dropping. His fingers itched with the urge to update his journal, but Algoma's eyes were on him. She'd never stand for it. He shifted uncomfortably under her stare. She chewed aggressively on a piece of gristly pork fat. He needed a drink.

"A toast is in order," he said, jumping up from his seat. His chair screeched as it scraped across the floor.

Algoma stopped chewing. "For what?"

Ferd held up his empty water glass in hopes of scoring a sip.

"To… us!" Gaetan ran over to the liquor cabinet "Civilized people have drinks with dinner. Kings have drinks with dinner. Vikings!"

Algoma rolled her eyes. "Your food is going to get cold. Sit down." She tried to fork an overcooked potato onto her plate, but it crumbled as soon as she stabbed it.

Gaetan surveyed his collection of half-filled bottles, every one of them a "donation" from the Club. He settled on a fat glass bottle of amber-coloured rum. Something warm and sunny to battle the bland dinner and the cold outside. He walked back into the kitchen and held up his glass to the swing lamp's light bulb.

"It's like sun, right?"

Algoma swallowed a forkful of grainy potato. "Aloha."

Ferd giggled. He stared at the pot of water-softened roots and meat on the stove and resisted the temptation to drop a note into the simmering mash. *Maybe later*, he thought, when his parents were watching television, which is about all they could stand to do together these days. Stalagmites of empty wine glasses rising from the coffee table.

Before Leo's accident, it had been normal for his parents to invite friends and family over for dinner, the sound of glasses clinking and card-game insults filling the house with a comfortable and familial din. But now no one came over, unsure of which version of Algoma or Gaetan they might find. How red-eyed from sadness or drink.

The phone rang. Neither Ferd nor Gaetan made a move to answer it. They knew better. Algoma hated phones—the uninvited noise, the intrusion. She wouldn't tolerate interruptions during dinner. One of her few rules. Dinner was for family.

The phone bleated out its final ring. Gaetan wondered if Bay was on the other end. In between bites of ham and limp onion he tried to imagine what a life with her would have looked like. Would things have turned out differently? Would she have had twin sons like her youngest sister? He was sure hers would have floated, not sunk like Algoma's.

While he tried not to, and while he knew it was wrong, Gaetan found himself at times blaming Algoma, at least in part, for Leo's death. She had not raised him hardy enough. She hadn't eaten the right things when she was pregnant. Things would have been different with Bay, but maybe not better. It could have been a parallel hell. Twin girls. He couldn't imagine what it would be like to lose a daughter. A tornado of ribbon and silk spiraling down toward the silt.

Throughout dinner, while Algoma and Ferd ate in relative silence, Gaetan cycled through all of Algoma's sisters in his mind. He pictured a wedding with each, the honeymoon night, the different combinations of children, what jobs he could have pursued with a different woman behind him.

With Cen, he was a carpenter, and they had a boy and a girl. With Steel, he was the proud father of three perfect black-haired girls that looked like him, and he worked as a teacher. Math maybe. But his imagination stalled on Bay like a flooded engine. He conveniently forgot the part where she hadn't wanted him.

Gaetan looked at Algoma. She was carefully rearranging the food on her plate so that it appeared she'd eaten more than she actually had. An old trick he'd given up trying to get her to stop. By the end of the meal she would just toss her napkin over the entire mess and announce that she was full and make a big show out of it. Her shoulders looked narrower than he remembered, sharp, as if the bone might slip through and relieve her of her skin at any moment.

After dinner, the family splintered off. Algoma to her sewing, Ferd to his room in the basement, and Gaetan to the living room to watch television. If someone stood in the centre of the house and listened—the television crackling, the sewing machine humming its way through repairs, and the muffled thumps of someone moving around downstairs—it sounded like a family. All the parts were there, but the web had been cut. One essential thread removed that had left them all speaking different languages.

Out of habit, Gaetan leaned over and picked up his weather journal again. He flipped through the pages and penned another entry for the evening. Sometimes, he took the journal with him to work or out for short walks to the end of the street, so he could report the weather in real time. His coworkers had nicknamed him "The Weatherman." He worried constantly that someone would steal his journal, his weather—twenty years of highs and lows—but he couldn't bear to leave it behind either. The back pocket of his jeans bore the distinct outline of his journal like a pack of cigarettes.

The thermometer remained constant at -11°C. He looked around the yard at what little he could see in the dark. The cedar hedges needed to be trimmed. He ran a hand through his own messy hair. He needed a cut, too. He'd have to wait until spring to prune the hedges, which were now over seven feet tall. When he and Algoma had first moved into the house, the hedges had been a series of thigh-high shrubs that stretched around the property in small puffs. Now they blocked the view of almost everything else. He found himself stranded on his own small green planet.

*10:13 p.m. -17°C. Wind NW, blustery.
Ice cube melting on the floor inside.*

Algoma stood outside Club Rebar, her scarf wrapped around her head like a turban. She pulled Barry out of her purse. She felt bad that Gaetan couldn't see her using it. It was the first thing he'd given her in a long time. She took a long drink of gin and coughed. The clear liquid burned her throat. Juniper berries. Like the bushes her father had asked her to stomp on when she was little, so that she could flush out the hares hiding beneath.

"Jump harder," he had yelled, holding his shotgun loose in his hand, "they don't even know you're knocking yet!"

Out of breath, Algoma had jumped up and down on the springy bush like it was a trampoline until he'd said stop. By the end of her stomping session, her socks were threaded with tiny needles that tortured her ankles for the rest of the day. But it didn't matter; she'd liked pleasing her father more than anything else. Every hare she'd flushed out had made her father love her more, she was sure of it, and would give her a leg up on Bay.

Algoma accidentally spilled some of the gin on her jacket. She'd only eaten a piece of toast earlier that day. Too tired to cook, she'd eaten whatever was easiest. Her brain felt gin-soaked—top-heavy—like she would tip over any minute. She leaned over and looked at her heavy winter boots and whispered, "Thank you." If drinking worked for Gaetan, maybe it would work for her, too. He seemed numb all the time and that was beginning to appeal to Algoma.

Even though she was the only one outside amidst the cigarette butts, she tried to look sober, focused. Through the thin walls, she could hear music, an occasional laugh, a shriek.

Times when she found the empty house unbearable—Ferd staying with one of her sisters or a friend and Gaetan working—she went to the Club. She rarely spoke to Gaetan while he was working, but she enjoyed his presence. The mutual silence. She liked the bar, which was little more than a tool shed with a pool table and a battered dart board. Seated at the bar, she drank free glasses of ginger ale and ice; outside, she spiked her stomach with shots of alcohol that warmed her entire body.

"Where's Ferd?" Gaetan asked. He poured a beer for a large man with a red beard and a matching red Mohawk, a skidder operator who found his way to the bar six days out of seven. While the skidder tipped poorly, he tipped on every drink, which was more than most did.

Algoma stirred her ginger ale with a yellow plastic sword. She pushed the ice cubes beneath the surface and then released them so they floated back up.

"He's at Cen's."

Gaetan nodded. Algoma pushed her glass forward for a refill. She liked the hiss of the soda gun, how the ice cubes popped and fractured when he dropped them in the ginger ale.

Before the accident, Algoma sometimes asked one of her sisters to babysit the kids while she went to visit Gaetan at the Club. She'd enjoyed the women who leaned over the bar trying to seduce her husband, their heavy breasts sopping up old beer spill. She liked Gaetan's deep laugh. How he would flirt for tips, with which he would buy her new old things. She liked how it felt like it was just the two of them, if only for a few hours.

The house was silent. Algoma shuffled across the floor in her socks, knocking into things as she passed. When she accidentally knocked over the spider plant that sat beside the phone, she knew she'd drunk more from Barry than she'd realized. The trouble with a flask was that it was impossible to tell how much you'd had to drink until it was empty. She stumbled into her bedroom and peeled off her shirt and tossed it on the floor.

Half-dressed, she turned out the lights, lay down on her bed, and closed her eyes. A moment later, she woke with a start. She hadn't set her alarm for work. In the darkness, she reached over to turn on the alarm, instead upsetting the homemade humidifier—a soup bowl of water—that sat on her bedside table.

Algoma groaned and got out of bed to clean up the mess. She switched on the bedside lamp and grabbed the shirt she'd discarded earlier to sop up the water. When she moved the table to clean up what had spilled down the sides, she found another note. Two hundred and fifteen, she tallied in her head. She'd set bowls of water around the house to combat the dry winter air and to prevent the bloody noses she was prone to. Because of Ferd, the bowls had a new use. They were like small mailboxes stationed around the house and Algoma was the collector.

She tucked the note into the pocket of her robe that hung on the door and went back to bed. She'd read it in the morning. Ferd's narrative was slowly growing inside her like a vine, almost convincing her at times that Leo was alive. Almost asleep, Algoma heard someone turn on the television in the living room. She tried to listen in, but couldn't make out the voices or which show it was. Gaetan must have come home. He would be up half the night watching reruns until he fell asleep in his chair with his head slumped forward, legs spread wide open, melted slush pooling around his boots. She often found him still sleeping there in the morning, the television still on. He looked like a noble soldier asleep in his bunker. At least that's how she tried to picture him, not as a husband minutes away from waking up to another hangover.

Unable to sleep, Algoma switched on the lamp again and dug through her bedside table drawer for a pen and paper. Maybe if she wrote a letter to Ferd from Leo the letters would stop. I'm fine, Leo would say. Happy. Not coming home. Miss you.

She wrote a few sentences, stopped, crumpled the paper, tossed it onto the floor, and tried again. There was nothing in the parenting books she'd read that could have prepared her for this. They'd covered imaginary friends, but not the undead. Maybe she would write her own book, she thought, if she ever figured out what to do. She threw her pen to the floor and lay back down. The world spun dizzily around her. A better idea would come. Tomorrow, she would know what to do.

1:25 p.m. 23°C. Wind S, light.
A scattering of stones and eggs.

The killdeer shrieked and scuttled back and forth across the gravel. It let one wing drag and exposed a patch of dark orange feathers at its tail. An evolutionary trick. The bird was supposed to appear wounded to attract attention from predators. Leo touched the birthmark on his neck, wondered what it signaled to others. The bird's antics, he knew, were a distraction to keep his interest away from the nest, which must have been nearby. He saw which direction the bird was heading and looked the other way. There, several feet behind him, hidden among the stones, a clutch of pyriform eggs.

Leo picked up one of the speckled eggs and held it in his hand. It rolled around in a tight circle in his palm, a clock gone mad. He carefully dropped the egg into his coat pocket and turned to look at the mother who was screeching even louder now, her wing dragging on the ground, the other flapping madly. Leo wanted to see the bright orange feathers on its tail close up. He raised the barrel of his pellet gun.

"What are you holding?" Ferd asked. He leaned against the door frame of the room he shared with his brother.

Leo tried to hide the bird behind his back. "Nothing," he stuttered.

Ferd flushed red. Older by minutes, he felt he owned his brother. There were no secrets between them because he did not allow them, always crushing the spaces where they could hide.

"Show me," Ferd said. He took a step closer to Leo.

"Leave me alone." Leo held the dead bird tighter in his hand, pictured its feathers, the pattern beneath its wings. He could still picture it clearly in his mind.

Ferd launched into his brother, tackling Leo's waist.

"No," Leo cried out, his hand involuntarily releasing the bird. The killdeer's soft body bounced on the floor, its glassy dead eye staring at both of them. Leo scrambled to grab it.

"No secrets," Ferd said, his voice more of a growl. He grabbed at his brother's leg, trying to pull him back.

The battle lasted only seconds, both boys reaching for the dead plover, before Ferd held up the bird and smirked.

"We can't eat this shit," he said. He tossed the bird back onto the floor, its neck now twisted at a painful angle. "Put it in the garbage now. Do it before Dad sees what you're wasting shot on," he said. "Do it before I tell him."

Leo picked up the killdeer and ran to the basement. He pulled a cardboard shoebox out of the kindling bin and put the bird inside the box. A perfect fit. He ran his fingers along the bird's feathers, the black bands on its neck. Gently, he pulled one of the wings back as far as it would go to mimic the bird's last moments, the emergency. "Safe, safe, safe," he whispered, placing the box on the floor. He opened the freezer door. Standing on top of an overturned milk crate, he moved frozen packs of meat around until he reached the bottom of the freezer. He made a space large enough for the box, which he carefully lowered down and buried beneath his family's appetite.

Leo walked back upstairs and looked into his bedroom. Ferd was gone. He walked over and opened the second drawer of his dresser. The killdeer egg he'd stolen was tucked inside a nest he'd made out of an old T-shirt. He petted the egg lightly with his index finger and wondered how long it would be before he became a mother.

"Hungry?" Ferd asked when Leo walked into the house. Their parents were playing cards next door with the neighbours, spending a rare night together.

"Sure," Leo said, surprised by his brother's sudden generosity. He took off his coat and draped it over the banister.

"Eggs?" Ferd asked.

Leo nodded.

Ferd rummaged through the kitchen cupboards for his mother's cast iron pan, the one seasoned with years of side pork, bacon, beans, and stews. With thin, winter-pale arms he hauled the pan up onto the stove and lighted the burner with a wooden match from the Redbird box. He turned the flame up high.

"Toast with your eggs?" he asked.

"Brown, please," Leo said, glad his brother was trying to make up for their fight.

"Mom doesn't buy white bread, idiot." Ferd laughed.

"Lots of butter."

"Whatever."

"And salt."

"You'll have a heart attack and die."

"Pepper, too."

Leo sat at the kitchen table, a small round table that was used more for card playing than for eating. Ferd and Leo were allowed to sit at the card table so long as they understood that they would be treated the same as everyone else. A bad play would cost them a seat at the table, maybe even a quarter or two, but they would learn fast.

Ferd put two pieces of brown bread in the toaster and pressed the square black lever down until it clicked. He waited patiently until the butter in the pan started to sizzle before he cracked the egg open. Holding the egg high over the pan, he dug his grubby thumbs into the fissure he'd created and pulled the two halves apart. Leo could hear the hot sizzle of the egg bubbling and popping in the pan. His stomach grumbled.

"Watch the pan for a sec," Ferd said, and he disappeared down the hall and into the washroom. "I just need to do something," he called out from behind the door. A click. The lock turned.

After several minutes, he heard the scrape of his brother's chair as he stood up. From the washroom where he sat on top of the closed toilet seat lid, Ferd could hear the sharp metal ting of the spatula hitting the floor and the sound of his brother's bare feet running across the kitchen, the door slamming behind him. Windows rattled. He waited a few minutes before he slowly unlocked the bathroom door. When he was sure the coast was clear, he walked back into the kitchen and waved away the clouds of smoke and turned off the element.

The killdeer fetus was no longer clear as it had first been when he had cracked the small speckled egg open. Instead, it was now a charred lump in the middle of the pan, smoke rising in thin plumes to the ceiling. "No secrets," he said.

4:04 p.m. -22°C. Wind N, blustery.
Varnish flaking off the bar.

Gaetan walked into the Club and leaned up against the jukebox, which was affectionately nicknamed "the local band." He looked around. At night, when the bar was low lit with blue and red lights (after nine o'clock), it was not impossible to pretend you were somewhere else. Somewhere more glamorous than Le Pin. Creative lighting hid the paint peeling off the cement floor, the ancient Goldilocks curls of fly tape suspended from the ceiling, the stained fabric on the chairs. In the afternoon, the white lighting, however low the wattage, illuminated every crease and crevice in furniture and patron.

Two regulars sat at the bar. When Gaetan arrived, they looked over their shoulders and nodded at the arrival of the next shift. Gaetan knew them as well as he did his co-workers, maybe better. In the far corner were a half dozen men that Gaetan recognized, but couldn't place. It was like that every shift, a mix of predictable and unpredictable variables, never knowing what they'd result in: a quiet night, or calls to the cops.

Two hours into the shift, the argument began. The sound of fists coming down onto the table and raised voices made Gaetan look over, but he couldn't hear what they were saying over the sound of the music. Every twenty minutes, or so, the shortest of them, a sandy-haired man with a deep scar on his chin that split his beard in two, came up for a new pitcher of beer. With each round, the argument got louder.

On his fourth time up to the bar, the man said something to Gaetan other than his order.

"Sorry, what?" Gaetan asked, as he refilled the pitcher.

"I was asking if it was your kid that drowned in the Charles a while back."

Gaetan said nothing.

Drunk, the man pressed on. "No, it was you right? The guys and I were wondering. Jos doesn't think it's you."

One of his friends yelled out from the other side of the bar. "Is it him?"

"So, is it?" the man asked.

Hoping it would end the conversation surrounding his macabre celebrity, Gaetan said, "yes."

"Sorry, man. You are one unlucky sonofabitch."

"I think we're good. Go sit down," Gaetan said, and handed him the full pitcher.

The man made it halfway to his table before doubling back. "It's just, I don't get it. Didn't you teach him about the river ice? If it'd been my kid—"

"Enough," Gaetan said.

At least once a month, a scene like this played itself out in the bar. Like an amateur reporter, a patron would bumble his or her way through the questions they wanted to ask about Leo's death. In some ways, Gaetan missed those first few months after the accident when everyone was too afraid to ask anything of him, let alone questions surrounding how Leo had drowned, how it could have happened. Now that some time had passed, people in town felt they owned part of the story, part of him. It had become a fable to warn their kids about.

The man seemed to finally sense Gaetan's impatience

and shuffled back to his table.

Gaetan looked across the bar at the men. They were likely fathers themselves trying to grapple with fears about their own children. He was about to look away when he accidentally caught the eye of one of the men. At first, he thought the man looked guilty, but then realized it was a look of pity on his face. In that instant he knew they saw him as less of a father, less of a man.

He couldn't stay and endure their looks. Gaetan picked up the phone and called Daniel, another one of the bartenders and close friend.

"I'm not feeling well," Gaetan said into the receiver. "Thought I was fine, but I'm not. I want to go home. Can you cover me tonight?"

Daniel and his wife had recently separated; Gaetan knew he could use the money.

Twenty minutes later, Daniel walked into the bar. "Ready for duty, sir."

"Thanks," Gaetan said. He stood there looking at his friend for a moment too long. Daniel had two children. Did Daniel pity him, too?

"You okay?" Daniel asked. His cheeks were still bright red from the cold. "You want some water? A beer before you go?"

"I'm fine. I mean, I will be fine. Thanks for coming in," he stammered.

He walked out of the bar before Daniel could ask anymore questions. He knew his strengths; he was good at being silent, not at lying. As the door closed behind him, Gaetan heard the first bars of a song he'd heard played a thousand times before. *It's Only Make Believe*, an old Conway Twitty tune. Daniel must be having a bad day, too, he thought.

The man with the scar-split beard was smoking a joint in the parking lot. On seeing Gaetan, he tossed his roach onto the ground and stepped on it. His eyes were red and glazed. "You should have told him about the ice. If you'd have told him about the ice, you'd still have him," he said, and started to walk back into the bar.

Wordlessly, Gaetan walked over and buried his fist in the man's face. Surprised at what he'd done, he stumbled back, slipped, and fell onto the ground.

The man stood there, his bottom lip badly split, drops of blood falling onto the snow. He sucked his bottom lip and winced. "Because that'll bring him back, right?"

Home was a fifteen-minute walk away if Gaetan took his time. Tonight, he walked in the opposite direction toward the middle of town. He wasn't ready to go home. The last person he'd hit was his brother. And it used to be that the bar was his refuge. More and more, he was finding there was no safe place to be. No quiet.

Darkness came fast this time of year. The street lights flickered on over head, one after the other casting yellow circles of light on the snow-covered sidewalk. The roads were mostly empty. Although the weather was warmer than it had been in past weeks, the air was damp and cold. A cold that ate at Gaetan's bones, awakened old injuries. A shattered ankle from a slap shot in his teens. A dislocated elbow. A testy knee that threatened to give out entirely one day. He limped down the sidewalk, the snow squeaking under the soles of his boots. Hungry, Gaetan stepped into the closest convenience store and walked through the brightly lit aisles. He assessed the rows of shiny bags of chips and chose one.

He tossed the bag onto the front counter and used the last of his change to pay for it. The cashier, a teenage girl with a tiny daisy tattooed on her left earlobe, scraped his change off the counter and tossed it into the till without counting it.

"Have a nice day," she said, her voice monotone.

"Night," he said. "Have a good night."

The girl rolled her eyes and turned back to the small television she'd been watching.

Outside, Gaetan walked along the unshoveled sidewalk and ate his chips with his bare hands until it became too cold for him to do so. He tossed the half-finished bag into an empty garbage can that had been left at the curb and pulled on his cold leather gloves. As he walked he clenched and released his fists until the leather was warm and soft again.

Before he knew he was even heading there, Gaetan found himself standing in front of Bay's house. The lights were out except for the porch light. She wasn't home, which made him both relieved and dismayed, although he didn't know what he would have done had she been home. Bay's house was like many in town: a stacked duplex. Someone lived upstairs, and someone below. Gaetan had always wondered who lived on the top floor of her house, the person willing to navigate the narrow iron staircase in winter. He had a hard enough time staying upright on solid ground.

Gaetan and Algoma lived in one of the few detached houses in town, even if it was only a one-storey with a basement. When they had signed the papers, friends and family told them they were being ridiculous and extravagant for a newly married couple; however, the extra sacrifice had been worth it to not have someone living above them. For a few extra dollars on the mortgage every month, Gaetan didn't have to hear another family's footsteps in his head all day long, tramping on his thoughts, his sleep. If he was going to be kept awake by children, they would be his.

He focused on Bay's house again, which he thought could be nice if a few repairs were made: a fresh coat of paint, new windows, the porch replaced. The mailbox was hanging sideways from a single screw, Bay's mail stacked in front of the door. Gaetan walked toward the house and climbed the three steps to the porch. He turned and faced the street like it was his house, to see what Bay saw every day; it was a mirror image of her side of the street. He half expected to see a carbon copy of himself standing on the porch opposite, but there was no one.

Gaetan turned to the mailbox. He held up the unscrewed end to where it should be secured, and let it drop again. It swung back and forth like a pendulum clock. He stepped back and looked down for the missing screw and found it wedged in the crack between the house and porch. Using the Leatherman he kept in his coat pocket—a gift from Algoma for their first anniversary—he screwed the mailbox back in place and tightened the other screw. Satisfied with his repair job, he looked around the porch. What else could he fix? He absently kicked one of the banisters, but stopped when he heard steps coming up the sidewalk.

"Gaetan? What are you doing here?"

Bay stood at the bottom of the stairs. Her glossy dark brown hair was pulled up into a loose twist. She never wore hats, even if it was dark and there was no one to see her.

Gaetan stuttered something about being in the area.

Bay looked around. "Where's your car?"

"I walked."

"Ah," Bay smiled. "This is the third time in a month I've

found you 'walking.'"

"I fixed your mailbox," Gaetan said. "It was broken."

"It was and now it's not. Look at that. Thank you." Bay put her key in the lock. "Do you want to come in for a drink? You know, to say thanks?"

Gaetan shook his head. "No, that's alright. I should get to work. I'm feeling better."

"You weren't feeling well?" Bay asked, still holding the door open.

From where he stood, Gaetan could see Bay's couch at the end of the hallway, a pair of grey slippers tucked under the end table. He was beginning to sweat despite the cold. "Yes. No, everything's fine." He ran down the stairs, waved without turning around, and hurried down the street like he was running away from something.

Bay let the door close and walked down the porch stairs. From her walkway, she watched Gaetan appear and disappear as he passed under the streetlights, like a flickering night light on the verge of burning out.

Algoma pulled into the driveway, car full of groceries, and wrinkled her nose. There was a six-pack of beer sitting in the snow on the porch. She parked, got out of the car, and walked toward the bottles. A white envelope was taped to the cardboard handle, Gaetan written on it in a loose feminine handwriting she immediately recognized. She ripped the envelope open and read the card: G. Now the mailman doesn't hate me anymore. Thank you. Feel free to paint the place next time you're around. There's dinner in it for you. B.

After a lifetime of knowing her sister, Algoma knew she could neither compete with nor deter Bay. It would only make things worse. All she could do was run interference and hope that her sister, as she almost always did, would grow bored and move on to the next thing.

Algoma stuffed the envelope and card into her coat pocket and picked up the six-pack. The beer bottles were an imported brand she didn't recognize. Green bottles that clanked as she carried them into the backyard where she hid them behind the cord of wood behind the shed. By the time Gaetan found the beer, the bottles would be frozen and broken, shards of glass buried in the snow.

6:01 p.m. -22°C. No wind.
Furnace rattling like fluid-filled lungs.

"We're going camping. Pack up."

"Um, Mom. It's minus a million outside."

"Pack up."

It was late Friday afternoon and Ferd thought his mother had finally lost it.

"Dad!" he yelled. "Mom says we're going camping. You know how to build an igloo?" He thought it was joke, but would find out soon that it was not.

Outside, snow was piled up high in huge drifts on either side of the street, every corner capped with a cold white pyramid. The details of the neighbourhood had been gradually erased as snow had risen like water over curbs, planters, and porches. Toys that had been left out on the lawn before the first major snowfall would sit beneath the weight of a season until spring released them into the hands of children who had outgrown them.

The week before, instead of going to gym, Ferd's class had been made to watch several snow safety videos. Even the most innocent act had been made lethal. Snowballs harboured slivers of ice and broken glass that could take your eye out. Go sledding and find yourself impaled by a tree branch. Build a snow fort and it could collapse and suffocate you. Play outside too long and a doctor would have to amputate your cold-blackened toes. Ferd had had nightmares for days after watching a dramatization of a snowplow clipping the legs off a dummy dressed in dark green snow pants like his own. He could not get the blue flashing light or the sound of the metal scraping along asphalt and ice out of his head.

"You go camping. I'll just stay here and guard the house," Ferd said.

Gaetan walked out of the bedroom. It was his day off. "What's this about camping?" he asked. He rubbed his sleep-crusted eyes with the palms of his hands.

"We're going camping. Pack up what you need. Bring a book, some extra socks."

"Algoma. Hon. There's at least three feet of snow out there." He looked outside. It was snowing again, large fat flakes. She'd finally snapped, he thought with a degree of relief. It was like an elastic band that had been aimed at his face for months had finally been released.

"We're not going 'out there,'" she said. A small smile played across her lips. "We're camping here. In the basement. Just like before."

Gaetan leaned against the side of the fridge. He watched his wife as she packed an odd assortment of food into an open cooler. Jars of pickles and beets, oatmeal, Cheez Whiz, sugar, tinned crab, and canned sausages. She reached blindly into the cupboards and packed whatever she pulled out.

She sing-songed everything she said. "Pack up, pack up, pack up."

Gaetan felt the hairs on the back of his neck stand up. "Why am I going to 'camp' in the basement, when I can sleep in my own bed, eat at my own table?"

"You just are," she said. Her eyes were flat now, her lips tightly pursed together.

Gaetan backed away from her slowly, as he would from a

badger, allowing her a wide berth.

Worried that her family was slowly and irreversibly falling apart, Algoma knew she needed a plan to pull them back together, to learn to be a family of three now, not four anymore. The dynamic now shifted and reduced.

They had always camped together. Every summer, the Beaudoins camped at provincial parks or on crown land. They spent weekends and extended vacations with dirt under their fingernails, their hands calloused from canoeing and kayaking, mouths hungry for more fire-split hotdogs. She would draw on those rituals to bring her family back together and the best part was that they wouldn't even have to leave the house this time.

Once Algoma had packed all the essentials, she consulted her checklist. Tent. Water purifier. Hatchet. Cast iron pan. Sleeping bags. A deck of cards. Candle lantern. Flashlight. Batteries. Flint. Every item checked off with erasable marker on her laminated list. The ghost checks of past trips had stained the plastic. Nothing was ever entirely gone.

The gear was packed into three large canvas backpacks, the kind meant for mountaineering, not weekend car-camping excursions. The smallest of the three packs was meant for Ferd, although it was still large enough to topple him. Every kind of weather had been accounted for, even though they were going to remain indoors. The bags were stuffed with raincoats, sweaters, and shorts. Long johns, bathing suits, and fishing hats. This time, she was prepared.

Gaetan reappeared behind her, holding an unopened beer bottle like a flashlight, pointing it at the packed bags.

"What, are we going to toast marshmallows in the basement or something?"

Algoma held three peeled sticks in one hand as she walked down the basement stairs, Gaetan and Ferd single file behind her.

"We're here!"

She threw down her pack and set about untying the tent from the bottom of it. "Ferd, you start putting your tent up. Get your dad to help you if you need to," she said.

Gaetan was already digging through the cooler, between the cans of tuna and frozen bag of peas, for something good to eat and finding nothing. "I have to work tomorrow. How does that fit into your camping schedule?"

Algoma struggled with a clasp. "You'll just come back to the site after work."

"It's cold down here."

"I turned the furnace off."

"What? The pipes will freeze."

"Build a fire if you're going to complain," she said, pointing at the wood stove.

Gaetan sighed and gave in. It was easier. He dug through the kindling bin for some good starter sticks.

"Why don't you show Ferd how to build a fire?" Algoma asked. She was working on the second clasp now.

Ferd already knew how, but Gaetan, again, agreed. It felt like Algoma was sleepwalking and that waking her could be dangerous. He nodded. "Sure. Get over here, kid."

Gaetan opened the heavy cast iron door of the wood stove and raked out the mountains of ash he'd meant to remove last week, or the week before, he couldn't remember. Inside, he made a small tepee out of the kindling. "Get me some newspaper," he said, his hand stretched out, waiting.

Ferd grabbed the business section from the kindling pile, pulled off the first sheet, and crumpled it in his hands.

"No. Not like that. Remember? We shred the paper, we don't crumple it." Gaetan grabbed the crumpled ball out of Ferd's hands and flattened it out on the floor. He folded the newspaper in half and tore off pieces in long thin strips that curled up at the ends and then threaded the paper curls through his kindling tepee.

"And you keep one for yourself to get the fire going." Gaetan held a limp strip of newspaper and lit the bottom with his lighter. He quickly tossed the lit paper onto the tepee, where the other paper and tinder caught flame. "Now blow on it."

Ferd crouched down in front of the small flame and blew on it until he was dizzy and ready to pass out. The smallest pieces of kindling caught fire first, then the larger ones. Once the fire was burning steadily, Gaetan added a quartered birch log to the mix. The white bark sizzled and crackled like chicken skin.

By the time the fire was roaring, Algoma had finished setting up the main tent, an old canvas military affair that took up half of the basement. The other tent, which had not been used since Leo's accident, was a newer piece of camp architecture. It was bright blue, complete with screened windows, proper venting, and a vestibule, so the boys would not have to bring their dirty shoes inside. A feature that had cinched the purchase for Algoma.

While Gaetan and Ferd admired their fire and tried to warm up in the steadily cooling basement, Algoma unpacked the camp cutlery and plastic plates, arranging them carefully on a beach towel she'd set out on the carpet.

"I need a nice low fire, boys," she said. "We're making chili."

She pulled out two ancient cans of Manwich that Ferd

recognized from the cupboard. He was sure the cans had been in the there since before he was born, maybe even before his parents had been born. When his father had tried to throw the cans out last year, Algoma had resisted. "It's emergency food," she'd said, holding the cans to her chest, refusing to acknowledge the well-passed expiry dates. "It's still good. I know it. Those dates are just to get you to buy more. It's marketing. A scam."

Ferd looked at the tins. Maybe this was the emergency she'd been talking about.

Just as they sat down to their dinner, there was a knock at the side door.

Gaetan stood up to answer it; however, Algoma stared him into submission. He sat back down and spooned another mouthful of metallic-tasting food into his mouth. They sat in silence for a few moments. The doorbell rang next.

"Are we going to get it?" Ferd asked, looking back and forth between his parents. Algoma shook her head and Gaetan shook his, but not in response to Ferd's question, rather at the entire situation. He felt defeated, things were out of control. He'd been sure that Algoma wouldn't be able to maintain the game through dinner, but she had.

The visitor knocked on the door one more time and then there was silence.

"There," said Algoma. "That's better."

She smiled and gathered the dishes to wash them in the laundry tub.

The basement was gloomy, darkness falling fast. Ferd looked up and saw the light bulbs had been removed from the light fixtures. When had she done that? He shrugged his shoulders and picked up a flashlight and went into the wood room. Algoma whistled in the background as she washed the dinner dishes. Ferd could already taste gritty detergent on his tongue.

At the end of the third day, Sunday, Algoma stood over the wood stove as she prepared a dinner of pancake and Vienna sausage sandwiches.

"You will eat it," she said to Ferd when he whined about what was for dinner. "Pancakes are bread and Viennas are meat. It's just like a regular sandwich. Don't act spoiled."

Ferd sat cross-legged in the vestibule of his tent with the screen zipped up. He stared at his mother, bored holes into the back of her skull. He was tired of this game—the bizarre meals, endless games of cards, and exercise sessions. He wanted to go upstairs, open the fridge, and have a real meal. He wanted French fries and hunks of marble cheese. He didn't even need to slice the cheese, he'd just eat it out of the package. The whole thing. All of it in one shot. Anything but this.

"I think there's meat in the fridge upstairs," Ferd suggested. "It's just—"

"It's just what, Ferdinand?" she said without looking at him. "It's just that you want to eat old lunch meat that needs to be thrown out? You'll get botulism."

Ferd looked at the clock, but it read, as it had since they had arrived in the basement, three o'clock. Either it had died, or his mother had taken out the batteries, so she could control time as well. I wish I could take the batteries out of you, Ferd thought.

Algoma turned and proudly handed Ferd a plastic plate with three blackened Vienna sausages sandwiched between two enormous undercooked pancakes.

"Do you want mustard with that?"

Ferd could barely watch his mother eat her "sandwich." She used a plastic knife and fork to cut it into small squares. Her face was soft and relaxed. She seemed happy, at least. That was something.

When she wasn't looking, Ferd slid his plate into his tent. He was looking forward to going to sleep soon, which was a first. By the time he went to sleep and woke up again, his dad would be home. If Ferd was lucky, Gaetan would have brought treats—jerky, peanuts, and pop—back with him, in secret, as he'd promised the night before. Real food, not the patchwork quilt of canned food and dry goods his mother kept pairing together with unbearable enthusiasm.

With every meal they ate in the basement, the recipes got worse. More inventive. Ferd opened up the lid of the cooler to see what was left: one can of flaked tuna, a milk chocolate bar, a single package of Saltine crackers, mustard, marshmallows, and a can of sardines. He shuddered thinking about tomorrow's breakfast. Maybe he would make a break for it during the night.

The next morning, Ferd woke with his face pressed into his cold leftover pancake and Vienna sausage sandwich. He fisted the dried mustard off his cheek, scraped bits of sausage off his neck, and tossed his plate, complete with destroyed leftovers, onto the carpet outside the tent. He knew what the day held already. It would start with jogging on the spot for half an hour and then move on to playing cards, which lasted until lunch.

He lay back down and wondered when this would be over. His father had told him that it would only be a few days and that, on the other side, his mother would be better, more capable. Whatever that meant. Gaetan had made Ferd promise that he would not go upstairs for anything—the illusion had to be maintained—however, with all his writing supplies up in the living room, it was difficult. It had been days since he'd written to Leo. How would he explain that he was being held hostage by their own mother and her terrible cooking? Every hour that passed put more distance between him and his brother. Without the letters to keep them tethered to one another, there was only cold, empty space.

Ferd looked forward to school. The water fountain beside the gymnasium. The janitor's sink in the utility closet. The stream in the woods behind the school, even though it would be buried under the snow. That it was all there comforted him.

Ferd sat still and listened. Everything was quiet except for the buzz saw of his father's snoring. His parents were still asleep. He quietly unzipped his tent and crawled outside. Beside his door, he found the dinner he'd tossed out and a plastic bag his father had dropped off when he'd returned home in the early hours.

"Awesome," he whispered. Ferd tore the bag open and chewed on a piece of jerky that was inside. He would wait until later to open the can of pop, in case the sound woke his parents. It was still dark outside, still early. He reached for the tin of peanuts, ripped off the lid, and ate them a handful at a time.

When the family had gone camping for real—packing up the car and driving for hours on end—Ferd and Leo had always been the first ones up. They liked to make breakfast, thinking their parents couldn't hear their stage-whispered instructions to each other. The memory gave Ferd an idea. He pulled the Saltines, chocolate, and marshmallows out of the cooler and unwrapped the previous night's horrifying leftovers, so that he could use the tinfoil.

Using the top of the cooler as a counter, Ferd assembled a half dozen improvised S'mores. He carefully placed the squares on the tinfoil, which now smelled like Vienna sausages, and wrapped it up carefully. Within minutes, he was able to coax the embers in the wood stove into a roaring fire. He touched the top of the stove to test the heat and burnt his finger.

He yelped and sucked on his finger, sure he'd woken up his parents, but they remained asleep.

Ferd sucked on his burnt finger and tossed the tinfoil package on top of the stove. He'd never made S'mores before, only seen them on television. He estimated that it would take about ten minutes for the chocolate to melt. By the time he took the packet off the stove, everything inside had melted into a chocolate soup. Undeterred, he carefully opened the tinfoil packet and scraped the melted chocolate, marshmallow, and burnt and broken crackers into a plastic bowl. He added two spoons and stood at the front of his parent's tent and yelled: "Breakfast!"

A smudge of chocolate still at the corner of her mouth, Algoma waved to Ferd as he ran to school. He didn't look back once. She went back downstairs to where Gaetan was still sleeping in the tent, his sleeping bag pulled up to his chin.

"Gae, go sleep in your bed," she said. "Go upstairs. Everything is good. It's all good. Everything will be all right."

FEBRUARY

4:47 p.m. -12°C. Dead calm.
Mannequin dressed in tuque and wedding dress.

Sometimes when Ferd skipped school, he went to his mother's work. She never faulted him for wanting her company, even if it was a school day. He could learn in the classroom, or he could learn on the floor. It didn't matter to her. When the school secretary called about his absences, Algoma always covered for him.

"He had an appointment. You must have lost the note. Look again."

She performed for the secretary so often that she began to believe her own stories. And soon, the secretary stopped calling.

While Algoma folded a pile of newly donated sweaters and Sandra was at the cash register, Ferd hid inside the warm centre of a circular clothing rack, a small woollen world all to himself. Some days, like today, he imagined the clothing racks were portals. He sat in the middle, imagined new galaxies, far-flung constellations. He could hear shoppers rifling through the clothes, circling like great fleshy spaceships flying around him, looking for the right size or a particular colour. When a woman's hand pierced the cotton barrier of his world, he imagined it was Leo's reaching out to him, so he grabbed it. The woman screamed and wrenched her hand free and he was alone again.

Ferd hadn't even made it out the door that morning before his mother had read his face.

"If you work on your homework, you can come to The Shop," she'd said. "I'll call in for you. A doctor's appointment."

"You told them I had one last week."

"Dentist, then."

The women who worked at The Shop, four in total, one or two at any given time, patted Ferd's head whenever they passed by him. At The Shop, he had a handful of mothers, someone to turn to at every corner. Warm waists and strong hands. The store was the only place he let people hug him.

Ferd exited the clothing rack. The woman whose hand he'd grabbed was now trying something on in the change room. The thin curtain billowed every time she moved, exposing flashes of pale skin. He tried not to look at her bare feet on the stiff carpet. The sight, for some reason, always made him sad. The vulnerability, the clothing strewn on the floor.

He made a beeline for the housewares section at the back of the store. The shelves were full of pots and pans and jam jars filled with cutlery. There were baskets of linens, a cluster of stand-up fans, and a couch with a $50 tag pinned to one of the cushions. He walked through the layers of drapes that hung from the ceiling, hands dragging along the smooth fabric. They were like flags in a medieval castle, retired jersey numbers hung from the roof of a hockey area, a poorly built maze.

The drapes still swaying behind him, Ferd picked up an old space heater from one of the shelves. He set it on the ground and plugged it into an outlet in the wall. He sat down and positioned the heater in front of him, turning both the heat and fan on high, and enjoyed the blast of a false summer breeze. The sound of the curtains rustling behind him was reminiscent of trees at the height of summer, or the sound of running water. He thought he could hear Leo speaking to him from across the river. He closed his eyes and tried to listen harder to make out the words, but nothing came.

The blinds drawn and the doors shut and locked, The Shop was bathed in complete darkness, a hermetic seal that would not be cracked until early morning by the key holder. The store was silent except for the creaks and rattles of an old building that was perpetually shifting, expanding, and contracting with the seasons. Its wear was beginning to show—cracked windows, loose floorboards, crumbling brick.

Outside, the temperature had plummeted. Ghostly roads coated in salt dust. Hoar frost crept along the windows, a slow takeover that only stopped when the sun rose, and even then, only a bit. What happened next would later seem like the building was trying to take back the night, bring a touch of August to the middle of winter.

A corner of one of the curtains in housewares touched the exposed element of the space heater and burst into flames. Fire, slick like water, travelled up the curtains and walls. Soon, a stratus cloud of fire spread across the ceiling. Just as quickly, the flames moved back downward, inward. They licked the hems of old skirts with outdated hemlines, blouses with faint perspiration stains in the armpits, ancient receipts in ownerless pockets.

The smoke alarm remained mute, its batteries having been removed months ago after the toaster oven kept setting it off.

"Need some good-goddamned quiet around here once in a while," Josie had said as she tossed the batteries into the junk drawer.

From a distance, the fire in The Shop's windows looked comforting and familiar. A cottage with fresh logs thrown in the fireplace. It was only when part of the roof caved in that someone noticed. A drunk reluctantly used his second to last quarter to call it in. The next morning, during a retelling of the story, he'd learn he could have made the call for free. The waste ate at his heart for days, everything seeming a single quarter out of reach.

When the firefighters arrived, they stood still for a moment, mesmerized by the sheer height of the flames. There was nothing to save. The brigade trained its hoses on the pulsating heart of the blaze for hours until it was only embers beneath a ruckus of awkward stacking and black smoke rising into pale morning.

Gaetan sniffed the air. The cigarette smoke in the bar was tinged with something heavier. Wood smoke mixed with the smell of burnt wires, plastic. The bar was quiet, almost empty. He put down what he was reading and stepped outside into the bitter February cold. Toward the north, he saw it—a subtle orange glow in the distance. He hoped it was an empty building and not a house. He crossed himself and went back inside.

Sitting on a stool behind the bar, he picked up the note he'd been reading. It was one of Ferd's. After reading it several more times, he put it back in the cigar box with the others. There were dozens, all stiff with water damage, brittle. He wished he could get his hands on the rest, the ones his wife was working so hard to keep from him, but there was never an opportunity, or he forgot when there was.

Before discovering that Algoma had been keeping

something from him, Gaetan thought her incapable of secrets, mistaking her for having no inner life. Yet, once he knew, he never let on that he did, wanting to see how far she would take her secret and what would finally make her show him the notes she'd collected. He approached her like the animals he hunted—watching from a safe distance, learning what he needed to know for future use when the time was right.

But the time, it seemed, was never right. He realized he'd missed the moment his wife had changed, when she'd doubled back. He'd followed one person and found himself face-to-face with someone he no longer recognized.

In the distance, sirens wailed. The smell of fire was thick in the air, giving rise in Gaetan the most basic instinct: flight.

7:15 a.m. -13°C. Wind N, light.
A spire of black smoke rising from the horizon.

The morning after The Shop burned down, no one called Algoma to tell her that her sorting services were not needed that day. As she drove toward work, the morning still winter dark, the acrid scent of smoke bit at her nostrils even before she could see what had happened. Gut seized with worry, she drove faster, blowing through stop signs until she could go no further. The roads surrounding The Shop were blocked off by yellow metal barricades the police had erected. Algoma abandoned her car in the middle of the road and walked toward The Shop. She approached the scene almost reluctantly, as if her actions could change what had happened.

The turn-of-the-century building—three storeys of stately red brick and concrete mouldings—was now unrecognizable. It was almost impossible to believe that only yesterday the building had held warmth and a loose degree of order. The far right third of the building, the section where The Shop had been, had collapsed entirely. The rest of the building, including Café Drummond, was still standing, but the windows were charred mouths of soot flanked by long, jagged teeth of ice. Algoma swore she could smell burnt coffee beans. The roof was missing, presumably incinerated, so that the morning sky was visible through the windows on the third floor.

"Almost pretty," she said, in a daze.

The building and most of the debris and surrounding sidewalk were covered in a layer of ice topped by the fresh water the firefighters poured onto the remaining hot spots. The water slid cleanly over the already formed ice, hardening at the edges. A crystalline lava.

Algoma watched a firefighter—indistinguishable from the others dressed in orange-and-yellow gear—spray a steady stream of water into a heap of blackened lumber that was still smoking. Tired, he knelt down on the hose to keep it in place, the thick brass nozzle propped up on a brick, the spray arcing over the mess.

Her lunch, the leftovers she had planned to eat again today, was now irreversibly overcooked and buried under rubble. She couldn't believe that at a time like this, she was thinking about her Tupperware. Algoma wiped off the cold mist of water that coated her face. A second fire hose was spraying water down from a crane high above the scene.

Where were her coworkers? Where was Josie? The street was surprisingly empty of onlookers. The only non-emergency services people on site were a handful of children who should have been in school. Algoma looked at them and shivered. She'd never liked children's attraction to devastation. They looked almost excited by the wreckage. Their wide, curious faces made her think of her son. Ferd. She had to see him.

"He has an appointment. I need to take him now," Algoma said, tapping her nails impatiently on the school secretary's desk.

The secretary, a woman of indeterminate age with orange-peel skin and darkly drawn eyebrows, shuffled nervously through the papers in her desk. "It's got to be—" she said.

"Forget it, I'll look myself." Algoma took off down the hallway in search of Ferd's classroom.

The secretary clipped along awkwardly after her in her too-tight skirt. "Mrs. Beaudoin, you need to sign in. I need a record for my files."

Algoma quickly found Ferd's classroom and opened the door with more force than needed, the doorknob denting the wall.

Ferd's teacher stopped in the middle of writing a math equation on the chalkboard. "Can I help you?"

The students in the classroom stared at Algoma who gripped the door frame with hard, bloodless fingers. Her hair was a fury around her small, tight face, and her denim skirt and wool jacket were still wet from the mist from the fire hoses. It was as if she had risen from the river to claim her sole remaining son. Or at least that would be the story that was passed from child to child until it had reached every parent in town by dinnertime.

"Ferd?" Algoma looked blindly around the classroom for her son. "Come here. Ferd, where are you? Stand up."

Her eyes settled on the empty desk in the back row.

Ms. Prevost looked at the desk. "He's not here," she said, slowly putting the piece of chalk down onto the ledge. "He left this morning."

"Yes, yes, he left this morning for school," Algoma said. "Where is he? In the washroom? Where is it? Show me. I'll go get him myself."

"Ferdinand came in this morning with a note that said he had a doctor's appointment. It was signed by you." Ms. Prevost pulled a piece of paper from her desk and handed it to Algoma who did not make an attempt to take it.

"He left an hour ago."

Algoma's face softened like a dam compromised, its mortar rotting, giving way. Her shoulders slumped and she left the teacher and secretary to calm the disrupted class, which was already spreading rumours about what had happened to Ferd.

At home, Algoma nervously thumbed the buttons on her stove, trying to reset the clock. For the past year, every clock in the house had displayed different times. The digital numbers of the alarm clock in the bedroom read 4:23 p.m. The black and white twelve-hour clock in the living room said noon or midnight, she couldn't be sure which. Her watch, dead for weeks on her wrist, had stopped at 3:01, yet she still wore it for the familiar weight on her wrist. The only clock she trusted was the ornamental sundial in the back yard, however approximate its timing was, but it was buried under snow.

She felt her life being taken from her, flash frozen and slowly melting away as the months dragged on. She could no longer remember the small differences between her twins. Which one wouldn't eat cheddar cheese, only marble. Who only liked to sleep with flannel sheets. Who had had chicken pox first, only days before the other. Which one had a mole behind his right ear. She only saw blank skin and Leo's birthmark. Her mind had amalgamated their identical bodies into one boy; blurry vision that had spontaneously cleared one cold winter evening last year.

Algoma wondered who or what she would lose next. Maybe she had already lost more things, small things that she hadn't noticed yet. How long would she be able to keep what she had left. She patted down her clothing for missing coins, pins, anything. Inventory, she thought. I should take inventory. But she didn't know where to begin or where the starting line was. Her breath was short and shallow.

She hadn't looked in on her husband that morning. It was late afternoon now. The bedroom door closed. Where was he now? The bar. It was the one thing she was sure of.

But where was Ferd?

Algoma considered calling Gaetan, but stopped short. What did it matter if he learned now, or a few hours from now, that their second income had literally gone up in smoke and that their son—their sole remaining child—was missing.

She promised herself that Ferd would turn up soon. The odds were in her favour. Who loses two sons? But then she thought of the muddied and bloodied faces of the mothers she saw on the evening news, women from war-torn countries who had lost everything. Their livelihoods, husbands, homes, children: gone. They had probably expected to keep something, but their eyes held nothing, and their arms, no one.

In the days after Leo's drowning, Algoma had not been able to turn on the television even though she would have welcomed the distraction. Images of her own tear-streaked face on the fourteen-inch screen were too much for her to bear. The sound of her own sobbing broadcast through thousands of television sets, an aural house of mirrors.

Media from southern Quebec and even Ontario had shown up in Le Pin. They loved the angle: twins. Reporters appeared on the playground at the school and tried to interview Ferd, who remained mute in front of the camera. He looked confused, they thought, at the suggestion that his brother was dead.

A day after the accident, Algoma turned off the television, unplugged it, and faced it toward the wall where its single, glassy eye could not stare at her anymore. Yet, from morning until night she scoured the newspapers for articles about the incident, hoping to find new details, something she'd missed, or had not been told. If she could find a discrepancy, there was hope. Body not recovered became her mantra.

"He's gone," Gaetan said, slumped on the couch, knees up to his chin. "You have to understand that. He's gone."

"There's no body," Algoma said.

"Ferd saw him go through the ice."

"It was dark and he was far away. He's young. He couldn't have known what he was seeing."

"Leo's gone."

"There's no body. There was no body."

For weeks, she received phone calls from strangers who said they'd seen Leo playing on the north side of town, or playing with other children at the hill, or even skating on the edge of the river. Each phone call sparked hope in Algoma, but in each instance, she would later discover that it had only been Ferd going about as the living do. After that, the phone was unplugged, too.

In the beginning, Algoma's sisters had come over every day. The house was filled with the voices of women and the smell of sautéed onions, great pots of soup bubbling on the elements. They'd tried to fill the empty space with food and company; however, Algoma shrank from their efforts and would not eat their offerings. Her body grew thin and frail until she did little more than sit in the living room and stare out the window. Her sisters' visits were eventually replaced with concerned phone calls and messages, which she mostly ignored, and then nothing at all.

Gaetan began to request extra shifts at the Club and stayed later than he was scheduled. In the early hours, he sometimes found himself on the other side of the bar, his hands cupped around a glass of golden liquid as the cleaner passed through with a wet mop the colour of an overcast sky. Ferd found his way to the dinner tables of other families who felt it was their duty to care for him during the Beaudoins' time of need. The mothers conferred with one another about his visits.

"He seemed quiet."

"Wouldn't you be? His mother losing her mind?"

"You would, too. He'll... they'll all be fine."

"I'm just saying keep him away from the river."

"Keep her away from the river."

"Don't even—"

"Rudy said he saw him at the river, just talking to the ice like it was nothing. Nothing at all."

"The poor mother."

The women began to pack extra treats in their children's lunch bags.

Ferd emerged from the woods to find morning recess in full swing. From a safe distance, he watched a pack of students rampage across the paved yard, wholly engrossed in a game of their own making. Two teachers, bundled in sober winter coats and thick knit scarves, patrolled the grounds.

To Ferd, humans were no different from animals. Here, two adult females watched over the juveniles in an organized attempt to keep them safe. The children were careless and curious, unable to understand the potential for disaster that existed beyond the perimeter of the schoolyard or even within it.

Using language he remembered from one of his nature guides, Ferd narrated the scene. "The two adult females do everything they can to ensure the children make it to adulthood, but not all will. At least several will succumb to illness or accident within the first ten years of their lives; however, as a result of the reduced numbers, the remaining children will receive more food and attention, thus increasing their chance of survival and reproduction."

Abruptly, the wind changed, and along with it several students lifted their heads, sniffed the air. Ferd lifted his. Smoke. The teachers followed suit and stared into the wind. Without thinking, Ferd walked off school property and toward the smell. The longer he walked, the stronger it became. Impatient, he ran the rest of the way until finally, breathlessly, he reached the source of the smoke. His heart was beating fast and furiously. He was already thinking about who he'd tell first and how he would tell it. It was like finding a pot of gold until he realized it was his mother's store. He froze and noticed the cold for the first time that day.

A dozen people were clustered behind the sagging yellow caution tape, as if waiting for a second fire to start, or for someone to emerge from the ashes. A single manifestation of everything lost. Those who had lost something, like Josie, stayed away. There was nothing to salvage or to gain from staring at the remains. She was probably already out collecting what she thought she'd need next.

Ferd weaved through the small crowd until he reached the front. He tugged on the coat sleeve of an elderly woman with a Dowager's hump who stood there holding a dog leash, her ratty mutt seated beside her feet.

"Where's my mom?" He asked, his lips trembling.

The woman shook her head slowly, her paper-thin eyelids fluttering.

He spotted a police officer and ran to him. "Have you seen my mom?" He was shouting now. "My mom."

The police officer, a short man with tired but understanding eyes, rubbed the back of his neck. "Listen, I'm sure she's fine. Why don't you calm down a minute?"

"But she works there," Ferd said. He pointed at the collapsed building. "She worked today."

"And no one was hurt," the officer said. "No one was there when it happened. Why aren't you at school?"

"My mom."

The officer pushed his hat up high on his wide forehead and sighed. "Let's take you home." He guided Ferd to his cruiser. "I'm sure we can fix this. Where do you live?"

Through the living-room window, Algoma watched the police cruiser pull up in front of her house. She stood up from her chair and watched as the driver took his time to perfect his parking job. The cruiser moved back and forth several times before coming to a complete and perfect stop inches away from the curb. Algoma chewed her nails viciously. There was no place she could hide—no ditch deep enough, no culvert long enough to hold all she held close to her from the coming winds.

The red and white emergency lights turned off and the driver's door opened. An officer emerged and took off his hat and adjusted his duty belt. When he looked directly at the house, Algoma collapsed to the living room floor.

"Ma'am?" The police officer held the back of Algoma's head with one hand, her chin with the other. He gently shook her face. "Mrs. Beaudoin. Algoma Beaudoin. Wake up. Come on now. Time to get up." He patted her cheeks and her eyes winked open.

"Ferd. What happened to Ferd? How did it happen?" she asked, her face ashen.

"He's right here," the officer said. "He's sitting in the kitchen. See?"

Algoma, still lying on the floor, propped herself up and looked more closely at the officer, her eyes tiny, suspicious slits. "In the kitchen?"

"Yep, right there," the officer pointed. "Look for yourself."

Algoma looked over and Ferd waved. He was sitting at the kitchen table, his legs swinging back and forth. He was eating from a bag of chips, his T-shirt littered with crumbs. "Look Mom, new flavour." He held up the bag.

Before she could ask any more questions, the officer threaded one of his arms through hers and lifted her up. "I think you hit your head on the coffee table. You should get it looked at."

Algoma touched her head and felt a sticky liquid matting the back of her hair. She pulled her hand back and looked at her bloody fingers. The room shimmered like heat waves over hot summer asphalt. "Maybe I should sit down." She watched the police officer's mouth move but she could no longer hear the words.

"Do you wanna try a chip, Mom?" Ferd asked.

"I should drive you to the hospital, Ma'am. Do you remember what happened?" The officer reached for his radio to call it in.

Algoma's vision flickered like a neon light about to burn out. "I can't see." She slapped her face, her hands like moths to a porch light.

Three nurses sat behind the Plexiglas barricade of the triage like stone-faced poker players who gave away nothing to the patients who sat slumped before them. Health cards and driver's licenses were laid face up on the table. Histories and allergies exchanged. Next of kin noted. "Just a formality."

The endless carousel of ragged patients, nurses, doctors, and paramedics was dizzying, all set to a soundtrack of sputtering coughs, beeping machines and the automatic doors whooshing open and closed every minute. Gusts of cold air filled the room. Flu-fuelled bodies, like small furnaces, trying to stabilize the temperature, their cheeks and foreheads bright red coals.

Seated on a gurney, Algoma buttoned up her shirt and gathered her purse. Her vision had come back hours ago, only minutes after she'd arrived in the emergency room, but the hospital staff had still asked her to stay. The gash, they'd pointed out.

"I'm fine now," she'd argued, but they'd ignored her and carried on with their poking and prodding.

She disliked the stitches the most, the idea of being held together by thread. For most of the hospital visit, Ferd remained in the care of an elderly volunteer who told him the history of the hospital. She showed him what wing she'd had hip surgery and the room in which her husband had died.

"It's a short walk from birth to the good Lord. Mine's just taking a little longer than Matthew's," she said while fingering the ancient wedding ring looped through her silver necklace. When Algoma tried to offer the woman a few dollars for watching Ferd, the woman waved her away with thick, arthritic hands. "Nice to be of use."

Algoma had her hand on the door, ready to leave, when

she saw the officer seated in the waiting room. He was flipping through a copy of *Châtelaine*. She walked over to him. "Did you call my husband?"

Startled, he coughed nervously, folded the magazine shut, and tucked it under the side of his left thigh. "I, well, I called the bar. They said he was out, so I left a message." He looked apologetic, "out" meaning so many things.

"Oh," Algoma said. She looked at the floor and started to chew on an already ragged nail.

Ferd ran up to them and began to recite from the book he'd brought with him, *The Field Guide to Eastern Region Trees*: "Bear oak. Much-branched shrub or sometimes small tree with rounded crown." He looked at his mother and then the officer. Neither said anything.

The officer stood up and stretched uncomfortably under Algoma's stare. "Well, I guess I'll let you two be if everything is okay."

"Everything is okay," she lied. Her head throbbed.

The officer nodded and tucked in the back of his uniform shirt as he walked away. He stopped at the door and turned his head. "Yeah, I bet he's on his way. Don't worry. You've got that one to take care of you," he said, pointing at Ferd.

Algoma looked at Ferd. "I should be taking care of him."

The officer smiled tightly, nodded and walked out the door. Algoma took a final look around the waiting room. Maybe she hadn't noticed Gaetan. Maybe he was waiting for her, worried. The waiting room smelled like a mixture of hand sanitizer and rubber. Some of the illnesses and injuries were obvious—a poorly wrapped gash on a teenager's forearm or a woman with road rash across her cheek, bits of pebbles still embedded in her torn flesh—while others were hidden in the body. An elderly woman fast asleep, her thin face pressed up against the wall, a curl of grey hair tucked into her half-open mouth.

Algoma watched as a paramedic tried to skirt past a gurney being wheeled in from an ambulance outside. The patient on the gurney was large and drunk, her cheeks flushed, lips covered in dried spittle. She flailed about, the gurney threatening to collapse beneath her, as the hospital staff tried to take her vitals. She let out a blood-curdling howl. "You're killing me! I hate you!"

She looked around a final time. Every seat was filled, but no Gaetan.

Algoma turned to Ferd who was staring wide-eyed at the woman. "How did we get here?" she asked.

"Cop car," he stuttered.

The drunk woman kicked a paramedic in the face. Algoma winced.

"Oh. Well, I guess we should—"

"Take a cab? There's one outside, let's go."

Maybe he will take care of things, she thought.

A wheezing pregnant woman got out of the cab. While she paid the driver, Algoma and Ferd climbed into the back seat. There were only a few cabs in town. They were lucky to have seen one of them.

"Home. We need to go home now," she said, and placed her hands on the driver's shoulder like he was family.

Ferd was in the middle of explaining the difference between a black spruce and a red spruce when the cab pulled up in front of the house.

"Well, I'll be damned," said the cab driver as he leaned back to accept a ten-dollar bill from Algoma.

"Please keep the change."

He nodded appreciatively and smiled to reveal a set of

bright white teeth, too many, she thought, to be in one mouth. Like a shark.

The elderly woman woke up with a start and pulled the strand of hair out of her mouth.

She didn't know where she was until she saw the bank of nurses, parked gurneys. The hospital. She exhaled and her shoulders slackened. She touched her knee. It still hurt from where she'd spilled a pot of hot soup on it at lunch. It all came back to her.

She licked her chapped lips. Her mouth was unbearably dry, a complication of one of her medications, maybe all of them. She got out of her seat and set out to find a water fountain and immediately spotted one at the end of the hallway that connected the emergency room to the diabetes care clinic.

The fountain was not one of the flimsy metal ones the hospital had installed a few years back that always had "Out of Order" signs taped to front with strips of surgical tape. This one was white porcelain, the same kind they'd had years ago. She turned the silver knob and a stream of cold water arced from the spout. It was only when she leaned down to drink that she noticed the folded note—white paper on white porcelain—blocking the drain, water pooling over it. She picked it up. Att: Leo, it read on the outside in a child's handwriting.

In the background, the woman heard her name called by an impatient nurse. She dropped the note back into the fountain where it spun in circles as the water emptied down the drain.

Algoma rummaged through the stack of board games she

had stored in the front closet. The doctor who'd treated her at the hospital had suggested she stay up for the next twelve hours.

"Just in case," he'd said.

Worried that people would think she was cursed with bad luck, Algoma kept her hospital visit to herself and didn't call any of her sisters. When the doctor had asked if she had someone to stay with her, she had said "yes." With no word from Gaetan, she relied on Ferd to keep her awake.

Algoma looked back over her shoulder. "What game do you want to play?"

"All of them!" Ferd had forgotten why his mother had to stay up. He was just excited to be the centre of her attention.

After their fifth game of Sorry!—four to one for Ferd—and before they had set up the Monopoly board, Algoma called the bar again.

"Well, where did he go?" she asked, on the verge of tears again. Gaetan was always reachable at the bar.

Daniel mumbled incoherently on the other end. "Yeah, soon I'm sure..."

She pressed the receiver hard to her ear, so that she would be able to hear what he wasn't saying. In the kitchen, Ferd poured his fifth glass of Coke. The foam overflowed onto the counter and he wiped it up with his sleeve.

"He said he was getting some smokes or a sandwich or something. I'm sure everything's fine, Al." The line crackled.

"Sure, thanks," Algoma said, not believing a word of it. She'd packed Gaetan's lunch (ham on rye) and he'd picked up two packs of cigarettes the day before. There was nothing else he needed, she thought, no reason to leave the bar. Something had to be wrong. She pictured him face-down in a snowbank, the victim of a hit and run.

Nervous, Daniel rambled on: "You want to come over for a drink? It'll calm you down. You can bring the kid, too. It's no problem. Nobody'll say anything and you'll be here when Gaetan shows up... I mean gets back."

Algoma carefully replaced the receiver on the cradle. Ferd was counting out brightly coloured Monopoly money, carefully tucking each money pile under the lip of the board.

Algoma sat down at the table. "I want to be the old boot."

*7:12 a.m. -16°C. Winds from all directions, raw.
Broken tree branches littering the snow.*

Thin rays of winter sun filtered through the living room window and illuminated the vase of plastic tiger lilies on the coffee table. The bouquet with its sharp and vibrant petals looked like a nesting bird. Algoma's eyes fluttered open. Her head throbbed a deep bass line. She reached up to touch the source of her pain and felt a crisp railroad of stitches across the back of her head. Confused, she sat up too quickly and a constellation of black dots speckled her vision. She tried to stand, but a wave of nausea overwhelmed her. She reached for the worn arm of the couch for support.

Ferd crested the basement stairs and found his mother on her knees, cleaning something up beside the couch. The smell in the air unmistakable.

Hearing his footsteps, Algoma stood up. "Hi," she smiled weakly, wiping her mouth with the back of her shirtsleeve. "Just excuse me for a minute.Stay over there. Okay?" She scrubbed the carpet a little more and then disappeared into the washroom, her face green-tinged.

Ferd went to inspect the shoe rack beside the side door. His father's boots were not there.

Algoma came out of the washroom, her face now dishwater grey. "Breakfast in a minute?"

Ferd nodded, "Sure."

But first she went into Gaetan's bedroom. She stared at the bed. Its tightly tucked corners were unchanged from yesterday and the decorative pillows she'd placed there were still in their careful arrangement. She sat down on the bed.

The Shop. Ferd. Stitches. Gaetan.

It all came flooding back to her at once. Nausea rippled through her body. She could hear Ferd rummaging through the pots and pans in the kitchen. He had been allowed to make breakfast for himself since he was eight. Unlike Leo, Ferd was a careful cook; he made precise measurements and movements. He navigated the kitchen with confidence. Most importantly, he always remembered to turn off the stove.

Algoma worried about fire almost as much as she worried about money. Before she left the house each day, she checked to make sure each element on the stove was turned off, the coffee pot and toaster unplugged, and the iron cold to touch even if she had not used it in weeks. Every morning, she toured the house and touched each item: Off, off, off. On busy days when she forgot her ritual, she was consumed by worry that she would return to find her house in ruins, her life in ashes. She sometimes pictured the entire neighbourhood burnt down to the foundations. Every last photo album, house pet, and fifty-year-old recipe card incinerated by her forgetful hand. However deep her paranoia ran regarding her home, the same care did not extend to The Shop—that was Josie's domain; however, she would never forgive herself for not checking everything before she'd left the night of the fire. She was sure she must have left a light on, maybe the radio plugged in, a loose wire that had sparked the flame. Somehow, it had to be her fault. She felt responsible for every bad thing that happened around her.

Algoma's stomach growled. The house now smelled of fried bacon and fresh coffee. She listened to the muffled thump of dishes being placed on the tablecloth, the splash of coffee being poured.

The side door creaked open. Algoma stood up too quickly, nearly falling over from dizziness.

"Hello?" she said, louder than she'd intended. Her voice echoed inside her skull.

Cen and Steel stood in the doorway, identical in appearance and demeanour. Long and lean like goal posts.

"It's Aunt Cen and Aunt Steel," Ferd said, his face breaking into a big grin. He dropped the spatula he'd been holding onto the counter and ran to hug Cen.

"Well, hello there." Cen's voice was deep and soothing.

"We heard about your fall," Steel said to Algoma. She put a cotton bag overflowing with groceries on the kitchen table.

Algoma shot a look at Ferd, who then hid behind Cen.

Steel walked over to Algoma and gently touched the side of her youngest sister's head. "Really, I just don't understand how you—"

"—always manage to get in trouble, Al," Cen finished.

Algoma smiled half-heartedly at her sisters in a weak effort to offer them some sort of assurance that everything was alright. Steel had let her straight blonde hair grow long until it was a pale cape across her narrow back. Cen, in an effort to be different, had cut her hair into a sharply angled bob. Still, it did little to separate them. They could not change their features. They shared the same wide-set almond eyes that seemed to take in every detail, long delicate noses, wide generous mouths, and high foreheads with only a small map of wrinkles. Elizabethan, Cen had said after learning the word in her high school English class. After that, their father had referred to them as his Renaissance girls, which pleased them as much as it did him.

Steel unpacked the grocery bag, placing canned goods

down on the table. Algoma immediately recognized the ingredients for her favourite dish: mushroom and wild rice casserole. "How did you find out?" she asked, rolling a large white mushroom between her palms.

"This morning from Bay who heard it from—" Cen looked over at Ferd. She picked up a can of cream of mushroom soup. "If we had known, we would have been there for you, you know. You don't have to always do that kind of thing on your own."

Algoma rolled her eyes, an old habit that still surfaced when her two eldest sisters were around. Steel grabbed Algoma by her shoulders and turned her around, her hands delicately searching Algoma's body head to toe for injuries. "You're sure you're okay?"

"I'm fine," Algoma said. "Just a few stitches." She ran a finger along the crisp ridges. "Do you think I'll have to go back to get these taken out, or will they just dissolve?" She hoped they would dissolve and not have to be ripped out of her scalp like twine out of a roasted turkey. She couldn't remember what the doctor had said.

"At least it's not on your face," Steel said touching Algoma's cheek.

Algoma brushed her sister's hand away. "Stop touching me. I'm good. Really."

Amid the concerned chatter, Ferd had finished eating the bacon and eggs he had cooked, put his dishes into the sink, and gone to the basement to write. The eggs, bacon, and dry toast he'd made for his mother sat cold on the table.

Steel and Cen worked on the casserole in tandem. While one opened the cans, the other emptied them out into a bowl. While one washed the vegetables, the other chopped. An endless partnership. It was no wonder they'd never married, Algoma thought. There was no room between them for anyone else.

"Oh, we should be quiet," Cen stage whispered. "Gaetan's sleeping, right?"

All six sisters accompanied Algoma to file the missing persons report. They ascended the steps of the police station with their arms linked, a solid front.

"Just give it a couple more days," Algoma had begged, but her sisters ignored her, as they always did. "He'll turn up. He has to. He has kids... kid, a kid."

Inside the station, Cen pointed out the duty sergeant and guided Algoma to his desk. He looked up from his paperwork. Algoma studied his face. He looked like he hadn't slept in weeks, his face grey and wrinkled. Sloppy origami. In that moment she decided he wouldn't be able to help her and tried to walk away.

"No you don't," Cen said, blocking her way.

"Yes?" the officer asked, twirling a blue pen with his right hand, although his eyes conveyed a profound boredom.

Algoma began to arrange the things on his desk, something she did when she was nervous.

He grabbed the snow globe from her hand. "Yes?" he asked again, drawing out the word.

"Someone is missing," she said.

"Tell him who," Cen pushed.

"My husband."

After an hour, Algoma had provided the sergeant with all the information he needed—physical description, clothing, routines—and made him promise he would follow up on it.

"We'll do everything we can," he said, sounding unsure.

The Belanger sisters gone, he looked at the photo of Gaetan that Algoma had given him, with the promise that he would return it. The photo showed the missing man standing in two feet of snow. Peculiarly, he was holding a length of green hose in one hand and a rake in the other. It looked like he was gardening in the middle of January. The officer shook his head. Gaetan's face was too obscured by his parka hood to be of any real help. If the man was still missing in a couple of days, the officer would call the wife up and ask for a better photo, but he was fairly certain he wouldn't have to.

7:34 a.m. -16°C. Wind W, calm.
Birdbath buried under snow.

Gaetan woke up early the morning of the twins' fifth birthday. He looked over at Algoma who remained fast asleep beside him, her mouth slack, her hair a bird's nest. She always slept on the half of the bed closest to the window because she said it was colder. She liked the draft on her bare feet, which poked out from beneath the comforter.

The work clothes Gaetan had taken off only four hours before lay in a heap on the floor. He pulled them back on, a yeasty smell of spilt beer with a top note of cigarette smoke and stale drug store cologne greeted him. It was like he'd never left.

Outside, he held his steaming mug of instant coffee to his lips and took a sip. The coffee was cheap and bitter, but he could already feel the caffeinated rush coursing through his veins. He looked up and could see the topmost part of the gas station's bright yellow and green sign through the trees. With the exception of the opening to the woods behind the house, the hedges were so thick that no one could easily enter or leave the yard, although last summer the boys had found a weak spot in the branches and had burrowed a tunnel to the neighbour's yard. Even the square of white lattice the neighbour had tucked into the branches to block the hole couldn't keep the boys out or away from his above-ground pool. The last time they'd jumped in, fully clothed and muddy, he'd threatened to empty the pool and fill it with cement with them in it if they ever came back.

Half the backyard was taken up by Algoma's garden. Even though the growing season was relatively short, Algoma made the most of it and managed to grow an assortment of vegetables. The radishes were Gaetan's favourite, salted within an inch of their lives. The boys were partial to pulling carrots out of the ground, but not to eating them. The food Algoma grew dominated their summer and fall meals.

From the beginning of his adult life, despite the incongruous world around him—the electronics and gadgetry—Gaetan had vowed that his future family would be able to provide for themselves, as he had been taught, and his father and grandfather had been taught. Algoma gardened while he took Leo and Ferd out into field and forest to harvest animals for their dinner table. Why should they rely on the pale and fatty meats of the grocery store when they could have fresh hare and lean venison? Just because it was easier to cruise through a grocery store with a silver cart, did not mean his family would do it. Not in my world, he repeatedly told anyone who would listen.

Gaetan's grandfather had hunted or fished every day of his life until he succumbed to a stroke when he was just fifty-three years old, poorly constructed hearts being also part of their heritage. Gaetan was not ready, nor did he think he ever would be, to modernize his life. He could handle the questions, and even the criticisms from his wife's family and friends over his hunting, and how he taught his children at an early age to handle firearms properly. "Better they know than not," he'd argued. "No more dangerous than riding a bike or driving a car."

In the middle of winter, the garden did not produce, it was just another place for snow to accumulate. It had been a year of impressive snow storms; there were no signs of the pumpkins from last fall. Algoma had grown so many, they hadn't been able eat them all and the neighbours had only taken so many for their Halloween exploits, so the rest had been left to rot. "Mulch," Algoma had defended.

Gaetan tossed his now cold coffee into the snow where it left a deep brown stain and placed his mug on top of one of the higher snow drifts. He hoped he would be able to find it later, but just in case gave it a two-finger salute goodbye. "You've served me well."

After digging his way into the shed, he collected the tools he needed—a large shovel, a trowel, a cultivator, two sheets of cardboard, and the garden hose—to build his sons' birthday present.

The night before, he'd instructed Algoma to keep the children away from the backyard and the windows that faced it for the day, if she could. He looked at his watch. Eight o'clock. He heard a window rattle and looked up. The blind in the kitchen had been drawn. They were awake. He had to work faster.

Chilled, Gaetan worked all morning to rearrange the snow in the backyard. With his shovel, he moved small mountains of snow, leaving some areas with only a few inches of ground cover, while others were host to piles several feet deep. He moulded and edged the piles with the trowel, erasing his mistakes with the rusty prongs of the cultivator. By mid-afternoon, he had finished construction. He screwed in the garden hose and turned on the water to coat sections with a thin layer of ice.

After a dinner of deer roast and baked winter squash dripping with butter and brown sugar, and before the vanilla birthday cake with cream cheese icing was introduced, Gaetan turned to Ferd and Leo who were still shovelling forkfuls of food into their mouths. "Your present is outside. Put on your jackets, let's go."

The boys stood at the edge of the backyard, Algoma and Gaetan standing behind them. The boys' eyes tried to adjust to the darkness. Leo desperately looked for the square silhouette of a present. "What did you get us? I can't see it," he said.

Ferd rubbed his mitts together. "I'm cold. Can you bring it inside?"

Algoma nudged Gaetan with her shoulder. "Turn on the light."

He reached inside the door and flicked the switch. The backyard was instantly saturated in sparkling blue light. Before dinner, Gaetan had switched the outdoor white light bulbs for two blue ones he'd picked up the week before.

The boys gasped.

Algoma yelped. "I love it!"

Gaetan beamed, near ready to collapse from fatigue or lack of drink.

The entire backyard was washed in a celestial light that reflected and refracted off the layer of ice that covered every inch of the backyard. As their eyes readjusted to the bright lights, a small blue planet of snow and ice was revealed to them.

Ferd was the first to step forward into the glow, his red wool mitt coming to rest on the back of a snow chair. The entire backyard was sculpted into snow slides, forts, benches, and animals. An English garden made out of snow. And all of it covered in layers of ice. Leo followed his brother into the yard. Like a tightrope walker trying to keep his balance, he walked with both arms outstretched until he reached the bottom of the steps of the snow slide. He ascended the five stairs slowly and carefully and then launched himself headfirst down the smooth sheet of ice.

"I have cardboard sleds, too," Gaetan said. He held up two flattened Jim Beam boxes, one in each hand, Leo's name written in blue marker on the left one, Ferd's on the right.

Long into the evening and well past their bedtime, the boys tramped and bellied across their hedge-bound ice floe like a pair of dark, bright-eyed seals. Their squeals and yelps, kicks and slips echoed off their father's ice architecture. Their laughter and screams muffled only by the slow moving clouds drifting beneath the black sea of a December sky.

*2:01 p.m. -22°C. Wind N, strong.
Single pane windows rattling in their frames.*

Ferd looked out the classroom window at the frozen playground. He daydreamed about showering, the spray of hot water and the clouds of steam. The classroom was cold and sitting next to the window made it even worse. The only time he felt truly warm in the winter months was in the shower, the steaming hot water insulating his body against the cold. But it was always over too quickly, his mother or father banging on the washroom door in an attempt to hurry him up, yelling that they weren't millionaires, that he was emptying lakes, that there would be nothing left for anyone ever again.

Ferd had resolved that when he was older and richer he would build a shower stall that had two shower heads, one at either end of the bathtub. He would never be cold again. But until then, he would have to rotate in the tub like a chicken on a spit.

"Water is a common chemical substance that is essential for the survival of all things on earth," the teacher said, not looking at any student in particular. Twenty-eight faces stared blankly back at her. None of them knew how someone so young could be so boring. Ms. Prevost pointed to a poster taped to the blackboard that showed the various states of water.

"Did you know that water has three states?" she asked. Every question she posed sounded like a sigh. She tapped on each state with her finger as she called them out: "Liquid, solid, gaseous." She turned to the class. "Repeat after me."

"Liquid. Solid. Gaseous," they said in unison.

Only Ferd smiled. Finally, something useful, he thought. There was little he could do with division or history, but this, this was useful.

During recess, while the other students were playing life and death games of tether-ball and engaged in epic snowball fights, Ferd easily slipped past the recess monitor's relaxed watch and ran across the street. He hopped the chain-link fence and landed behind the Save-a-Dime Laundromat. He took a deep breath, it smelled like summer, a warm mix of detergent and dryer sheets. After a quick search, he found what he was looking for. The dryer vent.

Ferd stood in front of the vent, pulled off his mitts, and put his hands directly into the warm steam. Beneath the vent was a half moon of asphalt that was barren of snow, the heat of several dozen loads a day kept the area summer warm year round. Ferd pulled off his backpack and pulled out a small notepad and a pen. He wrote quickly and folded the note four times. After rummaging through his pockets he found the penguin-shaped paperclip he'd stolen from his teacher's desk. Using the paperclip, he attached the note to the inside of the cracked plastic of the vent cover and stood back. He dreamed of his words floating up into the atmosphere, dispersing into the air.

Water is essential for all life.

Leo was like a fish now, all silver scales and slick motion, moving with the currents over rock bed and submerged tree trunk. He had found the lowest possible place to hide, dive.

Maybe their father had gone looking for him.

Through the kitchen window, Algoma looked at the backyard. What snow was there was not handcrafted into a winter playground. Gaetan had found the energy for two boys, but not for one. She drew the blind and bent over the sink. Another wave of nausea bubbled up inside her. She clutched her stomach and vomited onto the unwashed breakfast dishes. Worry, she thought, did strange things to the body.

Finally alone in the house after having convinced her sisters that she needed to rest, it felt like her body was emptying itself. Glad for their presence, but even more grateful for the silence after they had left, she no longer had to spend her time trying to reassure them that she was fine. That Gaetan was coming home. The reason for all the mystery that would be explained once he walked through the door. She'd had to force Ferd to go to school in the morning. He had wanted to stay home with her again, to try to convince her to drive through the streets looking for Gaetan, but she'd refused him.

"What if someone at school has seen him, or knows something," she'd said, dangling hope in front of him. He'd taken the bait.

Algoma put on her jacket and boots and went outside. She stood still and let the cold air seep into the cracks in her winter clothing, the openings at her wrists and neck. The cold felt good on her hot skin. She wanted to sit on her sliding swing, but the platform was snowed in, the rails frozen. Undeterred, she went into the shed and selected a tool.

Algoma knelt on the ground, and used her hands to dig away the snow and her pointed trowel to chip away at the ice. Soon, the swing was able to grind its way along the tracks. She put her trowel down and stepped onto the platform. The two benches were covered in a foot of snow, which she pushed off with her hands before sitting down. She shifted her body weight back and forth until the swing moved with her, the remaining chunks of ice crushed underneath.

Being on the swing was like sitting in a cradle, soothing to the point that she was close to falling asleep despite the cold. Her eyes fluttered, almost closing, as she allowed herself to drift off, to daydream of better times. However, in the middle of the yard, a slice of shine caught her eye. A small patch of ice in the snow that reflected the winter sun. She knew it was another note, this one pressed between a layer of snow and ice. She looked at the side of the house. The garden hose was out. At least Ferd had rolled it back up. She stood up and walked over to the note. Using the heel of her boot, she broke the ice and then tossed the shards away. At least she wouldn't have to dry out this one.

With the note tucked securely in her coat pocket, Algoma went to work on the yard. She moulded the grainy snow into a pitiful interpretation of Gaetan's crowning glory. It quickly became clear that her skills were lacking. Her snow stairs were built at a dangerous tilt. Her chair was little more than a crumbling heap with a flattened top. The fort had collapsed within minutes. Even her attempts to coat her creations in ice failed—the yard pockmarked with pools of water and abandoned garden tools.

Unlike Leo's disappearance the year before, there were no sightings this time—real or imagined—of Gaetan. He was gone, yet when she returned to the house the few times she'd left in the past several days, she systematically checked each room for changes, things missing or moved. She could spend an hour looking at the toothbrush holder, trying to remember if the red toothbrush had been the one closest to the sink, or the blue.

Gaetan had taken Leo's death hard. It was he who had taught his sons to be self-reliant, how to take care of themselves in and out of the woods, in all circumstances. In the months after the drowning, Gaetan had asked Ferd to repeat what he'd witnessed over and over again until the boy was brought to tears.

"Tell me again what happened. Slower this time."

Gaetan had been looking for a hole in the story, something he could slip and knot his hope through. In every retelling of Ferd's story, what was missing was why Leo would have followed the bear in the first place—an animal three times his size. "It's not something rational, healthy people do," he'd argued. The bear had obviously been ill. Maybe Leo had been ill, too. Something they had not seen muddying his blood and taking him away.

MARCH – APRIL

*8:24 p.m. 11°C. Wind S, blustery.
Bottles lined up as carefully as soldiers.*

Gaetan searched the unfamiliar bar for a bottle of Scapa, a drink he could never have served at Club Rebar even if someone had had the money to ask for it. He found the bottle and poured a dram of liquid over ice.

"Why don't you tip that bottle forward a little further and I'll tip you a little better," said the man who sat across from Gaetan at the bar.

The man was dressed in a T-shirt and jeans, but they were neatly pressed and looked expensive. Thick material, nothing frayed. Gaetan noted the thick, gold chain around the man's wrinkled neck, the dented wedding ring, and how everyone who passed by nodded at him. He filled the glass three fingers deep. The man gave him an appreciative smile, took a sip, and slipped Gaetan a crisp twenty-dollar bill. This city and its people, the occasional random extravagances, didn't make sense to Gaetan, but he accepted them more than he did most things he understood back home.

It was in between shift changes at the police headquarters across the street, which afforded Gaetan a break from an otherwise busy night. He leaned against the glossy mahogany bar and marvelled again at how he'd found this place—all dark wood and brass trimmings. An everyday pub with royal leanings.

Club Rebar offered only a selection of five domestic beers, two imported, and an embarrassment of low-end rum, vodka, whisky, gin, and crème de menthe (a local favourite). The Brass Ring was stocked with no fewer than a hundred bottles of fine spirits and liqueurs. None of the patrons—most of them police, retired police, office workers from the station, and security guards—were ever forced to choose from among fewer than a half dozen brands of their favourite drinks.

Although he'd worked at the bar for a while already, he still had trouble finding the right bottles during a rush. Old physical memory kicked in and he grabbed rum when he meant vodka.

Gaetan found the bar the day he'd arrived in Toronto. He'd left the bus station and walked through the city until he found himself standing in front of The Brass Ring. He walked in for a drink and by the time he reached the bottom of his glass, he'd been hired. The owner had been filling in for a bartender who'd called in sick for his shift for the last time.

"Fucking hungover is what he is," the owner said, as he poured Gaetan his drink. Rum and coke, no ice. "That'll be five-fifty."

Gaetan said thank you and tipped the man generously with money he shouldn't have spared and immediately regretted it.

"You're from somewhere else, aren't you?" the owner, Hal, asked. "I mean, you have an accent."

"Quebec."

"Yeah, that's it. Bet it makes people feel like they're somewhere else when they're talking to you, hey? Like they're in goddamn Paris, or something. Where'd you learn English? School?"

"My cousin used to live here," Gaetan said. "I used to visit a couple times a year until she moved to Miami with her husband. He was from Scarborough."

"Well, this ain't no fucking Miami or Scarborough neither. It's better. Middle of it all."

The day after Gaetan's first shift, he'd gone to a bookstore and bought a drink-making guide. Never in his former life had he been asked to make the strange cocktails and potions that customers at The Brass Ring asked for. These were people who'd been around the world and returned home with new palates and cravings for the drinks they'd had abroad, each of them trying to outdo the other in asking for something the bar "couldn't possibly stock." Gaetan liked it best when they just ordered a beer, even if it wasn't domestic. Nevertheless, he'd spent a solid week studying the geography of the drinking world and sampled everything the bar had to offer, so he knew exactly what he was pouring, or so he said.

The man who'd ordered the Scotch had almost emptied his glass and was already eying the bottle.

Gaetan took the cue. "More?"

A slow, sleepy nod of approval. More people passed by, touching the man's shoulders like he was a good luck charm. He didn't even turn to look at them, only nodded into his glass. Gaetan poured two shots into the glass.

A large group walked through the double doors at the front of the bar. They were already drunk and one of the men was wearing a bridal veil over his baseball cap. The night was getting busy again. Gaetan was glad for the bar, the hard wood that separated him from everyone else, with the exception of the three other bartenders who moved fluidly around him, barely speaking until closing.

Gaetan had quickly learned the silent physical shorthand of working behind the bar. The bartenders saved their smiles, jokes, and flirting for the tipping customers. Where there had been empty booths only twenty minutes earlier, the bar was now standing room only. The waitresses busted through the kitchen doors with heaped plates of nachos, fries, and wings.

The people who came to The Brass Ring seemed to spare no expense. Gaetan wondered where all their money came from. No kids, probably. The drinks were overpriced and the food mediocre, even if there was a lot of it. The short-skirted service didn't seem to hurt, either. The women, some hardly more than girls, were required to dress in black polo shirts and black-and-red kilts. Hal made sure he only ordered the uniforms in size small and hired his staff to match. The waitresses were a tough lot. Carrying trays loaded with drinks, they skillfully weaved through the inebriated ranks mostly managing to avoid the slaps on the ass with which some of the men tried to "tip" them.

Gaetan looked up from the pint of Guinness he was pouring. One of the girls, Aasha, was unsuccessfully trying to excuse herself from a booth.

"I'll be right back with your beer," she said, with a large fake smile, teeth as white as ceiling paint.

"I love you," the sergeant slurred leaning close to her chest. He was only a half hour off duty and already drunk.

The waitress staggered back and held her tray in front of her like a shield. "Do you want something to eat maybe? Coffee?"

The man tried to playfully bat away her tray. "No, no, no. Just you and that beer I ordered." He knocked his empty beer bottle over. "You wanna sit down with me?"

"How about some bread?"

The sergeant smiled and then his face crumpled, his eyes

watering. He grabbed Aasha's forearm. "Even when I'm an asshole, and I'm an asshole, you keep coming back to check on me and ask me what I need."

Aasha tried to wrench her arm free and catch the attention of the doorman or one of the other waitresses.

"It just means so much to me. Thank you. I love you. I completely love you."

With that profession, he shut his eyes and fell sideways out of the booth and onto the floor. Aasha screamed and dropped her tray on him. People turned around and laughed. Hal stomped across the floor, unceremoniously elbowing his way through the crowd. Luckily, the sergeant's friends arrived at the booth before Hal did and scooped their fallen friend up by his arms.

"We'll take him home. Sorry about that," said the largest man in the group. "It's not like we won't need the same favour sooner or later."

Another one of the friends handed Aasha four twenty-dollar bills. "Cool?"

Aasha nodded at the forty-eight-dollar tip. "Inconvenience fee," the man said, and smiled. "Hey, do you know where his shoes are?"

She shook her head and watched the men drag their barefoot friend out of the bar.

As soon as they were outside, Gaetan watched Aasha reach under the booth and pull out the man's boots, his socks still tucked inside. She looked around to see if anyone was looking and walked toward the kitchen and tossed his boots in the trash.

Algoma wouldn't have let those boots go to waste, he thought. They'd have been plant holders by the end of the day.

He leaned against the cold glass of the beer fridge. Although he hadn't left home that long ago, it already seemed like years. After Leo had died, the days seemed to repeat, varying little from one to the next. Even the weather became predicable. His grief did not lessen or change into something more manageable. He felt unleashed, while everyone and everything around him was an anchor.

Each day, he'd had to contend not only with his own loss, but with Algoma's as well, and Ferd's increasing flights from reality. And the notes. He'd read and reread them, looking for the message within the message, the date the madness would end, or how he could stop it, but the answer never came.

Unplanned, and in the middle of a shift at the bar, Gaetan had gone out for a smoke. Once finished, he tossed his butt into the snow and walked until he reached the highway. He only had to walk for ten minutes along the soft shoulder until someone picked him up and he was on his way. With each kilometre, he felt lighter, the distance between himself and everything else he knew growing greater by the minute. By the end of the week, he'd started working at The Brass Ring and living in one of the owner's apartments. "Investment properties," he called them. It had been like living in a mining town, most of his earnings went back to his boss for rent. But at least there had been no questions. Hal hadn't cared about Gaetan's life, only that he showed up for work. A perfect arrangement.

If asked, Gaetan would not have been able to explain why he'd left Le Pin, or if he would ever return. He felt calm and light now, completely unburdened, under a new sky. Everything had been left behind—Leo's death, Ferd's notes, his weather journal, his wife, his life. While he knew he would miss his family, his need to escape the eyes of the town had been stronger. At the twenty-four-hour grocery store on Chestnut Street, no one asked him with wide, pitying eyes how his wife was coping; they just bagged his groceries. When he went to have his hair cut, the barber didn't slap his back and say, "I'm sorry, man," for the sixth time in as many months. Back home, he'd not been able to escape the town's memory of his loss, but here no one knew to ask. They passed him on the street like he didn't matter, like he was not there at all. It was perfect.

Ferd could take care of himself. He had made sure of that early on. And Algoma would be okay, she would adapt, this much he knew. She'd fill his empty space, so that it was as if he'd never left. She would cut and restitch his memory into something new that she could use. While his new life did not feel like it was his own yet, it was something different and that was enough to allow him to sleep after a hard shift at work—and they were all hard shifts—something he hadn't been able to do in a year.

Most of the regulars at The Brass knew Gaetan only as the quiet guy they liked, the one with the accent who poured any drink they asked for no matter how many they'd already had. He poured generously and they tipped him well. At Club Rebar, Gaetan had no longer known if the men were tipping for good service or out of pity.

Gaetan looked around the bar. None of the women looked like his wife, here they were hard and shiny, leather and platinum. Some were cops' wives, and others wannabes. And a few, whom Gaetan could easily pick out, were on the force. He liked them best. They exuded purpose and precision, but could also throw drinks back like the rest of the guys, looking like little could faze them. Algoma, under her veil of scarves and used furs, always looked like she was on the verge of imploding, disappearing entirely under the weight of everything around her.

The media had been captivated by Leo's death and the bear for weeks, focusing just as much airtime on the animal as they did the boy. Animal experts and hunting guides were interviewed. Long distance shots of school children crying made the local news. Everyone was an expert. Everyone knew someone who knew someone. Gaetan wondered if anyone had mourned the loss of the bear. He had not, but whenever he thought of Leo, he thought of the bear. The two were as entwined in his mind as Leo and Ferd had once been. Inseparable.

The night was a blur of drinks and exchanged cash until people in the bar started leaving, piling into the cabs outside. Gaetan looked at his watch. It was five to two. He could go home soon.

After a few drinks with the closing staff after the doors had been shut, Gaetan left the bar. Outside, the sky was already changing. He could see the light blue glow of morning bleeding into the black. He was tired. Cabs slowed down beside him as he walked home, but he didn't look their way, so they drove off to the next person. He liked that about Toronto, the city was never entirely closed, the streets never completely empty.

Close to home, Gaetan passed a homeless man seated on the sidewalk. The man was older and had a cardboard sign resting in his lap that said "Just had open heart surgery." A German shepherd slept to his right. Gaetan dropped whatever change he had into the man's crumpled coffee cup and kept walking. The man looked like his father. The resemblance was so strong that he struggled not to think it was his father shored up and broken against the brick.

When Gaetan arrived at his apartment building, there were two young men in the elevator who were only partially successful in holding one another up. They were drunk and arguing about food.

"Nothing's open this late and I'm starving," the blond one whined. "We should've picked up something earlier."

The other man starred at Gaetan, his eyelids fluttering, blue eyes rolling back: "Do you know if anything's open around here? I mean for delivery?"

Gaetan shrugged his shoulders and looked at the floor and mumbled, "No." Then he thought of that steak on a bun place on Yonge he liked, but didn't say anything. He stared at the closed door. When the elevator arrived at his floor, he turned to wave at the men as a sort of apology for not being able to help them, but they were now deeply kissing, the food ordeal forgotten.

"Sizzlers," Gaetan said quietly.

He put his apartment key into the lock, one of only three keys he had now, and opened the door. His place was clean and empty except for the usual kitchen appliances, an orange-and-brown floral print couch that one of the waitresses had given him and a futon bed he'd bought after sleeping on an air mattress for his first three weeks in the city. He planned to get a small TV next, something to have on in the background, but for now the balcony provided him with all his entertainment. He sat out there for hours after work when he knew he should be sleeping, sitting in his lawn chair until the sun peeked over top of the apartment buildings and the glass shone like mercury.

Gaetan changed out of his work clothes and tossed them into a corner with the other dirty clothes. The pyjamas he'd purchased the day before—new and full price—sat on his unmade bed. He tore open the cellophane wrapping and pulled out the matching shirt and pants. They were too large. Regardless, he put them on and shuffled out onto the balcony like a child who didn't want to go to sleep. He sat down, lit a cigarette, and, despite the chill, listened to the two women talking on the balcony below. He couldn't make out what they were saying, or why they were up this late (or early). He just hoped they wouldn't stop.

Three fat pigeons were perched on the window sill, cooing and murmuring, as they had been for the past hour. Gaetan tossed a pillow at the window where it thumped against the glass.

When he heard the birds fly away, the flap of their wings, he lay back down and closed his eyes. He needed to pick up one of those plastic owls to scare them off. Better still, he wished he had a pellet gun.

Unable to fall back asleep, Gaetan sat up and wiped his eyes. Sometime during the night, he'd taken off his pyjamas and now sat naked on the edge of his bed. There were no curtains on the windows, but the sun was in his favour—no one would be able to see him. He opened the drawer in his bedside table (a curb-side salvage) and pulled out a package of postcards. He shuffled the postcards in his hands, writing side up, and randomly selected one. Toronto landmark tarot. He flipped the card over: the CN Tower surrounded by blue sky and too-perfect clouds.

He looked outside. The early afternoon sky was clear, bright, and cold. Winter's last gasp. The windows were not rattling as they normally did, which meant there was no wind. He jotted a note on the back of the postcard, wrote down an address from memory, and tossed the pen and the rest of the postcards back into the drawer. He leaned back, head on his pillow, postcard resting on his chest, and fell back to sleep.

When Gaetan woke up again it was night. His windows were black except for the occasional sweep of a spotlight high above. He switched on the light, thinking curtains would be helpful now. However, there was no curtain rod, and that was enough of an excuse. The room was cold, the single-pane windows doing little to keep the heat in. He pulled on a long-sleeved T-shirt and a pair of jeans and grabbed his wallet. It was his night off, and he was going out. He felt like he hadn't been heard or seen by anyone in months. Tonight, he'd change that, even if he didn't know just how yet. He was sure the city would provide the opportunity if he just looked.

Even though Gaetan had lived in Toronto for months, he'd seen very little of it, already tethered to his new schedule and routines. Tonight would also give him a chance to adjust to the tilt and keel of this new city of cement, grease, smells, and sirens.

Instead of turning right at the end of the driveway as he did when he was going to work, Gaetan turned left. Within a couple of blocks, he'd walked past several stores and half a dozen restaurants. Had there been a Korean barbecue back home? He couldn't remember but doubted it. The only restaurant that Algoma had ever wanted to go to was House of Chips—a diner with photocopied menus in Plexiglas holders that sat on the round, Formica tables. The waitresses were quick and the prices cheap. On Good Friday, the diner sold a lake's worth of fish and chips. Gaetan had enjoyed the first visit, but the charm wore off after half a dozen years of weekly visits, the same menu each time.

On the main street, a half dozen scraggly young maples pierced the sidewalk of each block, each raised on an anorexic diet of car exhaust and rain runoff. When Gaetan looked down the side streets he saw one-hundred-year-old oaks and maples towering above the frayed rooftops. If even one fell, he thought, it would take out several homes and businesses, maybe a car or two. Nostalgia, he realized, was a potential liability.

After he'd been walking for some time, Gaetan found himself on the sprawling campus of the University of Toronto. Dark and gothic at its centre, it felt like another world. When one of the campus police trucks drove past him, his heart beat faster. He thought about the letter he'd sent to Algoma to ensure he would be left alone; however, every day he half expected someone would come knocking on his door, ready to drag him back to Le Pin. But no one ever came. Maybe they didn't care. Maybe his leaving had been a blessing.

Walking along a side street that ran parallel to Spadina Avenue, Gaetan stared at houses, a new favourite pastime. Some were massive and probably once beautiful, but they were now in a state of disrepair—half-rotted fences, clutches of bicycles chained to any available pole, mailboxes overflowing with yellowing fliers. Every window had a different type of covering, most improvised. He saw tinfoil and newspaper, Bristol board, and even a collage of McDonald's hamburger wrappers. Everyone living with the wallet they had been born with. His father had once told him that you could tell everything you needed to know about a person by looking at their curtains. The house in front of him, likely rented to students given its proximity to the university, had five windows that faced the street. The main bay window was covered with a pink and white striped sheet. He could see the faint outlines of plants and possibly a cat sleeping on the inside ledge. There were three windows on the second and third floors. White lace, tin foil, dark green mini-blinds. The window in the front door was covered by a triangle of fabric, dark green with a large, gold pattern. Gaetan noted the drawstring dangling in the middle. A woman's skirt. It was the closest he'd come to wanting to go back home.

A quick right turn, another left, and Gaetan found himself in the middle of Chinatown. It felt like a new city, the street overflowing with people, lumbering streetcars, fruit and vegetables spilling over onto the asphalt, piles of empty wood crates, mountains of garbage. It was near impossible to manoeuvre the sidewalk, so he walked along the curb, cars whizzing past him.

Almost every storefront was a restaurant or market. On the sidewalk, permit-less vendors sold homegrown vegetables, fake designer handbags, phone cards, pirated DVDs, and potted herbs, all showcased on overturned cardboard boxes or card tables. The smell of the neighbourhood was a mix of sickly sweet rotting fruit and fried food, which Gaetan found oddly pleasing. Between the constant noise and pervasive smells, it was impossible to hear one's own thoughts. It was perfect. His stomach grumbled. It was time to eat.

He made his way across the sidewalk and stepped into one of the restaurants, taking his place at the end of a short lineup of people who were waiting for tables. He watched as waiters expertly manoeuvred silver carts of food through the restaurant, dropping something off at every table they passed. Within minutes, he was ushered to a seat by a crisply uniformed waiter who had a sheen of sweat coating his face; a laminated menu was put into Gaetan's hands.

"I'll have the whole deep-fried soft-shelled crab," he said when the waiter came around again.

The waiter wrote down Gaetan's order on his yellow notepad. "And…?"

"That's it. One whole deep-fried soft-shelled crab. And hot sauce if you have it."

The waiter shrugged his shoulders and left.

The restaurant—Gaetan hadn't caught the name on the way in—was packed, patrons sitting elbow to elbow. It was hard to see where one table ended and the next began with the exception of those seated at the planet-sized tables in the middle of the restaurant. Family tables. Gaetan was the only person who sat alone, his extra chair immediately scavenged.

"Can I take this for my boyfriend? He's just over there. At the back, see?" The girl, maybe eighteen or nineteen years old at the most, already had her hands on the arms of the empty chair. She had a sprinkling of acne at her temples and her eyebrows were drawn in too darkly. She was wearing cowboy boots and a floral wrap dress. Her right forearm was covered in a large tattoo of a dancing bear. Gaetan looked at the tattoo and then over her shoulder at the boyfriend, a wiry man in a three-piece dark-blue suit who was leaning up against the back wall. He was looking at his watch, which, even from a distance, looked expensive. He looked too old for the girl and Gaetan almost said as much.

"So, can I?" the girl asked again, her fingers tapped rhythmically against the chair.

"Go on, take it," Gaetan said, "but can I ask you about your tat—" he started, but she squealed a thanks and hoisted the chair up and walked off before he could finish.

Gaetan watched the girl set the chair down beside a small table where her things were. She motioned to her companion to sit down, but he looked at his watch and shook his head. The girl kicked him in the shin.

The waiter arrived in that moment and interrupted Gaetan's view of the squabble. A large plate of crab, huge and radiating heat, was set in front of him. "Thank you," he said. "Maybe a glass of beer?"

The waiter nodded and disappeared.

When Gaetan looked over again the girl and her companion were gone, their table already occupied by a middle-aged couple. Out-of-towners, he guessed by the nervous way they kept looking around the room, the woman holding her oversized purse protectively on her lap.

Gaetan wondered about the girl and her bear tattoo, its significance. Since Leo's death he made note of any bear reference he came across and there were many. He didn't understand everyone's fascination with the animal, their reverence. It was made out of meat and bone like any other. He'd hunted them with his father when he was younger, and they'd ended up in the stew pot like anything else. No special meaning or divinity—just dinner. And to the bear, maybe that's what Leo had looked like: just dinner. An easy meal.

Gaetan wiped the sweat from his forehead with his shirtsleeve. The restaurant was as humid as a rainforest. Even the walls were beaded with pearly drops of condensation. Only the ghostly shadows of passersby were visible through the fogged glass. The neon lobster that hung in the window blinked on and off like a broken streetlight. He reached into his back pocket for his weather journal, frowning when he realized it was not there. He longed for a barometer.

Three waiters simultaneously descended upon the table beside him with fresh plates of fried rice, chop suey, and a large, steamed fish. Chopsticks darted through the air as the family snapped up the food, chatting back and forth as they ate. Seven people sat at the table. They seemed inseparable, all part of the same effortless machine. Gaetan wondered what it would take to break up the group. A divorce? Infidelity? A car accident? A missing child? It wouldn't take much, it never did.

Belly full of crab and beer, Gaetan pulled out his wallet to pay the bill. He took out a twenty and a ten and set them on the table. Thirty bucks. Algoma could do a lot with thirty dollars, he thought. She could feed a family for a week with that amount, and well. In that moment, he knew what he was going to do. He looked around. His waiter was taking an order on the other side of the restaurant. Gaetan stood up slowly and put on his jacket, willing himself to look normal, relaxed even. He picked up the money from the table and stuffed it into his coat pocket. His blood thumped a nervous beat against his temples. A woman at the table next to him looked over. Gaetan smiled, sweatily clutching the bills in his pocket.

"Another beer, sir?" the waiter asked.

Gaetan jumped, surprised to find the waiter beside him. "Sure, sure," he said. "Just going to the washroom."

The waiter arched his eyebrow and stared at his jacket.

"I'm cold."

"One beer," the waiter said, looking at him sternly.

Gaetan nodded. "Where's the washroom?"

The waiter pointed to the back of the restaurant, the furthest possible place from the exit. Gaetan said thank you and walked over.

Inside one of the stalls, he leaned up against the walls and shut his eyes. When someone walked in, he walked over to the sink and washed his hands. "Thirty bucks," he whispered to his reflection in the mirror. "Thirty bucks." When he exited the washroom, he took a deep breath and looked around. His waiter was at the bar, his back partially turned to him. Gaetan sped toward the door, opening it just in time to hear his waiter call out, "Mister!"

He ran down the street until he tasted blood at the back of his throat and he was sure there was no one following him. He felt exhilarated. Not only had someone noticed his absence, but he had thirty dollars to show for it. He pulled the bills out of his pocket and stared at them. He shook and smiled. He felt alive.

Several blocks south of the restaurant, Gaetan stepped into a shop that sold everything from pesticides to nylons. Still buzzing from his run, he spun the carousel of postcards around until one caught his eye. Mixed in with the new postcards was a throwback, something from the '80s. Maybe someone had found an old box in the basement and was trying to sell them. The postcard had the Ontario parliament building on the front, sober brick set against an oversaturated neon blue sky.

"Pretty dry," he said, trying to joke with the woman standing next to him, her arms rifling through a bin of discounted underwear. She rolled her eyes and walked away. He took the postcard to the cashier. "Wait a minute," he said, and grabbed a birthday card from a display on the counter, "this, too." When he asked for stamps, the woman sold him a half-used book of stamps out of her own purse.

Outside the store, leaned up against the building, Gaetan wrote on the back of the postcard and pasted a stamp onto it. He put the postcard in his back pocket and grabbed the birthday card. He put thirty dollars into the card and addressed the envelope to Algoma.

The closest mailbox he found was covered in a collage of local band and fruit stickers, Sharpie tags, and posters for events that had already happened. Even the door had been ripped out, so that letters and bill payments were readily available to anyone with a good reach. He looked in the box and saw a pop can and some trash mixed in with the envelopes and wondered if anyone actually came by to pick up the mail anymore, but dropped the postcard and birthday card in anyway.

8:11 a.m. -3°C. Calm.
Tangle of hair caught in the drain.

The pressure from the shower head blew the plastic liner inward where it wrapped around her legs. Algoma reached down to peel the plastic from her calves and re-affix the magnets to the inside of the tub. She stood up and rubbed her pregnant belly, which was now hard like a gourd, but smoother.

With Ferd spending a significant amount of time out of the house, staying with his aunts, Algoma had less and less to do and no one to take care of, except herself and whatever child was adrift in her womb. She was out of work, both at The Shop and as a mother and wife. She felt like an incubator.

While The Shop was under construction in a new location, it was a slow process that was compromised by the delays that came with inclement weather and a lack of finances. Josie spent her days trying to barter for what she needed—the walls, windows, and doors—hoping for the deal that would salvage her livelihood. Algoma hoped the rebuilding wouldn't take long. She was lonely and desperately missed the feel of fabric in her hands. The ka-chunk of the price gun she used to tag every shirt and shoe. She missed seeing Josie every day, her one constant in the past year. She wanted her life back, even if it was missing parts.

Still, there were times when she allowed herself to imagine a knock at the door, Gaetan arriving with Leo's hand in his.

"I went looking for him," Gaetan would say.

Leo's head would poke out from beneath his father's arm. He would say, "Hi, Mom."

During her daydreams, Algoma felt her body's chemistry respond to her imaginings, a soft electricity that ignited her fingers and tingled along her scalp. As soon as she opened her eyes, the feeling was gone.

The police had ceased any efforts to find Gaetan after Algoma received his letter. He'd written very little, saying only that he remained in the country and needed some time away from everything. He'd ended with a promise that he'd be in touch again, but not when. No return address had been included. The letter had left Algoma devastated, but she carried on with the hope that he'd return. She stored his letter with Ferd's notes and washed Gaetan's bedsheets every week, so they'd be fresh for when he came home.

Home.

Algoma now slept at the centre, on the couch, so she could see everything that came, everything that went. Nothing would escape her watch.

Her sisters had not been so agreeable about the idea of her husband's return.

"You should have your locks changed," said Cen. The constant protector.

"Your last name, too. Be a Belanger with us again," said Lake.

Gaetan was no longer welcome in Algoma's sisters' lives. They'd cut him out as instantly and severely as he had himself.

After receiving the letter, Algoma had focused on Gaetan's handwriting and what it might reveal. The deep ditch his pen exacted in the paper. The slant of his letters.

How much space left at the top and bottom. She should have been paying attention earlier, before all this. There must have been signs.

Tired, Algoma sheltered her growing belly against the hard spray of the shower and hoped for a girl.

"You're going to boil the baby," Ferd said. He bit into an unripe pear and spit out the chunk into his hand.

Algoma had come out of the bathroom wrapped in an oversized robe, her face, hands, and feet bright red coals. As she walked into the kitchen, she tripped on the terrycloth hem.

"Be careful," he said, pointing at her belly.

In Gaetan's absence, Algoma had appropriated most of his wardrobe. At first it was just his robes (three of them) each floor-length and made of heavy, durable terrycloth. Gaetan had insisted on variety in colour and style for his morning wear. At the time, Algoma told him he was being extravagant, even if it was one of the few purchases he'd made during their marriage; however, when she'd pulled on one of his robes for the first time, she'd understood. It had felt heavy on her shoulders, like someone was standing behind her, a familiar weight on her shoulders and hips.

Soon, she found herself wearing pieces of Gaetan's clothing to do errands, to drop Ferd off at school. Large and loose, his clothing became her pregnancy wardrobe. She wore his oversized plaid shirts unbuttoned over her own tank tops and T-shirts and completed most of her outfits with an ankle-length denim skirt, so that no part of her was exposed or vulnerable.

"Breakfast for two?" Algoma asked, patting her modestly distended belly. "Well, two and a half." She tried to look capable around Ferd, even happy, but he eyed her with suspicion. "Just give me a second to get changed, okay?" Within several minutes, she returned wearing a new assortment of odds and ends.

Even though his mother now dressed in more clothing than she ever had, Ferd thought she looked smaller. Her belly was the only place that he could hold on to and she held it every moment her hands were free, as if she was afraid she might lose it. The rest of her seemed as fragile as a bird skeleton, hollow bones ready to blow apart under a hard wooden wheel no one could see coming.

Algoma took a carton of brown eggs out of the fridge. "Eggs?"

Everything had become a question. She didn't trust herself anymore.

Ferd nodded and Algoma cooked.

At the table Algoma leaned over her plate of heavily peppered scrambled eggs and buttered toast. "This was a good idea. Don't you think, Ferd?"

Ferd mashed his eggs with his fork and took a sip of his orange juice. "Sure," he said. He sounded unconvinced. Eggs were all they ate anymore. Easy, inexpensive, familiar. And boring. He wanted to tell her that they weren't dead. Instead, he put down his fork and watched his mother eat. He was confused by her new habits: how she carefully piled a forkful of egg onto her toast and ate an equal portion of bread and egg with each bite. She was so consumed with her rituals, she didn't notice him staring. If she finished her toast before she finished all her eggs, she would put another slice of bread in the toaster before taking another bite. She sought balance, equal input on every front.

"Festival of the Nations 1994," he read off her T-shirt.

"Come taste the world." The world map on her T-shirt stretched tautly across her stomach, most of the borders disfigured.

Algoma finally realized Ferd was staring at her.

"Are you thinking of a name?" she asked.

He shoved another piece of toast into this mouth. "No."

"Well think of one. Without your father around, I need your help." There was no skirting Gaetan's absence. He had been there one day, gone the next. Even Ferd's notes to Leo had begun to chronicle the details of his father's absence: Have you seen him?

Ferd poured another glass of orange juice. "Leo," he blurted out.

Algoma breathed a deep and heavy sigh. "I think it's a girl."

Ferd slammed his fork down onto the table. "It's not," he yelled.

Startled, Algoma dropped her fork. "We can talk about this another time—"

But Ferd ran down to the basement and slammed the door behind him. Pictures rattled against the wall, a puff of plaster dropped from the ceiling. He'd grown.

Ever since Algoma had announced her pregnancy to him, he'd seemed unhinged, and the frequency of his note-writing had increased ten-fold. It took a great deal of work for her to ensure she'd collected them all, at least the ones that were in the house; there was nothing she could do about the others. When the school had called to discuss the matter, she'd simply hung up the phone. Algoma had hoped that word of a new baby would have put an end to it, but it had only been the beginning of something else.

"Will Dad come back now?" he'd asked, hopeful. "I

mean, to see the baby and all." His dark brown, almost black, eyes had bored holes into her trying to extract the answer he wanted.

Algoma had turned away guiltily. She had no answer.

From that day forward, Ferd was fascinated by her growing belly and her well being, constantly asking her if she needed anything, if he could do anything for her. He started making his bed in the morning and doing the dishes before she asked him to. Even his nails were trim and clean.

"What does it feel like for the baby inside," he asked her one night. He poked her belly with his finger half expecting it to pop like a balloon.

"Like a pool of warm water."

"Like at the Community Centre?"

"Yes, but with less chlorine."

Her joke missed its mark. Ferd mouthed the words, mentally taking a note: Less chlorine.

She would later realize that water had been the wrong answer.

He was sure the baby was a boy. He was sure it was his brother.

After a months-long campaign of notes and letters, Ferd believed that Leo was finally coming back to him. He had no doubt and began to plan for his brother's return. Leo would have to grow up and learn everything all over again before he could tell him what had happened in the year after he had gone through the ice. Ferd promised himself that he would be a better brother this time, or try to be. At least he had a chance of being a better shot.

Ferd read Algoma's baby books like they were user manuals. Before bed, instead of allowing his mother to read to him as he sometimes allowed in his weaker moments, Ferd read chapters of the baby books to her.

"You need more folic acid. You shouldn't let it sleep on its back. You could use cotton diapers."

After the initial outburst, Algoma rarely had the heart or energy to correct Ferd, to tell him the baby was not Leo, that it couldn't be, that it was a girl. With the exception of her sons, girls were all her extended family produced. So many girls, her mother had joked that they might run out of girls' names and would have to start dipping into the boys'. Or at least another shipping company.

Algoma got out of her chair and put another piece of bread in the toaster. She was not going to let Ferd's unfinished eggs go to waste. She glanced at the clock on the stove. It was almost time to go to Josie's.

There was a trick to entering Josie's driveway, a long, narrow gravel road that suddenly opened up into a large space the size of a grocery-store parking lot. In the past, the lot had been used to park farm equipment, but now it was mostly empty except for her pick-up truck. The entrance to the driveway was flanked by two deep ditches that visitors drove into from time to time, despite the reflectors she'd posted on each side. The front ends of their cars smashed, foreheads bleeding, tow-trucks called. Inspired, Josie had come up with a simple solution: she'd painted two antique milk canisters bright orange and posted them on either side of the entrance. Visitors were so scared about scratching their cars on the cans, they took their time coming in. No one had landed in the ditch in months.

The house was large and old, but well cared for. Even if there wasn't a new coat of paint on the wood siding—ancient white paint curling up to reveal a dark green past—the porch was swept clean and the sidewalks shovelled. The focal point of the backyard was a huge bonfire pit that was surrounded by a triangle of church pews Josie had scored a few years back when a church two towns over had been decommissioned. Once a summer, everyone from The Shop and a few of Josie's best customers and traders came over for an all night bonfire. They'd arrive early and put their tents up on the lawn, break out the coolers of beer and wine, and not leave until the following evening. Breakfast would be made in huge cast-iron pans over the remaining embers. For those who were invited, it was one of the highlights of the year.

Josie took a small key out of her pocket and unlocked the padlock on the barn door that led to her workshop. She'd purchased the property because of the barn, so she could store all her larger barters, the things she didn't take directly to the shop for Algoma to sort through and clean. Things she knew would be worth something to someone someday. Today it was worth something to her. Just as she walked inside, she heard someone coming up the driveway, the pop and crunch of gravel beneath car tires.

Algoma.

Josie and Algoma manoeuvred their way past the antique furniture and mysterious shapes that were covered in faded moving blankets and old quilts.

"I didn't think I'd be having any more kids, so I donated all of their baby furniture." While her mouth was upturned in a smile, her eyes were flat and expressionless. She peeked under one of the blankets and quickly dropped the corner of the blanket back down again, a cloud of dust colouring her jacket.

Josie tried to think of something to say. "Well, there's

enough stuff here that you're set even if you have quintuplets."

Algoma laughed sincerely. "I'm not a cat, Jo."

"We'll it's a good thing because a litter of kittens can have more than one father," Josie said, proud as ever of her random trivia. "More than two and I'd be suspicious."

"You're so full of it."

"I'm serious. You come take a look at my two cats and tell me they came from the same father. I'm thinking of hitting up one of the barn cats for child support."

By the time they left the barn, Algoma had settled on a set of matching white baby furniture that had been stored in an old goat pen. Josie carefully loaded up the pieces into her truck and followed Algoma home where she unloaded the pieces and then said she was off to check on how construction on The Shop was coming along.

After Josie left, honking her horn as she turned the corner, Algoma and Ferd set about wiping down the furniture with a mixture of white vinegar and water.

Since Ferd had slept on the pullout couch in the basement for the past year, his and Leo's old room had remained relatively untouched except for when Algoma slept in it. When the boys were born, Gaetan had painted the walls dark yellow, the colour of late season corn left to stand against grey winter. Algoma had asked for something brighter, but Gaetan had insisted they'd grow into it.

In the room were two single beds separated by a large wooden dresser pushed up against the wall opposite the door. Above the dresser was an antique, oval mirror Algoma had rescued from a neighbour's trash bin. Any image reflected in the middle of the mirror warped, so the boys had only been able to see their reflection along the beveled edge, a sliver at a time. Along the inside of the door frame were two lengths of masking tape. Once a month, Algoma had asked her sons to stand up straight and put their heads back against the tape where she measured their heights and wrote it down. Most times, the lines she drew for the two boys overlapped one another. She had stopped the ritual after Leo died. The twins' heights remained a matching three feet and four inches tall. Drunk one night, Gaetan had used a black marker to measure his slumped height, a man reduced.

Algoma retrieved the empty cardboard boxes she had picked up from the grocery store and brought them into the room. Together, she and Ferd packed up everything and stored the boxes beside the holiday decorations in the basement. Snakes of Christmas lights and stacked foam snowmen. And now most of the boys' belongings. Once the room was emptied, the beds dismantled, and the dresser pushed into the hallway, they opened the windows and brought in the brushes and paint cans.

Years later, it would be easy to spot who had painted what part of the room. Algoma's sections were precise, coated evenly in robin's egg blue paint. Ferd had painted quickly and with an overloaded brush. His sections of the wall appeared veined.

By the end of the weekend the room was complete, the new furniture arranged and waiting for the baby. While Algoma made Sunday dinner, Ferd went into the basement and cut open one of Leo's boxes. He dug through the newspaper packing and grabbed a handful of things: a T-shirt, an old shotgun shell, and curl of birch bark Leo had torn from the neighbour's tree. He stuffed his brother's things into an empty pillowcase he'd brought downstairs and took them up to the baby's room. He wanted Leo to be comfortable when he arrived, surrounded by familiar things.

As Ferd rummaged around the house, Algoma took a moment to look out at the empty street. She picked up Gaetan's weather journal from the window sill and recorded the details of the day: 5:14 p.m. 11°C. Wind unknown. Sore back. Empty cupboards. You're still not home.
   She recorded the weather every day so there would not be a gap in Gaetan's journal when he returned. So he would know what snow had fallen while he was gone, how the temperature had risen and fallen like the peaks and valleys of a heart monitor. He would not have missed a single day.
   His cursive sat above hers on the page like oil over water. Her words looked like small, squat buildings, each word carefully printed out in block letters, while his blue ink was a fine yarn that held everything together until it was abruptly severed the day he'd left.

2:14 p.m. 4°C. Wind W, strong.
Tin roof of the barn rumbling like thunder.

En route home from the grocery store, Josie drove straight past The Shop, not even so much as glancing in the direction of the construction. There was enough to do at home to keep her from staring at what wasn't yet finished, but The Shop had become an easy excuse of late. Any time she didn't want to do something, or wanted to be alone, she said she was going to look in on The Shop. Her trump card, whatever the real reason.

She pulled her truck into the driveway and drove past the house, parking beside the barn. Drops of rain hit the windshield. The temperature was rising, a couple more degrees and all the snow would melt. When the temperature dropped again, everything would be covered in ice. She got out of her truck and unlocked the padlock on the side door of the barn. Inside, it was cold and dark. Even with the light switched on, only a small area was lit up, the corners still black and shapeless. Josie grabbed her flashlight and walked up to what used to be the hay loft. She couldn't have imagined what farmer would have made a go of it this far north, or what he would have farmed. She was just grateful to have the storage space, and she was always finding things tucked away under stairs and floorboards. The barn was a treasury of rusted parts and machinery that was either half taken apart, or half put together. She couldn't tell which.

Even if The Shop was not up and running, Josie had not

stopped collecting or sorting what she already had. If anything, her accumulation had increased, so that she could replace what she'd lost in the fire, and the barn was her warehouse. Upstairs, she'd fashioned herself a temporary sorting area; downstairs, she'd set up a washing machine and dryer to clean any clothing that came in. That was the secret to the success of The Shop: everything was clean. The store never smelled like the others in town, a sickeningly sweet mixture of ancient sweat and must. Every piece of clothing that Josie sold had been cleaned and pressed. The furniture she collected was stored in the west side of the main floor of the barn—like with like, and all diligently cleaned, some refinished. Everything left the barn in better condition than it had arrived in.

Josie switched on her small, silver radio to the only station that would come in. She reached for one of the black plastic bags of clothing and gutted it with her thumb, clothing and a handful of costume jewellery spilling out onto the floor. From the pile, she pulled out a black and white striped dress. She unzipped the front pockets and reached in to look for anything that would bleed in the wash or tear the fabric and narrow her margins—packets of gum, tissues, pens, or pins—and instead found a puzzle ring.

She held the six interlinked bands in the palm of her hand and tried to picture their undoing. The owner of the dress had gone out, drunk too much, shown her ring to a friend, how she could easily put it back together, but couldn't. Drunk fingers fumbling unsuccessfully to reassemble the silver bands, the knots and curves, until she'd given up and tucked it into her pocket and never thought about it again. That, or it had been an unwanted gift that she'd "lost."

Sometimes working at The Shop was like working in a

Cracker Jack box. There was a prize in every pocket, purse, and locket. In her bedroom, Josie had an antique jewellery box where she kept all the treasures she found. There were silver dollars and old coins tucked into the velvet folds of the ring holder, charm bracelet charms hanging from the necklace hooks, wallet-sized photos of strangers' girlfriends, children and parents taped onto the doors. It was her personal lost and found box.

Josie looked at the ring in her hand. She was good at puzzles, at putting things back together again. Maybe she could fix this. If she could, she would give it to Algoma. A bonus for her hard work, she thought, like those years of service pins and watches that big companies gave out. A reward.

Algoma had been wearing Edith Renaud's clothing the first time Josie saw her. Josie immediately recognized the turquoise and white pinstriped jumper with matching white shoes, but said nothing. It was like meeting an old friend even if Josie hadn't known Edith personally—she'd been dead when Josie was introduced to her wardrobe.

In the days after Edith's untimely death—a fall down her front steps that should have resulted in a few scrapes and bruises had killed her—Josie had come to know her closets and wardrobe boxes intimately. She'd been called in by Victor, Edith's husband. "Please just come and take it away," he'd asked. "It's too much, too much."

Josie arrived within the hour and began the tedious task of sorting through eras of clothing—eighty-seven years of seasonal wear. Apparently, Edith had never settled on one style and stuck with it as so many other people did. There were denim bell bottoms and red polyester pants, full-length gowns and a carton of jeans.

Like paramedics or the coroner, Josie was often one of the

first people to know about a death. She was a first responder, her name synonymous with someone who could take away the things that pained those who had been left behind. Closets stuffed like Christmas turkeys with once-worn holiday clothes. Shoe boxes full of overexposed photographs, 1-2-3-cheese smiling faces, most of the names already forgotten. Entire collections of cast-iron frying pans with fifty years of meal memory hardened like thin layers of coal over iron. To call Josie in was civilized. Loved ones' belongings would not end up destined for the local landfill for a half century of slow rot; instead, they would be cared for, washed, folded, and given new homes. Some widows and widowers called Josie before they called anyone else, wanting to avoid earth-shattering fights over who got what hutch, candle holder or scarf. They gave or sold everything to Josie who saved them from the embarrassments of their own families.

Algoma had come into the store for a job. She'd nervously twirled one strand of her hair around a finger as she handed over her woefully brief résumé. Josie hated nervous tics, but immediately forgave Algoma hers.

Josie scanned the résumé. Among her qualifications, Algoma had listed "mother to two boys and sister to six." Within ten minutes Algoma was hired and scheduled for her first shift the following day.

"What should I wear?" Algoma asked.

Josie nervously fiddled with some receipts. "Something old, something new, something borrowed, something blue," she said.

The next day, Algoma arrived at The Shop ten minutes before nine o'clock dressed in the same turquoise jumper (cleaned and pressed overnight), yellow plastic sandals that Josie recognized from the dollar store, a blue patent leather belt wrapped around her thin waist, and thick black eyeliner. "I'm ready, boss."

During her first week at The Shop, Algoma named the mannequins in the front window: Esmeralda, Eleanor, and Eloise. "They'll work harder for us if we name them," she told Josie after adding their names to the schedule. Their hours were listed from 12:00 a.m. to 12:00 a.m. every day of the year. When the store burnt down, everyone mourned the loss of the girls.

Josie hadn't minded when Algoma had taken to decorating the wall above the sorting table like it was her home or locker—everything important to her on display so there was no question about her priorities. Photos of her family were tacked front and centre and beside it a perfume advertisement ripped out of a magazine. The model in the ad had Algoma's long neck, high, flat cheekbones, and thin hair. When Algoma stood in front of the paper, it turned into a mirror.

For the first month of her employment, Algoma mostly worked for things in trade with which to fill her home. Every hour she spent at the cash register, she earned what she needed to make a life for her and her family. By the end of her first week, she had filled an entire sheet on the debit board. Her shelves were filled with strangers' knick-knacks, a pair of silver candelabras from someone's twenty-fifth wedding anniversary celebrated thirty years earlier, a plush reclining chair that no longer reclined, and a pine coffee table that was high enough to eat at comfortably. She also ensured that she had sufficiently filled her closet with enough clothes to see her through two solid weeks of work—a franken-closet pieced together from more than a dozen women's wardrobes.

By the end of her first year at The Shop, Algoma's home looked like an antique shop, old farm tools displayed with as much pride as collectible plates. In a pinch, she could stretch a fence, saw barn boards, or curry a horse. Once a month, she oiled the metal on each of the tools and polished the wooden handles until they shone. Any time Josie went over, she felt instantly and completely at home, Algoma's home having become a simple extension of The Shop.

Josie polished the ring bands with the bottom of a concert T-shirt of some metal band she'd never heard of. Her sorting abandoned, she was now sitting on the floor completely focused on the ring and putting it back together again. She turned the bands around and around trying to figure out their secret. When she tried to force two of the bands to interlock, she bent the metal ensuring the ring would never go back together again.

7:29 a.m. 7°C. Wind NW, light.
Thin curls of smoke coming out of the toaster.

Ferd stood on his tiptoes and reached for his toast. He grabbed both slices with one hand and quickly dropped them onto his plate. The toast was charred black. If his father were here, Ferd could have turned the darkness dial down a couple shades and popped in two more slices of bread. Gaetan liked cold, burnt toast and tea, but he was not here. He was eating cold, burnt toast somewhere else.

Ferd opened the cutlery drawer and grabbed a butter knife. He stared at a smudge of jam hardened onto the dull blade. This kind of thing had been happening more and more lately. Whenever his mother did the dishes, he found greasy thumbprints on the plates, lip marks on the glasses, bits of food on the cutlery, but he didn't say anything to her. Instead, he rewashed the dishes, dried them, and put them back in the cupboards, so she wouldn't notice. He flicked the jam spot off the knife with his thumbnail and scraped the burnt parts of the toast into the garbage. Black snow on hills of crumpled tissues.

Aside from what his first note of the day to Leo would say, the biggest decision Ferd made every morning was what to put on his toast. There was less choice these days, but still enough to allow him pause. Strawberry jam or Cheez Whiz. They'd run out of peanut butter, his favourite, a month ago, but his mother had never replaced it. He walked over to the fridge for the ancient oversized jar of spreadable cheese that lived on the bottom shelf. He made to open the door, but stalled. There was something new on the fridge. An ultrasound photo.

Ferd slid the magnet over, pulled the photo off the fridge, and flipped it over. A date from last week was penned onto the back. He turned it back over again. Leo. It was the first time he'd seen him in over a year. His heart ached as much as it was overjoyed. He was sure his mother had left the photo there for him to discover. She'd known he'd find it. A truce. He carefully studied the black and white photo. It looked like the maps of northern Canada that were posted in the halls at school; thousands of kilometres—every tree, person, animal, and road—reduced to water or land.

Algoma called out from the boys' old room and asked Ferd if he could put down two slices of toast for her. She'd slept in again. "Jam, please," she said, her voice thick with sleep. "Not too much."

He told her he would and folded the ultrasound photo and slid it into his back pocket. It was the first time in his life he wished he had a wallet. Men put photos of their families in their wallets. He would be a man soon. Roles had been reversed: he was the older brother now. He needed to start acting like it.

Later that day, during afternoon recess, Ferd sat on the front steps at school and looked at the photo. The image was bisected into four parts from having been folded in his pocket all day. He studied it with the eye of an archaeologist, mining one square at a time until he knew every part. Around him, even though there were still clumps of snow about, other kids were skipping rope and playing something called "first-base baseball," a modified baseball game they'd created to play during the twenty minutes they had outside.

Hunched over and focused on his brother, Ferd did not notice Adrien Plamondon come up beside him.

"Hey, Ferdinand," Adrien said.

Ferd looked up long enough to see Adrien's fist bear down on his face. He reeled off the side of the steps, his arms covering his face, and landed hard on the asphalt. Adrien walked over to Ferd and grabbed the photo from his hand.

"What's this?" he asked.

"Give it back," Ferd said. His left eyebrow was split, a thin rivulet of blood ran down the side of his face. He touched his cheek and looked at his bloodied fingers.

Adrien asked Ferd what the picture was of. "Your mom pregnant or something? I thought your dad was gone."

Ferd struggled to stand up. "I said give it back to me."

"Oh shit, did you knock up someone with your little pecker? Gross."

The other kids stopped what they were doing and stood around the two boys in a circle. No one said a word. There was no question about who would win the fight, if it continued, which most hoped it would. Adrien never lost and he was a full foot taller than Ferd.

Adrien, fists raised, threatened to hit Ferd again if he didn't tell him whose ultrasound photo it was.

"It's Leo," Ferd said, taking a step back out of striking range.

Adrien took a step forward. "I'm sorry, I didn't hear you. Can you say that again?"

"It's my brother. It's Leo. The photo is of Leo."

Adrien cocked his head. He was confused. "Like before he was born?"

"Like now," Ferd said.

The teacher who was supposed to be supervising the students during recess stepped out just in time to catch Adrien straddling Ferd and timing his punches with each word. "Say... it's... not... your... brother."

The teacher mentally reprimanded herself for having taken the time to arrange a doctor's appointment when she should have been outside. She could be suspended for this kind of thing. She yelled at Adrien to get off Ferd. "What do you think you're doing?" Her voice was shrill.

Adrien turned around. He was flushed, his cheeks burning bright red. "Tell him it's not his brother in the picture. Tell him he's a liar."

The teacher walked over to the crumpled photo on the ground and pulled it open. She turned to Ferd who could barely stand up straight and touched his bruised face. "What is this?"

Ten minutes after the final bell rang, Ferd stood on his toes in front of the mirror in the boys' washroom. It hurt to stand, his ribs ached from where Adrien had punched him. He hoped they weren't broken. The split over his eye was crusted over and the skin around it swollen and bruised. He touched his face and winced. He thought about Ms. Prevost's face, the sadness in her eyes, when he'd told her the photo was of Leo. She looked disappointed in him. Worst of all, she didn't give him back his photo. He watched as she tucked it into the top drawer of her desk.

Ferd pulled a make-up compact out from his backpack and tried to camouflage the damage to his face, so his mother wouldn't notice. After the fight, the girl who sat to his right in class had passed over her compact with a sympathetic smile. "Keep it," she'd said. "It's just my mom's."

Using the sponge from the compact, Ferd applied a thick

layer of foundation to the area around his eye. The cover-up was several shades too light for his skin and filled the ridges of his cut like spackle, making it even more noticeable than before. He examined his work and figured it was better than nothing. There was nothing he could do about the swelling. He'd have to make something up.

Make-up packed away, Ferd opened the washroom door a crack and looked down the hallway. His teacher was closing the classroom door. Ferd had never seen her with her glasses off. She looked naked and vulnerable. He felt embarrassed for having seen her this way and looked down at the floor. He could hear her digging through her purse for her keys. After she left, he waited an extra ten minutes before leaving the washroom, in case she returned for something. When he was sure there was no one else in the hallway, he ran to his classroom.

Once inside, he shut the door behind him and tossed his bag on the floor. He pushed Ms. Prevost's chair to the side and opened the drawer.

The ultrasound photo was sitting on top of other confiscated items—rubber balls, a small pen knife, matchbooks and about ten packs of gum. He grabbed the photo and tucked it back into his pocket. He slid the drawer shut and hoped his teacher would forget she'd ever taken it. He had no idea what he'd say if she brought it up.

There were steps in the hallway. Ferd froze for a moment before crouching behind the desk and looked around the corner at the door. Through the frosted window pane, he watched someone, maybe another teacher, walk by. It looked like a man. He crawled across the floor toward the door and sat down beside it, hunched over. A deep ache still lived in his ribs from Adrien's blows. He barely breathed as he listened to the steps pace back and forth until they finally disappeared outside. With the sound of the door closing, Ferd let out his breath. It was time to go home.

Even from the end of the street, Ferd could see that there were no lights on at home. His mother was still at work, and knowing that she'd only be an hour or two late, she hadn't arranged for a babysitter. She'd been working longer hours lately, earning whatever she could to pay the bills. Ferd knew this because she told him. She'd had no one else to talk to, so she was starting to tell her secrets to her son. The only thing she did not speak about were the offerings that were occasionally being left outside the house.

Word had spread that Gaetan had left, and that meant that strange things were happening in the minds of a handful of single men who thought Algoma was a romantic possibility, pregnant or not. In the past month, Ferd had returned home from school to find a variety of gifts left on the porch.

Yesterday, there'd been a small red-and-white plastic cooler with a frozen moose roast inside. When he'd shown it to his mother, she'd simply taken the roast and put it in the fridge to thaw. "Put the cooler back on the porch," she'd said, not meeting his eyes. She wasn't about to waste good meat.

11:56 p.m. 4°C. Wind W, steady.
Carpeting on stairs puckering like sagging skin.

Algoma pulled the envelope out of the mailbox and ripped it open. This time, there was forty-five dollars and another birthday card. She tossed the card into the trash and pocketed the bills. It wasn't her birthday, and wouldn't be for months. The card was just a way to disguise the cash Gaetan was sending. Last week, there had been two envelopes totaling seventy dollars, and the week before, thirty dollars.

When the first envelope had arrived, she'd sat and wept, clutching the money in her hand like a love note. Even though her bank account was suffering, she did not spend that first thirty dollars. Instead, she kept it tucked away in her jewellery box along with her valuables.

Algoma shuffled downstairs in the slippers, nearly tripping over them on the last step.

"Shit," she cursed, tossing her slippers off into the corner.

She walked into the back room and opened the freezer. It creaked like an old door and was nearly empty. There were only a few packages left, meat that Gaetan had butchered with saw and cleaver. She pulled out a pack of venison steaks. They would last her the week. The money in her pocket would not.

As she was shutting the freezer door, she noticed the shoebox, its frost covered edges. She put the package of steaks on the floor and picked it up. It was lighter than she expected. The box had been for a pair of Leo's running shoes, white-soled ones he'd needed for gym class. She set the box on the workshop table and opened it.

The bird looked like it was sleeping, its feathers crisp and bright, its beak an ice pick. How long had it been there? Hollow-boned sleeping beauty. Algoma closed the lid and carried the box upstairs, forgetting the steaks on the floor, which would create a bloodstain in the carpet she'd never be able to fully remove.

The next night, once the bird had thawed, Algoma plucked its feathers and cleaned it as she'd observed Gaetan do so many times, although never with a killdeer. Never with something so small. She tossed her knife onto the counter and turned on the stove. She sat patiently at the kitchen table with a glass of wine as the oven heated up.

Dirty plate abandoned in the sink, Algoma sat down in Gaetan's chair, firmly holding the armrests as she lowered herself down. The chair creaked under her new weight. Was it still his chair now that he was gone? How long until ownership reverted? In her worst moments, she thought it made it easier to simply pretend he was dead, the result of an illness or accident. A car accident. Something destined and uncontrollable. Something she could bury with good conscience that would allow her to miss the good things, allow her to move on. She propped her swollen feet up on the coffee table, shut her eyes, and fell asleep.

In her dream she sat cross-legged at the bottom of an outdoor swimming pool. Schools of small children swam around her, their cool, silver fins fluttering against her as they passed and disappeared into darkened corners. She drew deep breaths of water into her lungs, felt the cool liquid flow through her body, the sharp sting of chlorine in her throat. A dropped shoe slowly sank to the bottom, a slow motion bounce. The sodium lights above the pool went out and she was simultaneously overcome with pain in the palms of her water-puckered hands. She looked at her hands and Leo emerged from the right, Gaetan from the left. Both were dressed in swim trunks, flip flops, and had rosaries around their necks. And from their open mouths, long strands of seaweed swirled toward the surface.

Algoma woke up cold.

The room smelled like Gaetan. She sat up and was blurry with sleep and hope until she remembered what she'd done: sprayed one of his shirts with his cologne and stuffed it under the chair cushion. That way it always smelled like he'd just left. Like he was out picking up some forgotten ingredient and would be right back.

6:23 p.m. 0°C. Wind SE, light.
Neighbour's garbage bag opened by raccoons.
Shredded diapers and potato peels everywhere.

Bay ran up the stairs to her door and tripped. The toe of one of her black leather peep-toe pumps caught on the extended lip of the top step. She heard a loud crack when she fell but couldn't tell if it was the porch or her knee. As she stood up, she saw her dry cleaning and the Chinese takeout she'd been holding were now hopelessly mixed together.

"Fuck."

Her knee bled profusely under the ragged web of torn nylons. A run like a railroad track went all the way up her thigh, beneath the hem of her pewter-coloured silk skirt. She palmed away the mix of dirt and blood. There was no one on the street except for the feral cat that had adopted the neighbourhood as its home. Bay felt her stomach lurch when she thought about the litter of hares she'd found under her porch the year before, the explosion of fur and blood that had replaced them.

Bay reached into the mailbox and pulled out a stack of bills and magazines. Her knee throbbed. Most of the mail, and all the magazines, belonged to her upstairs neighbour. She tucked the latest issue of a tabloid magazine under her arm. She'd return it later. When she put the mail back into the box, she noticed something she'd missed on first look.

Another postcard.

She kicked aside her now stained laundry and spilled

takeout. She'd deal with it later.

The apartment was airless, dust motes suspended in the lamplight. Bay opened up a window, but only an inch. Living alone on the ground floor, she had nightmares about intruders, even in a town as small as Le Pin. You never knew. The dream was always the same: she returned home after work to discover that someone had broken into her home, destroyed it and stolen her favourite things, right down to the expensive chef's knife she had bought for herself in Montreal last Christmas. Everything she valued, gone. But everything was always there when she woke up. If anything, she had more than she needed.

Bay fell back into her couch, tossed her keys onto the coffee table and picked up the postcard. They were arriving more frequently now. A new one every other day. She knew the weather in Toronto better than she did in her own town these days. There was never a salutation or a sign off, but Bay knew the postcards were from Gaetan. His perfect handwriting, as efficient and unromantic as a teacher's. She read the card once and put it down.

Distracted by the pinch of elastic at her waist, Bay wandered into the kitchen and peeled off her destroyed nylons. She threw them onto the heap of take-out containers in the trash. The floor was covered in a fine grit that stuck to the bottoms of her bare feet; it desperately needed to be swept and washed, but she was hardly ever home. She accepted every extra shift the hotel offered her. Anytime someone wanted a night off or called in sick, they called Bay. Within the hour, she would arrive at the hotel, push through the heavy oak doors and take her place behind the front desk.

The hotel, La Belle Fille—no longer a shiny young girl—was a grand old dame who showed her wear at every turn, one who was expensively dressed from another era with little replaced or repaired along the way. The Persian carpets in the lobby were threadbare in places. The wooden banisters, while polished daily, sagged and some of the dowels were missing. The front desk bell rattled more than it rang. It had once been the hope of the hotel's founder that La Belle Fille would be the flagship hotel of a chain that would take over North America, but he never stepped outside county limits. The hotel's clientele was mostly lumber executives visiting the mill or tourists on fishing, hunting, or snowmobile vacations.

For hours on end, Bay would stand behind the counter, the corners of her mouth pulled into a tight work smile. She thumb-polished her Hostess tag when no one was looking. During her breaks, she often unlocked one of the unoccupied suites and laid down on top of the made bed with her heels still on. She tried not to think of the past guests, the bodies that had slept and sloughed in the beds. Instead, she focused on the crisp and clean sheets, the drawn blackout curtains, the television that was always set to channel three. The detail and order were soothing, something she never achieved in her own life. When her coworkers asked her where she spent her breaks, she brushed them off.

"I was out," she said, though there was no real place nearby to go.

She would immediately point out a failing on their part to distract them. An untucked shirt, messy bun, or eyeliner smudge. "Don't you care about yourself?" She was a master at shifting focus, deflection.

The postcard.

How many CN Towers did this make? Ten? Twenty? She went into her study, which was always locked when she wasn't at home, and sometimes even when she was if her twin, Port, was visiting.

"It's just storage space, a mess," Bay had told Port.

Port had jiggled the loose handle. "I could help clean it," she said. And she meant it. She'd always relished any opportunity to organize someone else's mess, especially her twin's.

Bay picked up a blue push pin from her desk, pinned the postcard to the wall, and stood back. The effect was astounding. The walls of her office were covered in row after row of Toronto landmarks. A concrete, brick, and neon rainbow of tourist attractions.

A row of Casa Lomas.

CNE shots.

Royal Ontario Museums.

CN Towers.

Parliament Buildings.

City Halls.

Old City Halls.

Ontario Art Galleries.

Toronto Islands.

And her favourite: Royal York Hotels.

Bay removed one of the dozen Royal York Hotel postcards from the wall and flipped it over: 2:15 p.m. 3°C. Strong N wind. The doorman's red mustache like a train's cowcatcher.

She cared little for the weather. She wanted details: the thread count of the sheets, how plush the towels, the precise perfume of the palm-sized soaps, what coffee was served in the morning. She sniffed the postcard. Nothing.

Bay knew it was wrong to accept the postcards, to display them like she did, but she couldn't stop. Quite simply, she liked them and the attention. She was careful to keep her collection from her twin, her friends, and her family—especially Algoma.

What difference would it make, she rationalized, if Algoma knew? The knowledge would not make Gaetan come home any faster, if he ever planned to. And besides, what would she tell her sister? She didn't even know where he was living, only the city—the largest in the country. He would remain lost as long as he wanted to.

Bay had studied the faint postmark tattoos on each card for a clue to his whereabouts, but they offered little information. She would tell Algoma if she had to, but she could not think of one reason that would make it necessary to do so. Most importantly, she didn't want the postcards to stop coming. She was already eager for another to fill in the gaps on her wall that stood out like missing teeth.

JULY – AUGUST

9:09 p.m. 17°C. No wind.
Fridge motor ticking in time with the clock.

With Ferd already passed out on the living room couch, Algoma went into the boys' old room and turned on her ancient radio. She adjusted the dial to the second lowest volume notch, so the music was hers alone. The radio was preset to a station that catered to the miniscule German community in the area. Algoma was sure they couldn't have more than five listeners a day, yet they carried on as if they were broadcasting to all of Germany. She did not understand a word and that was the appeal. It was as close as she could get to instrumental music in Le Pin.

During the past year, Algoma had found it difficult to fall asleep. She often lay awake thinking about several worries in great detail until early morning, a focus exercise gone horribly wrong. She recalled a television show that said humans tended to obsess over three things at any given time, that the thoughts were cyclical and unending until new obsessions replaced the old ones. Algoma was able to see the perfect geometry of her obsessions. All three corners. It did not make a difference if her eyes were open or closed. Her obsessions were accommodating, patient, always waiting for her. She wondered if Gaetan was actually sleeping wherever he was, or if he, like her, was just performing sleep, a twisting, turning, slack-jawed night dance. Before Gaetan had left, Algoma used him as she did the radio. As a distraction.

"Tell me a story."

"I don't know any stories."

"Tell me a story anyway. Anything."

"Once, long, long ago, there was a bar in a forest..."

Gaetan's stories were often a mix of fairy tale and what happened at the bar the night before. Drunks were cast in the roles of child-devouring witches who didn't pay their tabs and trolls who asked you to solve their relationship riddles before they would let you pass. There were evil step sisters who wore too-short skirts to get free drinks from innocent townsfolk and an evil king who watered down the vodka.

"Another," Algoma asked.

"There was a rich bar owner who had a good-looking daughter who made fun of all the logger suitors—"

"Wait, you told me this one last night."

"It has a different ending this time."

"Oh."

"This time the fiddler is only a fiddler."

And sometimes people just left to leave and you had to let them because there was no alternative. That Gaetan was deliberately staying away baffled her, tore her insides apart, but she had no choice but to accept it. She didn't know where he was, and even if she did, she wouldn't drag him back. For what?

Growing up, several of Algoma's friends hadn't seen their fathers in years. They had blurry memories of what their fathers looked like and received the occasional birthday card postmarked from other provinces. She recalled oldest daughters forced into co-parenting with their overworked and overtired mothers. All-female households with unique hierarchies. The town, for reasons unknown, did not produce many males, and those who were born typically left for work or school and never returned. Gaetan used to joke that the town needed to introduce new bloodlines to make things interesting again, worth staying for.

In five or ten years, what memory of Gaetan would Ferd have? A strong nose. Sunken cheeks. Sweet rye breath. Already, Algoma was forgetting details, while other things became more clearly defined. Crystalline. While she had forgotten his blood type—what ran through him now a mystery—she remembered what glass was his: a simple tumbler with the Olympic rings etched into it. Something he had purchased from a gas station years before and used for everything from gin to milk.

Algoma heard the television turned on in the living room, the volume quickly muted. Ferd was up. Even with the sound off, she could hear the low whine the television emitted, a sound she'd once tried to explain to Bay—a hornet, a dog whistle, a laser—but her sister had never understood.

She got up and walked into the living room. When Ferd saw her, he scrambled to switch off the television. "I was just thirsty," he said guiltily. He pointed at the half-empty glass of water on the coffee table.

Algoma made a mental note to remember to check the kitchen sink drain before she went to bed, knowing there would be a note stuffed down the pipe. "You forgot a coaster," she said. She picked up the remote and switched the television back on. "What's on?"

Into the early hours, they watched a cycling race. The brightly coloured peloton cycled through foreign countryside, repeatedly pulling apart and joining back together again like mercury.

"Ferd, call the police. Someone's trying to break in."

Ferd woke with a start from where he'd fallen asleep on the living room floor. The television flickered in the background. "What's going on?" he asked, voice sleep-slurred.

"Call the police," Algoma whispered. She crouched down as far as she could on the couch. "Someone walked by the window twice. I think he went around back."

Ferd scrambled for the phone in the hallway. Just as he was about to dial, there was a knock at the door. He and Algoma looked at one another.

Algoma grabbed her sewing scissors from the coffee table. "Go into the bedroom, shut the door, and keep the phone with you," she said.

There was another knock at the door, this one louder than the last. Ferd went into his old room, but didn't shut the door. He watched his mother slowly approach the door, holding her sewing scissors as a makeshift weapon.

"Hello?" she called out.

She almost jumped at the sound of the furnace firing up.

"It's me," said the man on the other side of the door. His voice was deep and familiar.

For a split second Algoma's heart leapt at the thought that it was Gaetan, but he wouldn't knock and the silhouette was taller and leaner than her husband's.

"Come on and let me in," the man said, now impatient. "I can see you standing there."

Ferd was standing beside Algoma now. "Do we let him in?" he asked, holding the phone to his chest. "Maybe he knows where Dad is."

Algoma turned off the hall light, hoping it would allow her to see who was at the door, but she couldn't make out the man's face. She desperately tried to place the voice. A family member? A neighbour? A customer at The Shop?

"Who is it?" she asked. "The cops are on their way."

"It's Simon," the man said.

Algoma opened the door to see her brother-in-law standing there. "Simon?"

While no one had ever called Simon handsome, he was interesting to look at, almost regal in his ugliness—a turkey vulture. He stood in the doorway, head cocked to one side. "Hi Allie, it's been a while."

"Come in, come in," Algoma stuttered.

Ferd stepped back into the kitchen.

"What's going on? Everything okay?" Algoma asked.

Looking around the house, Simon asked where Gaetan was. "He owes me a hundred bucks."

Algoma laughed, tears springing to her eyes. "Is that all? You may have wanted to wait until morning to tell me that."

"What's so funny? He owes me money."

Algoma kept laughing until her brother-in-law began to look uncomfortable.

Simon tried to regain control of the situation. "Is he at work, because I can go there, too."

Algoma choked out a response in between gusts of buckling laughter. "He left months ago. And why didn't you ask for it last time you saw him?" she asked. "Hoping to collect interest?"

Simon looked at Ferd. "What the fuck is going on here? Is everyone crazy? Where's your father? Is he at work?"

Ferd nervously picked at a ragged fingernail. "Dad's gone, Mom's pregnant, and we're broke."

Simon smiled involuntarily. "That asshole."

"Hey," Ferd said, ready to defend his father.

Algoma wiped the tears from her eyes. "Do you want

something to drink? I can explain everything, at least the parts I know."

"I want my hundred bucks," Simon said.

"Well, how about you accept a cup of coffee and a sandwich as a down payment?"

Seated in Gaetan's place at the kitchen table, Simon took a bite of the sandwich Algoma had made for him.

Algoma had never seen Simon look so thin. He didn't look healthy, his eyes red-rimmed, his skin sallow.

Ferd climbed onto the chair beside his uncle. "Are you my godfather?"

Algoma set a glass of water beside Simon's plate and shot him a look.

"I can be if you want," he said.

Algoma took the seat on the other side of Simon. "Why do you need money so badly? When did you get into town?"

Simon told her that he'd hitched a ride. "A friend," he said. His girlfriend had broken up with him and kicked him out of the apartment. "Her dad owns the building, so what could I do? And she was letting me borrow her truck for work, so—"

"So," Algoma continued, "you have no job."

Simon took a sip of his water.

Algoma picked up Simon's sandwich and took a bite. "A hundred bucks, which I don't have in the first place, isn't going to help you. Why don't you stay here until you're back on your feet?" She looked at Ferd. "We could use the company, right? There's room at the inn."

*10:37 a.m. 21°C. Light breeze.
Paint-speckled floor.*

Piles of clothes were shored up against the wall like snowdrifts. It felt strange to be inside a new building that held old things—a museum of the ordinary and discarded. Josie had somehow found the means to finish the building, and The Shop had reopened the minute the paint had dried. It was smaller and no longer part of a larger structure, but it was open for business. Algoma found the sharp corners and the smell of new drywall unsettling. She immediately sought out the warm and musty comfort of the boxes of used clothes that needed sorting. She had no idea how one small town accumulated so many things they didn't want when it was so hard to find them in the first place. At what point did something once prized become worthless to its owner? Loved one year, bagged and dumped the next.

Although she was in the business of repurposing things, it always pained her to come across the same piece of clothing two or three times. Like a Christmas kitten returned to the pound by Easter, some things were not meant to have a home. Simon was like that. He bounced around from town to town, taking on odd jobs when they came his way. The only constant in his life was instability. The only reason she'd invited him to stay was that she knew there was an expiry date on his visit. He never stayed anywhere long.

She already doubted the details of his story. Maybe there had been a girlfriend, maybe not. Whatever had happened, he needed money and a place to stay, and she'd offered. And whatever the consequence, she would deal with it.

Algoma opened a box and pulled out a fistful of material and dropped it onto the table. While she no longer had to sit on the hard floor to sort clothes, she resented the long steel sorting table Josie had installed in the back room. Rayon blouses fell off the slick surface; belt buckles sounded like ceremonial gongs when they hit the cold metal.

Although the burnt-out remains of the old shop had been demolished, removed, and a new building erected, Algoma swore she could still smell fire. She worried that there was fire in the walls burning up the building from the inside out. A slow burn. She looked up at the smoke detector. Were there batteries inside? Did it work at all? She put a chair under the detector and awkwardly climbed onto the rattan seat. Her pregnant belly threw her off balance, she struggled to remain upright. A tightrope walker with only the platform and no rope. Once steady, she reached up to the detector and pressed the test button. A shrill beep pierced the air.

"Shut it off," Josie yelled from the front. "You do that one more time, you're fired. I mean it this time."

Algoma got off the chair and looked up. Was it really working? Maybe the test had been a fluke. I should test it again, she thought.

"Don't do it, Al," Josie called out knowing the extent of Algoma's self-doubt.

Boxes and black garbage bags of unsorted clothing were piled into a heap at the end of the sorting table. She could never be sure why any of it had been donated, where it had all come from, or how it all ended up in the back room, but she was grateful because it meant she had a job. She pulled a tangerine skirt out of one of the bags. Maybe the previous owner had outgrown the style, or size, or wanted to be rid of the history the piece was a part of. Reminders of who she was at one time now passed. So easy to stuff all that anxiety into a black garbage bag and toss it into the open mouth of the collection bin and never have to look at it again.

Sundays were the highest drop-off days. Josie and Algoma would unlock the back of the bin and a tidal wave of bags and loose clothing and would spill out into the parking lot. And sometimes, empty beer bottles. Saturday nights were long and lonely times. Josie called the Sunday morning take "the great wine-purge."

Last Sunday, Josie had ripped open one of the smaller bags to find a man's outfit inside complete with button-up shirt, undershirt, jeans, socks, and black leather boots. She'd held the shirt up to her face and sniffed. "Good cologne." In the back pocket of the jeans, she found a pack of cigarettes and a silver lighter. She and Algoma had sat quietly in the parking lot while Josie smoked one of the cigarettes. It was impossible to know people's motivations. They could only work with what they were given.

Algoma left her sorting and walked into Josie's office. The outfit they'd found was folded on top of the filing cabinet, the boots neatly placed on top of the pile. Simon had not arrived with a bag, only had the clothes he'd been wearing. She picked up the bundle and carried it back to her station. She carefully refolded each piece and tucked them into her cotton tote bag. If anything would make Simon feel comfortable, it would be not having to wear his brother's clothing.

7:12 p.m. 18°C. Wind NW, breezy.
Rusting pick-ups and hatchbacks lined up like dominoes.

Josie's cousin Kristin said that Josie would barter her own mother's bones if she thought she'd come out on top in the deal. If there was ever a war, apocalypse, or epidemic, Josie would be king. But even so, she prided herself on never taking advantage of others' needs, especially immediate ones. That her bartering provided for her, she did not deny or take for granted. She'd traded virtually everything she had stored in her barn to rebuild The Shop, and now it was time to rebuild her supply, her savings account of furniture and household items that would always be needed by someone.

"Next up is an antique baby scale, hospital grade. Maybe your grandmother or mother were weighed on it," said the auctioneer in his gravely voice.

Josie sat forward in one of the metal folding chairs that had been set out for people attending the auction. The flimsy chair creaked every time she moved. It punctuated each breath with a squeak.

"It can weigh babies. It can weigh fruit. It can weigh that ten-pound pickerel you landed and tell you it's only seven pounds. Bidding starts at ten dollars. Ten dollars."

The crowd laughed. Josie raised her blank recipe card.

"We have ten dollars. Do we have twenty? Twenty dollars for this white enamel baby scale that weighed your grandmother. Maybe your grandmother's grandmother."

An elderly woman who could very well have been

weighed on the scale herself shakily raised her card. Josie found herself in a bidding war with one of the oldest people in town. She was sure that at least half the people in Le Pin were related to the woman in some way.

"Twenty dollars. Do we have thirty? Thirty? Know the weight of everything in your home, including your wife. Well, at least her foot."

A spattering of laughter from the men.

Josie raised her card again. She pictured the baby scale in Algoma's newly painted nursery. Something old, something new. Josie had never attended a wedding, but was sure the adage was appropriate for babies. It would be the perfect gift, something Algoma might keep forever.

"Twenty-five dollars."

The bidding for the scale topped out at fifty dollars. Josie tucked the recipe card into her back pocket. She only had a twenty dollar bill on her, but she wasn't worried. Billy, the sixty-something auctioneer, had just complained to a mutual friend that his apartment was so damp the covers of his books were starting to curl. He worried that there was mould in the walls and under his carpet, a toxic black bloom beneath his mattress. Josie would trade Billy the extra dehumidifier she had at the store for the scale. A more than fair trade. At first she'd felt bad about taking the scale from the old woman, but it became apparent that the woman was bidding indiscriminately on everything, but not high enough to actually win anything, pulling out at the final moments. It was the thrill of raising her card, making other people sweat with no risk. She probably went home to dinners of canned vegetables and powdered milk. Maybe she could use the recliner that came into the shop last week, Josie thought guiltily. The woman's hands looked like gnarled driftwood.

Josie shook her head and focused on the bidding. Billy's auctions were her favourite because they were by invitation only. Someone had to die or move away before a new person was invited in. She'd never asked who she'd replaced. After the owner of PlasiTech cut work down to only the day shift, Billy had approached him to use the space one night a month. The owner had agreed and in turn he received the pick of the lot from every third auction held. While a plastics factory was not the ideal space for the task—there was little room to set up chairs and it always smelled like burnt chemicals—people enjoyed the novelty, being so close to the sometimes dangerous machinery. Newcomers were always shown the press where David Ypres had lost two fingers on his left hand. People who knew him argued whether he played his guitar better or worse since the accident. It was an even split.

"Next up is a case of top-shelf red wine. The previous owner was waiting for the perfect occasion to drink it and now he's dead," Billy hollered. "Twenty-four bottles of Merlot for your special occasion. Bidding will start at one hundred dollars."

Josie looked at the floor around her. It was covered in hardened white dollops of plastic that looked like melted ice cream. Her forehead was beaded in sweat. Even when the machines were turned off, the place was unbearably hot, which meant the bidding was fast, reckless. She was sure that Billy turned up the heat before each auction for that very reason.

"We have one hundred dollars. Do I have one fifty?"

There were more than fifty people at this month's auction, lured by the promise of "fresh" goods from a newly acquired estate, everything from boxes of personal family photos to a drawer full of mixed cutlery, silver, and stainless steel. Old televisions and an ammunition box. A quilt. Six coolers. A war medal. A brand new fridge.

"Two hundred dollars. Two hundred dollars. Do I have two hundred and fifty dollars for the most special moment of your life? Just don't die first."

Josie wondered if she should leave to retrieve the dehumidifier while the auction was still going on. Maybe drop off the recliner at the old woman's house. She could be back in thirty minutes flat. Maybe Algoma was still at The Shop. She was working longer and longer hours lately now that Simon was around to watch Ferd every day.

"Three hundred dollars to the man with the great palate in the blue sneakers at the front."

The man pumped his arms in the air and woofed, his face red and bobbing like a buoy in rough seas. "Drinks at my place afterward," he yelled. "It's my good-goddamned birthday!" People cheered.

Billy allowed his assistant, the eldest of his sixteen grandchildren, to remove the crate of wine from the display table.

"And the final item of the evening folks will solve all of your problems," he said in a low, serious voice befitting a church.

Billy's grandson Scott, a reedy twenty-something with prematurely grey hair, had a difficult time lifting the item up onto the table even though it didn't look heavy. The metal detector looked homemade—part computer, part vacuum. Josie's stomach lurched. She lifted her card.

"Hold your horses, Jo. I haven't even started the bidding yet," Billy chuckled, then leaned over and gave into a coughing fit.

Josie continued to hold her recipe card in the air. "Fifty bucks," she said.

Billy wiped his mouth and waved his hands over top of the metal detector like he was a magician. "We have fifty beans for this contraption. What have you lost lately? How much is it worth to you to get it back? Better yet, what are you going to lose next?"

"It's beautiful, Josie. Where did you get it?" Algoma traced the white porcelain-coated edge of the baby scale. The scale face was so large she first mistook it for a clock. The time: high noon. Or midnight.

Josie crossed her arms across her chest and leaned back against the counter. "A guy," she said noncommittally.

Algoma grinned. "Who died and what do I owe you?"

"You pay me back every day by staying," Josie said. "In all this time, you're the only one who hasn't quit. See that girl over there?" Josie pointed at the stout girl who stood behind the cash register.

Algoma nodded.

"I don't even know her last name. When did she start? Did you hire her?"

"Nora. Her name is Nora Heriot. You hired her a week ago. She's your neighbour's kid. Nice try."

"You stop trying to keep track when they keep leaving," Josie said. "Can't we just give them all the same name? The illusion of consistency?"

Algoma held the scale in front of her and pressed it up against the bottom of her belly. "What does it say?"

Josie leaned down to read the needle.

"Well, what does it say? Are you going blind or something?"

"Bake at 350 degrees for 45 minutes."

Algoma pushed Josie's head away. "Liar," she said, laughing.

Josie stood up, but her face had gone from relaxed to troubled. "What are you going to do, Al?"

"Today? I'm going to sort the bags and wash and tag the stuff that came in on the weekend. Maybe clean the kitchen, too. I—"

"I mean when the baby comes. How are you going to do it? Two kids."

"I've had two kids before, if you haven't forgotten," Algoma said, more caustically than she'd meant to. "You mean how am I going to do it alone, right?" It wasn't a question.

"Yeah," Josie muttered. She lifted her head slowly, but only high enough that Algoma could see her eyes. "I'm just saying that if there comes a time that you need more—more help, more space—I could help. The farm, it's big. Ferd would have all the space in the world. And you. The baby. And I could help. I'm just saying."

Algoma paused, then embraced her boss as she would Cen or Port, tightly and with utter abandon. She held on to Josie like the last piece of wood in a sinking boat, releasing her at the last moment.

6:52 a.m. 19°C. Wind SE, light.
Open tool box on the kitchen table.

"You don't have to do that, Simon," Algoma said.

Simon stood at the sink, washing the dishes from the night before. "Just eat your breakfast and be thankful," he laughed. "I don't do this for everyone."

"Just people who are housing and feeding you?" Algoma joked.

"Exactly, so never."

"Then carry on, kind sir."

Since his arrival, Simon had been cleaning non-stop. The other day, Algoma had returned home from work to find him scrubbing the baseboards. "You really need to get out more," she'd said. And it was true: he spent all his waking hours indoors either cleaning, watching television, or watching Ferd while she was at work. She was glad, at least for the time being, to relieve her sisters of their babysitting duties. The only time that Simon left the house was before dinner; he walked two blocks to the corner store to buy a pack of cigarettes and returned immediately. While he cooked most meals, he refused to go to the grocery store. "Bad back," he'd said. "Those bags would do me in."

"How's your breakfast?" Simon asked, looking over his shoulder.

Algoma forked the last piece of French toast onto her plate. "Great." She enjoyed having someone help with the daily cooking and cleaning. Gaetan had been diligent with all matters outside the house—the roof, the lawn, trimming the trees—but she'd never seen him wash a dish or put in a load of laundry. With Simon around, her work was halved and she even found some time for herself. She also benefited from the adult conversation in the evenings that she'd been missing since Gaetan had left. For the first time in months, she felt some control over her life, even if it was by giving someone else part of it.

"Coming home after work?" Simon asked.

Algoma nodded. "But I'm having lunch with my sisters today—Bay and Port."

Simon grunted. A dish he'd been drying slipped and clattered onto the counter, but didn't break.

"What's your problem with Bay? You've never liked her, not even in the beginning." Algoma thought back to several particularly bad arguments Simon and Bay had had early on.

Simon mumbled something.

"Sorry, what was that?" Algoma said.

"I said her motives are flawed. Always have been."

"What does that mean?"

"Exactly that."

Algoma picked up her empty plate, walked over, and put it on the counter. "Any luck looking for work?"

"Your pipes are leaking," he said, pointing to a thin stream of water dripping from the cupboards beneath the sink. "That's my job today."

11:43 a.m. 21°C. Wind SE, light.
Pink soap dripping out of the soap dispenser.

The design of the bathroom did not make sense. It only had three walls; the sink and toilet were installed at the wide base of the triangle, the door at the narrow end of the room. The door barely opened enough to let someone through, let alone someone who was pregnant. Algoma didn't know how the new shop had passed code. It seemed everyone in town—at every level—had owed Josie a favour that she'd collected upon.

Another month, Algoma thought, looking at her belly, and she would not be able to use the bathroom at all. She dug into her purse and pulled out an old tube of lipstick. Coral. Weddings, funerals, and meeting up with Bay were the only times she ever wore lipstick. She dragged the oily stick across her lips and pressed them together. She felt like a teenager trying on her mother's make-up. Someone knocked on the door.

"In a minute," she yelled over her shoulder.

She could barely turn around in the washroom and managed to knock her elbow on the hand dryer when she tried.

"Shit," she said and held her elbow protectively.

Algoma prayed silently for a small baby. Five pounds would be good. She pictured a small rump roast on a raised bed of halved onions, sliced carrots, and whole mushrooms. She was hungry. Bay had better not be late. She ran her hands through her hair, dragging her fingers through the tangle. After another several minutes of primping and two more knocks at the door, she surrendered her looks. There was nothing else that could be done.

Waiting in the back room for her sister to show up, Algoma noticed the hem on her skirt had let out in the back. The skirt hung significantly lower in the back than in the front. That wouldn't do, not with her sister. She dug into her purse for a safety pin, dragging her fingers along the worn leather for the small tongue of metal.

"Lose something?"

Startled, Algoma accidentally pierced her finger on the safety pin she had been looking for. "You're early," she said, sucking on her finger and tasting blood.

"Work was slow," Bay said. "Thought I'd drop by—you know, see if you were ready."

Algoma tried to pin the back of her skirt, but she couldn't pull it around to the front far enough.

"Here, let me get that so we can get going," Bay offered in a way that wasn't a choice. "We need to pick up Port along the way." She gracefully crouched down in her tight pencil skirt and deftly pinned the hem. She pulled a second safety pin out of her own purse and preemptively pinned the front of Algoma's skirt. "There. That'll stay for the afternoon, but you need a seamstress."

"Should we get going?" Algoma said. The skirt was pinned much shorter than she would have liked, but she didn't say anything to Bay. Algoma looked down at the forest above her knees. She'd forgotten to shave.

The day was bright, sunlit in a way that sharpened the edges of everything. Algoma struggled to get out of the car with a modicum of grace, Bay watching her every move. When it became apparent that she needed a little help, Bay held out her hand and Algoma grabbed it.

"You're huge. Bet you're ready to be done with all this."

Algoma sighed. "I hope we can still get a seat."

"Or two," Bay said, looking at Algoma's stomach.

Algoma crossed her fingers behind her back and prayed for a bomb threat, anything to end the lunch early.

The restaurant was new, which was why Bay had recommended it. Unlike most other restaurants in town, Mocha Mocha had a small patio. Flower containers and homemade wasp traps (mutilated bleach bottles containing a mixture of pop and antifreeze) hung from the railing. While the restaurant had been open for several months, the "Just Opened!" banner was still hanging from the door. Even though it was the middle of the week, the patio was full of people enjoying the subtle summer warmth, which always seemed to leave too soon. Bay and Port had to sit so close their legs crossed over one another's. Algoma sat on the other side of the table.

Bay immediately ordered drinks for everyone. Mimosas for her and Port. Orange juice for Algoma.

"Perfection," she said, downing her mimosa in one shot, as soon as it arrived.

"Maybe you want some water with that," Port said sarcastically.

"What? It's Friday, or will be tomorrow. I'm tired." Bay looked at the waiter whom she appeared to know better than she let on. Even though he was taking orders from another table, she yelled out: "Another round, Mitch!"

Mitch nodded and returned with a fresh round of drinks only minutes later.

Algoma drew her finger along the condensation on her

glass. Her sisters ignored her and spent the next twenty minutes catching up. Algoma shifted in her seat. She had to use the washroom, but dreaded trying to walk through the packed patio. It could wait. She stared at her sisters, waiting for the break in the conversation that would allow her to leave. She could walk back to The Shop, if need be.

Port looked like the casual Friday version of Bay. She swapped nylons for bare legs, heels for flats, and flat-ironed hair for a loose ponytail. Algoma picked at her shirt self-consciously. While it pulled at her armpits and belly, the fabric ballooned at the neck and bust line. Her already short skirt had ridden up even higher on her thighs when she sat down. She was grateful to be facing her sisters and not another table. She was keenly aware of the scuff on her left shoe, her pinned hemline, the cheap fabric of her shirt. Her clothes felt like an awkward second skin that she had shed but could not lose.

Mitch set down a third round of mimosas in front of Port and Algoma and another orange juice in front of Bay, who quickly carouseled the drinks to the proper owners.

"Can I take this extra chair for another group?" Mitch asked Algoma, pointing to the chair beside her.

She nodded. Her entire life, people were always expecting a second version of her to show up and assume the place beside her. When they realized no one was coming, they seemed disappointed, like they'd been tricked.

Mitch was about to pick up the chair when Bay's hand shot out. "Wait, I need it." She tossed her oversized purse onto the empty seat. "There, now it doesn't have to sit on the floor."

Algoma looked apologetically at the waiter and shrugged.

Bay stared at her youngest sister while her twin told a tedious story about the parking ticket she'd received the day before. Since they had arrived at the restaurant, Bay had been waiting for a reaction. She was waiting for Algoma's intuition to kick in. Before she had left that morning, she'd put Gaetan's latest postcard in her purse, one of Riverdale Farm that showed two jersey cows fenced into a miniature field. Somehow, she'd expected her sister to sense it, but Algoma hadn't even looked at the purse. She should be looking at it, Bay thought, noting Algoma's cotton bag, the blue ink stain in the bottom corner. Her own purse had cost her three hundred dollars, a small fortune.

"Did you know there's a farm in the middle of Toronto?" asked Bay, interrupting her twin's description of the police officer's handwriting. "Cows and everything. Even those pretty ones—what are they called?"

"Jerseys?" Port offered.

"And the restaurant at the top of the CN Tower rotates. Some woman put her purse down beside her and it disappeared, but then it came back ten minutes later with everything still inside. Can you even believe it?"

Algoma shifted in her seat. Her tailbone ached from sitting still so long. "Are you planning a trip?"

Bay, realizing that she'd said too much, pressed her lips together. "No. Well, maybe."

"Maybe she's going to move there," Port said. "Work at one of the big fancy hotels like The Fairmont York."

"It's The Fairmont Royal York."

"Royal," Port drawled, mocking her sister. "Whatever, she goes on and on about it like it's a person or something."

Bay rolled her eyes.

"I have to get back to work soon," Algoma said, looking at her bare wrist.

The twins tag-teamed Algoma and convinced her to stay

long enough to have some food. "You still haven't told us why Simon is living at your house," said Bay. "I wouldn't even have let him in the door, let alone sleeping in my bed."

"He's sleeping in the basement," Algoma said.

"Has he said how long he's staying? I hope he's giving you money."

Algoma said she'd stay for lunch on the condition that Bay lay off Simon. "He's family," she said.

"He's Gaetan's family," Bay snapped, her face reddening at even the mention of his name.

Mitch arrived at the table. "Ready to order?"

After their meals arrived, the sisters performed their individual food rituals. Algoma removed the pickles from her burger and placed the ketchup-covered dills on the edge of Port's plate. Port plucked every black olive out of her heaping Greek salad and placed them on Bay's Cobb salad. Bay spooned the grated cheddar from her salad onto Algoma's fries.

"Have you heard from him?" Bay asked Algoma, forking a salted wedge of egg into her mouth. She was tired of waiting.

Port elbowed her twin in the ribs and glared. "Bay."

Algoma felt a wave of nausea. "Nothing except for the envelopes," she said, referring to the cash.

Bay nodded sympathetically and asked her twin what time it was. The mailman would have already passed her house. "Time to go soon, yes?"

3:15 p.m. 21°C. Wind SE, light.
A pack of cigarettes resting on the toaster.

As soon as Algoma had left for work, Simon had picked up the newspaper she'd purposefully left behind on the table for him, and tossed it into the garbage. He'd already read the paper the day before; there were at least a half dozen jobs he was qualified for, but he wasn't interested. It would mean he would have to leave the house, and he was not ready to be seen yet.

Le Pin was the town of his youth; he'd undoubtedly be recognized within minutes. Even the thought of being in town fatigued him. Instead of looking for a job, or a new place to live, he'd crawled back into his unmade bed downstairs. If he slept, he didn't have to think about why he was back in the town he said he'd never return to.

It was mid-afternoon by the time Simon woke. He went upstairs to smoke. Afternoons had become his favourite time of day. If mornings were his anxious times, afternoons were when he busied himself with problems that were easily resolved and not his own. Algoma's house was an embarrassment of riches when it came to things that needed repair. Everything, it seemed, needed fixing. It almost felt like after Gaetan had left, the house had given up, though he was sure the issues were a result of several years of neglect. Like a geologist, he felt like he could pinpoint the exact year the cataclysmic event had happened: the year Leo had died.

When Simon's cousin Louise had called to tell him what

had happened to Leo, he'd immediately called his brother. They hadn't spoken for some time, but Simon felt that his brother needed his support and might even accept it. He'd been wrong. As soon as Gaetan heard Simon's voice on the other end of the line, he'd hung up.

Simon opened up the kitchen window and lit a cigarette. Algoma forbade smoking in the house, but if he smoked close to the open window when she was gone, she was never able to tell, or at least she never let on that she could. Since he'd first met Algoma when she'd started dating his older brother, he knew she could keep secrets. He wondered how much she was keeping from herself. Her life was built on an outdated routine that she kept performing like a caged animal who didn't, or refused to, see the open door.

He leaned over the counter to exhale the smoke out the window and did a mental calculation of the cash he had left. Eighty dollars. A week of cigarettes. Instead of worrying about it, he set about his work for the day—fixing the pipes under the kitchen sink—but first he had to take everything out of the cupboard. Simon butted his cigarette on a dirty dish in the sink and sat down on the linoleum he'd scrubbed the day before. He opened the cupboard doors and began to remove everything inside, placing the items on the floor around him. Bright, glowing bottles of cleaner, heaps of dingy rags, and an assortment of brushes and scouring pads. When he grabbed the bucket behind the S-pipe, he saw a cardboard shoebox. He tossed the bucket behind him and grabbed the box, which was half-destroyed from the leaking pipe, and set it behind him.

His working space around the pipe clear, Simon went downstairs to get his brother's toolbox to fix what should have been his brother's problem. He couldn't deny that part of him was happy to be doing it—cleaning up his brother's mess. Somehow it made him right in the end, about everything, every argument he'd ever had with his brother now recalibrated.

Once the pipes were cleared, replaced, and tightened, Simon began to put everything back under the sink. When he picked up the shoebox, the still-wet cardboard buckled and ripped in his hands. Folded pieces of paper fell into his lap and onto the floor. Most of the notes were written on paper, but some were written on scraps of cloth, leaves, and pieces of torn wallpaper. Simon rested the shoebox in his lap. He picked up one of the notes and began to read.

*3:12 p.m. 19°C. Wind N, gusting.
Lightning charred oak still standing.*

Ferd found a large boulder to sit on and laid his shotgun down with the barrel facing into the woods, the safety on. The wind was coming from the north. There was a bite to it, which made it feel like the beginning of fall, not the end of summer. He took off his canvas backpack and searched through it for his lunch. A tinfoil-wrapped turkey sandwich with two thick slices of mozzarella cheese and three slices of dill pickle. No butter or mustard. It was only when he made his own sandwiches—as was the case more and more these days—that they remained whole, uncut. His mother was partial to cutting sandwiches into four squares.

"It makes lunch seem smaller," he'd argued.

His mother said it was more "civilized." How butchering something was more civilized, Ferd didn't understand. When left to his own devices, a knife never saw his sandwiches. They were simple hunks of bread, cheese, meat like he imagined Vikings or voyageurs used to eat, without the pickles, of course. After he unwrapped his sandwich, he flattened out the tinfoil and laid it down on the rock, so he could sit on it.

It was the first time that year that Ferd had gone hunting. It had taken him an entire afternoon to find his gear in the basement and the shed, to clean it, and ensure it was all in working order, just like his father had shown him. It was also the first time that he had gone hunting alone. Without his brother, the woods seemed denser, the air colder.

From his perch, Ferd faced the railway tracks that he'd walked along all morning in search of hares. Shining parallels of rail that went clear across the province, north to south. The hunting was hard going without another body to walk along the bottom to flush out the hares, but he kept pressing on, hoping that, either perseverance or luck, would prevail. It was not like he could ask any of the kids at school to join him. He listened to their stories about their mothers' lasagnas, pizzas, and taco dinners. At Ferd's house, it was hare stew, moose steak, and tourtière made with ground deer meat, complete with sides from his mother's garden. The kids at school would sooner starve than harvest their own dinner, but then again, Ferd had thought that an avocado was a type of car until his teacher brought one into class one day. He'd readily admit that there were things his classmates didn't know about him and he didn't know about his classmates. But the one thing he knew for certain was that an avocado, whatever it was, was not a meal.

As he sucked on his juice box, he heard a train approach. It sounded its horn several times. He had no idea who they were warning. There were no houses around for miles.

"Twenty-six," he said out loud. He guessed the train would have twenty-six cars. It was a game that he used to play with his brother, a game Leo always won. Ferd had suspected his twin had better eyesight, but Leo tried to convince him that he was psychic. As the cars passed with their freight, he counted each one. Every other car was covered in graffiti. It was like code, sent from one city to another. Spy messages hidden in plain sight. Thirty-two cars was the final count. He was wrong again.

Ferd balled up his tinfoil seat, tossed it into his backpack, and resumed his hunt. He was ready, but still careful. A year ago, Ferd had heard a story about a hunter in town who'd been surprised by a hare that had run right across his feet. The hunter had reacted too quickly and fired off a shot. He'd killed the hare dead but the meat was blasted apart and useless. And so was his foot.

Focus.

The day was overcast, the sky cluttered with thick grey clouds, but it was the cluster of darker clouds on the horizon that worried him. He didn't want to get caught in the rain. His rain jacket was the one thing he'd not found the day before. His sweater would keep him warm so long as he didn't get wet. He crossed himself as he saw his mother sometimes do when things became dire. The wind picked up and tree branches creaked eerily. The only bird Ferd could hear was a crow off in the distance, a persistent, urgent caw. He looked both ways down the tracks. No train. He carried on.

When Ferd had hunted this spot with his brother and father, Gaetan had walked the rails.

"It's dangerous," he'd said. "Too dangerous for you." He'd made the boys walk along either side of the track, doubling his chances.

"Hunting is all about luck," he said with false humility. Whenever someone asked Gaetan about his take for that day, he would respond: "I was lucky."

"It's never good to piss people off," he'd taught his sons. "They know the real score. But you never tell them the truth and you never tell them your spot. 'I was lucky,' you say. 'Thank you,' you say."

Ferd heard the chatter of a red squirrel in a tree close to the tracks. He pointed his shotgun at the small animal, aimed. "Pow," he said, pretending to shoot. The squirrel ran down the tree and back into the woods.

A hare darted across the track. Ferd swung his shotgun around, took the shot, and nailed it. He put his shotgun down on the ties and ran over to retrieve the animal, a smile plastered across his face. At least he would have something to go home with. There was nothing worse than going home empty handed, even if no one was expecting anything. All that effort for nothing. Admittedly, he also liked to impress his uncle with his abilities. Every time he brought home a fish or animal, Simon seemed genuinely impressed.

Just as he was about to pick up his catch, a man walked out of the bush—a game warden. Ferd froze, his stomach a bowl of ice. The warden was taller and broader than his father, his shoulders seeming to take up the sky.

"I'll be taking that," said the warden, pointing at Ferd's shotgun.

Ferd fought the urge to run. He'd never make it, not with his shotgun, and he wasn't leaving it behind, or his hare.

The warden leaned over and picked up Ferd's hare. "Nice shot but wrong season," he said, "Where's your guardian?"

Ferd remained mute, his heels dug into the ground.

The warden used a plastic zip tie to attach the hare's feet to his belt. "You want to hand over the shotgun now and any shells you have in that backpack there? I'm not asking again. Where's your orange vest?"

Ferd handed over his shotgun and all the shells he had. "I have an apple left. Do you want that, too?" he asked earnestly.

"Let's go," the warden said. "My truck's just over there." He pointed toward a cluster of trees.

Ferd hadn't known about the utility road that ran alongside parts of the rail tracks—he'd always kept to the tracks. The road was used by workers from the rail company, but the Ministry used it to track hunters in the area to ensure everyone was on the up and up.

"What's your name?" Ferd asked nervously.

"You're a little young to be toting a firearm alone, don't you think?"

Ferd said nothing. When they arrived at the truck, the warden cut the zip tie and tossed the hare into the truck bed where it landed with a padded thump.

"Go on, get in. It's unlocked."

Ferd climbed into the cab of the truck.

The warden sat in the driver's seat and turned on the ignition and they were off, but Ferd didn't know where to.

"How did you learn to shoot like that?" the warden asked. He kept his hands at the ten and two position as he drove.

Ferd ignored the question and looked out the window.

"That a Browning?" the warden persisted. He tried a different approach. "I have a black lab named Browning. Another one, a golden, named Trigger. I've got two girls, too—your age, you might know them—but neither are interested in hunting. But the wife, she got her firearms license last fall."

Ferd didn't turn once toward the warden, his view a blur of leaves and mud. Fat drops of rain hit the windshield. At least he didn't have to walk home.

When Gaetan had been around, Ferd and Leo had never been bothered by the Ministry. One of the top guys had liked drinking at Club Rebar too much to ruin it for himself, so he left Gaetan and his family to do as they pleased, and Gaetan was generous with his pours. As long as they weren't hunting too close to houses, they were left alone.

But with Gaetan gone, the rules had changed. Suddenly Ferd was just a twelve-year-old with a shotgun alone in the middle of nowhere.

Ferd took in the warden's uniform, the yellow foam floater he had on his key chain, his overly gelled blond hair that was combed back so you could see his pink scalp in the spaces in between. He thought about his father and what he would do in this situation.

Ferd tugged on the warden's shirtsleeve. "Can I at least keep my hare?"

Algoma ran inside the house, eager to get out of the rain. She was hungry and headed straight for the kitchen with her shoes still on, squeaking as she crossed the floor. "Ferd, you home?" she asked. There was no answer, but she heard movement in the basement. He was home. There was a note from Simon on the table: Gone for smokes. Be right back.

She grabbed the loaf of bread from the counter and a plate from the cupboard. When she turned to get a butter knife from the cutlery drawer, she saw a teacup on the kitchen windowsill. She leaned over, looked in, and dropped her plate into the sink where it split into two neat halves. The teacup—one of her mother's—held a roughly cut hare's foot, a small amount of blood dried at the bottom. How many more good luck charms, she thought, would she find there without finding any luck at all.

1:29 p.m. 24°C. Dead air.
Wind whistling in the tunnels like an old man's tune.

The hulking booth attendant offered a strained smile when Gaetan waved at him as he passed through the turnstile, flashing his transit pass like it was a backstage pass to the city. A flight of stairs below, commuters stood elbow to elbow, breathing in one another's coffee breath, and trying not to look each other in the eyes. Gaetan took his place among them.

In recent weeks, he had become very familiar with the subway system, its web of routes and stops. On his days off, he took transit to different parts of the city to find new restaurants that did not know his agenda: eat and run. In only a month, he'd hit restaurants in Little India, The Beaches, Parkdale, and the Danforth. Some days it was easy and he walked out of the restaurants without anyone noticing. Other times, he found himself running down unfamiliar streets looking for the right turn or open door that would save him.

When Gaetan hit a restaurant, he never chose anything expensive, and he limited himself to one beer to ensure his senses were not dulled when it was time to leave. He always made small talk with the server, asked how his or her day was going. He tried to act normal. He tried to be forgettable. Mostly, he wore good shoes. Running shoes.

That he could have opted to prepare his meals in his apartment and send the money he saved home crossed his mind, but it wasn't the point. He felt a shiver of pride every time he dropped an envelope for Algoma into the mailbox. It was also the thrill of the kill. No longer able to hunt, he had found a new way to earn his dinner.

Gaetan took the subway to Spadina Station and boarded a southbound streetcar. He exited the streetcar at College Street, the beginning (or end) of Chinatown and continued to walk south on foot, careful to stay on the opposite side of the street of the first restaurant he'd dined and dashed from. It was a perfect day—bright and sunny—and the sidewalks were filled with midday shoppers. He took his time considering the restaurant he'd hit next. Some, he felt, were too small, while others didn't have enough people already inside. He'd be too noticeable. Finally, he settled on a restaurant that specialized in dumplings. Through the plate glass windows, he could see that most of the tables were occupied and there appeared to be only one server. He went inside and took a seat close to the door and smiled at his waiter. "What's the special?"

When it came time to leave, Gaetan stood up and walked out the door without so much as a glance from his waiter. The man, along with one of the cooks, was yelling at a baseball game on the television. Once outside, Gaetan looked over his shoulder, but the men were still watching the game, oblivious to his departure and the money that was still in his pocket. Without even thinking about it, Gaetan walked into another restaurant only three doors down from the last one. He wasn't hungry, he was bored. The last restaurant had been too easy. This time, he sat in the back and grabbed the menu from the waitress's hand before she could even give it to him.

"Sir," she said, reprimanding him with a nervous laugh.

"Be nice."

"I'll have number 4C and a Labatts," he said.

The woman jotted down the order, smiled, and turned on her heel.

"And a number 15B," he yelled after her.

While he waited for his order, he thought about Algoma. He imagined his wife opening the envelopes and discovering the money inside, but when he tried to think of what she would do next, he drew a blank. He didn't know her life anymore, not even what bills the money would go to first. He recalled the winter the heat had been turned off. Algoma hadn't been working because she'd broken her leg, and the boys were very young, maybe four years old. They'd barely had enough money to begin with and with Algoma not working, their financial problems compounded. During that month, the wood stove had been their constant companion, both keeping them warm and the pipes from freezing. Algoma had turned it into a game for the boys. Camping. She'd never complained once. He thought about their more recent bout of basement camping, the fervour with which Algoma had approached it, the desperation to knit a new unit out of the three of them. It had worked, for a time. But now his leaving had unravelled it again.

The waitress interrupted his nostalgia when she put his beer on the table. Gaetan took a swig from the bottle and tried to imagine Algoma's face.

When the waitress returned with his leek and pork dumplings, he powered through his meal almost mechanically. He stuffed forkful after forkful into his mouth until there was nothing left on his plate except for a mix of vinegar and hot sauce.

Seeing his empty glass, the waitress walked over to him.

"Another, sir?"

"No," he stuttered. "Just the bill."

The waitress nodded and went to the cash register. As soon as her back was turned, Gaetan stood up. Seeing how far away the exit was made his stomach turn. He'd made a bad choice sitting at the back, but he was still confident he could make it. Fueled by his past successes, he made for the door, his shoulders square, back straight. False confidence. When he heard the register chug out his receipt, he sped up his pace. "Sir," he heard the waitress call after him. "Your bill, sir!"

Gaetan ran the last few steps and threw the door open with such force that the brass bell at the top snapped off and fell to the ground. Outside, the sidewalk was still packed with shoppers. He pushed his way into the centre of the crowd that was flowing south and tried to blend in, however, when he looked over his shoulder, he saw his waitress's face in the door of the restaurant. She was talking into a cell phone and staring right at him.

"Shit," Gaetan said. He ducked down and tried to make his way through the crowd. When that became too difficult he made his way toward the street and jogged alongside the curb hoping he wouldn't get clipped by a car. The next time he looked back, he couldn't see the waitress. He slowed his pace, but only a little. Once he got down to Queen, he thought, he would hop on a streetcar and disappear east. He wouldn't be returning to Chinatown anytime soon. Digging into his pockets for change, he found exactly what he needed. Maybe his luck was changing.

"There he is," he heard a man shout. Gaetan turned to see the server from the first restaurant about fifteen feet behind him, but when he tried to run, he ran right into the barrel chest of another man, the cook the server had been watching the game with.

"Walk with me," the cook said, guiding Gaetan back up the street.

"I can explain," Gaetan offered. "I'll pay double what I owe, just let me explain." He tried to think of a story that would placate them.

"Just walk."

When they reached the server, Gaetan offered to go to a bank machine. "Just tell me how much you want. Please."

"Let's go," the server said.

When they passed the second restaurant Gaetan had been to that day, Gaetan saw the waitress standing in the window, a big smile on her face. She gave Gaetan a small queen-like wave, her hand barely moving. Had she called the men? How had she known? His mind reeled trying to make the connection.

When they walked past the first restaurant Gaetan had hit, the one where the server and cook worked, Gaetan knew he was in more trouble than he'd first thought. They were not bringing him back to the restaurant to call the cops. They were going to take care of the matter themselves.

"Where are we going?" Gaetan asked, his voice edged with worry.

The man responded by tightening his grip on Gaetan's arm.

Not wanting to discover where the men were taking him, Gaetan wrenched his arm free and ran. He made his way toward an opening between two buildings, hoping it would lead him to Kensington Market where he could duck into one of the bars or shops. When he turned the corner, he instantly regretted his decision. It was a dead end. A tall chain-link fence blocked his escape. Before he could backtrack, the two men turned the corner into the alley behind him.

"Listen, whatever you guys want," Gaetan pleaded. "Just let me explain. My wife—"

"First you rip me off and then my sister?" the server said. "You're lucky our father is out of the city. He doesn't take kindly to being taken advantage of. He's owned those restaurants for more than twenty years and you're not the first asshole we've had to deal with."

Gaetan could not believe his bad luck. Resigned to whatever fate the afternoon was going to offer him, he closed his eyes and let his shoulders slump.

The cook stepped forward, but the server stayed him.

"No," he said and picked up a piece of a broken wooden pallet. He stepped forward and struck Gaetan on the side of the head.

The darkness was immediate.

3:55 p.m. 22°C. Wind W, light.
Bird seed scattered on the lawn, birdbath overflowing.

The grackle dropped dead on the lawn, its head twisted at an unnatural angle.

"You got it," Leo shrieked.

Gaetan slapped Ferd on the back. "You did it. Good eye!"

Ferd beamed.

Leo leaned against the cupboard. "Will the finches build another nest?"

"Not sure," said Gaetan. "We'll have to wait and see now."

A week after the family had discovered a finch nest in their backyard, they'd watched a grackle destroy the eggs, nosing pieces of shell onto the lawn below. Leo had cried the entire afternoon.

While shooting a gun—even a pellet gun—inside town limits was prohibited, Gaetan ignored the law when it came to "bad birds," which included grackles, sparrows, red-winged black birds, and cowbirds.

"They take over nests that are not theirs and destroy the eggs. They're asking for it."

The hedge that wrapped around the backyard provided them with the privacy they needed to carry out their vendettas. Algoma clapped every time one of them shot a starling or sparrow. The Beaudoins' "bird pail" was three-quarters full with feathered layers. Feral cats circled the bin like sharks.

Gaetan looked at his boys, who eagerly waited his instructions.

"A dead bird scares off live ones," he said, waiting for the boys to figure it out.

Leo and Ferd fought over who would get to shoot the next bird and who would have to retrieve the grackle.

Afternoons when there were no birds, Gaetan and the boys practiced their aim on lawn ornaments. Their favourite was the already bullet-riddled wooden duck. They took turns shooting at it from the kitchen window. Gaetan was the best shot, followed by Leo, and Ferd a surly third. Ferd believed he was a better shot than anyone—even his father—but there were factors that worked against him. It was always something else that ruined his shot: a sudden gust of wind, Leo's heavy breathing, or the sun in his eyes, even on the cloudiest day. Ferd's shots were often non-lethal, hitting the duck's tail or legs. Leo had mastered the kill shot. Immediate death.

Ferd ran outside to get the bird and tossed it into the bird bin.

"Three points," he yelled.

"Wait," Gaetan called out. "I have an idea."

In his basement workshop, the boys watched their father cut a length of wire from a large coil on his worktable. Gaetan pierced the grackle's still warm breast and carefully threaded the wire through the bird's body, up to and through its head. He used wire cutters to snip off the excess wire that poked out, so that it barely showed.

"Here," he said, handing over the franken-bird to Ferd. "Go stand it on the lawn and then get your mother."

"Mom, there's a bird. Come and take the shot," Leo yelled. Algoma closed the washing machine lid and ran up the stairs, happy they were including her in something.

"Here," he said, handing her the pellet gun. "It's already loaded."

It was her first time holding the gun. It was lighter than she had imagined, the weight of a broom.

"There," Leo pointed. "By the bird feeder."

Algoma slowly slid open the kitchen window.

"There," Ferd hissed. "See it? Shoot! Shoot!"

"Shhh—"

"Now! Shoot it!"

Algoma raised the gun and let the barrel rest on the window sill, a trick Gaetan had taught the boys when they were younger and too small to keep the barrel steady on their own. She carefully lined up the sight with the bird's head.

"Stay still, stay still," Leo coached. He sat cross-legged on the counter. "Don't even breathe."

Algoma bit her lip and pulled the trigger.

The bird shook but did not fly off or fall down.

"It's not moving," she said. She was confused. "It's not even scared."

"Shoot it again, Mom! Shoot it again!" Leo could barely contain his laughter.

Algoma took several deep breaths and leaned into her shot. Breathe. Exhale. Take the shot. She pulled the trigger again. The bird bent over at a gravity defying angle, but did not fall down.

"What the—"

Gaetan and Ferd stumbled out onto the lawn, doubled over with laughter. Ferd ran over to the bird and punted it with his running shoe. "Goal!" he yelled lifting his arms above his head. The bird sailed across the yard and over the hedge into the neighbour's yard.

3:48 p.m. 25°C. No wind.
Tin of pellets forgotten on the sidewalk.

Both pellet guns looked the same. Even though they'd had different owners, there was little to differentiate them. Ferd couldn't recall how he and Leo had always been able to tell them apart, but they had. He wasn't so sure anymore. He sat cross-legged on the lawn and assessed the two rifles. Both had been gifts from their father—hand-me-downs—break-barrel air rifles that he'd had at the same age. Years of immaculate care meant that the guns had lasted, but Ferd had always believed that his shot a couple centimetres to the left, which was why Leo was always a better shot when it came to target practice.

Leo had laughed at Ferd's theory. "Let's trade rifles then," he'd said, but Ferd never accepted the offer. He would know the truth now.

He unlocked the shed and squeezed in behind the lawnmower to where the cardboard targets were kept. Behind the targets, he found what he was looking for.

Immediately after Leo had gone through the ice, Gaetan had removed the black bear pelt from the spare room wall and put it in the shed. He said he couldn't look at it anymore. The pelt had been a gift from his father after a hunting trip they'd gone on when Gaetan was a teenager. Until it had been removed, the pelt had been a fixture in the house; and once it was gone, its spread-eagle silhouette remained on the wall like a ghost.

Ferd picked up the pelt and shook it out a like a rug. It was old and brittle, the hair missing in patches where it had fallen out. He looked over the pelt and decided to use the small bald patch above the bear's nose as his target, so that his shots wouldn't get lost in the fur that remained. Sure his father was not coming back, and even if he did, he'd hardly be able to punish him, Ferd took the pelt and nailed it to the side of the shed. Target ready, he took his position on the other side of the yard.

Ferd picked up the first gun, broke the barrel, and loaded the pellet into the breech. Once he'd tipped the barrel back into position, he was ready to shoot. He pressed the walnut stock against his shoulder and carefully lined up his shot. A sparrow flew down and perched on the bear's nose, and for a second, Ferd thought he might have a live target, but it flew away. He took several deep breaths and, on the third, he slowly exhaled and pulled the trigger. The shot went two inches wide and struck the bear's nose. He took another shot and the pellet struck the bear several millimetres away from his first shot. It was definitely his gun.

Swapping guns, Ferd put down the first gun and picked up the second. He loaded his pellet and switched off the safety. This time he would hit the centre of the bald patch. He wished he'd drawn a proper target on the exposed hide. A target within a target. Even if there was no one to see it, he would know that he'd been the better shot all along. While he loved his brother, he didn't think it was fair that he'd left with the title of best shot in a contest that had only ever existed between the two of them. Since his mother had asked him to stay out of the woods until the incident with the game warden calmed down, he'd had a lot of time to practice in the backyard. If he wasn't the better shot before, he was now.

Ferd adjusted his grip on the rifle and focused on the target. Again, he took several deep breaths and, like clockwork, took his shot on the third exhale. He put down the rifle and ran over to the target, sure his shot was dead centre. Instead, he found a third hole beside his previous two. Impossible, he thought. Both guns shot exactly the same. He was crushed.

Simon called out to Ferd from the side door. "You want to come in here for a minute?"

Ferd threw down his gun and walked to the house. Inside, he found his uncle seated at the kitchen table with a box sitting in front of him. "Where's Mom?" he asked.

Simon opened the lid and pulled out a piece of folded paper. "She's still working."

"What's that?" Ferd took a step forward.

Simon took a deep breath. "That's what I was going to ask you."

He'd held onto the notes for days trying to figure out what to do. In the end, he decided it was just like fixing the sink—something his brother should have taken care of, but now the job had been left to him.

Simon pulled out one of the notes and began to read. "Dear Leo—"

Ferd's face fell. "What are you doing? What is that?"

Simon continued. "Dear Leo... I can't wait until you come back. Everything will be better then. Don't stay away too long."

"Stop it," Ferd said, tears coming to his eyes. "That's not yours. It's Leo's."

Simon read on: "I miss you a lot. Sometimes I pretend you're still here—"

Ferd ran over to Simon and ripped the note from his

hands. "I said stop it. How did you get that? It's not yours."

Simon pushed the shoebox towards Ferd and sat back in his chair. "There are dozens more in the box. Look for yourself."

Ferd rifled through the box, looking at the notes. He immediately recognized his own handwriting and even some of the paper the notes were written on. A bill envelope he'd stolen from his mother, a grocery store receipt, a slip of birch bark. Had he been wrong all along? Had his brother not actually received any of his letters? The idea was impossible to him. He shoved the box off the table, the notes tumbling onto the floor.

"You're a liar. You made all this up," he choked.

Simon spoke calmly in a low, slow voice. "He's gone. I'm sure you're breaking your mother's heart with these letters. It needs to stop. Leo's dead. He's not coming back."

"I hate you," Ferd said. "Leo is coming back."

"Then why do I have these letters?" Simon asked.

Ferd didn't understand what was happening. He felt hollow, gutted of purpose, but he refused to let go of the only thing he had: Leo.

"I don't care," he spat. "You're wrong." He bent down and started ripping up the letters. "You did all this. You made this all up."

Algoma walked in the door with a bag of take-out in her arms, a special surprise. She looked and saw Simon sitting at the table, head heavy in his hands, and Ferd crouched on the floor ripping up pieces of paper. When she saw the empty shoebox, she understood.

"What you have done, Simon?"

*11:13 p.m. 5°C. Wind S, breezy.
Crunch of gravel underfoot.*

Simon was the only person to arrive at the bar on foot that day. Two rows of cars and trucks gleamed under the parking lot security lights. When the lights automatically switched off in the morning, a half dozen cars would be left behind to be collected later. The air was crisp and cool, the sky blanketed with stars. It was already beginning to feel like fall. He was so shaken up by his encounter with Ferd earlier that day that he'd left without his jacket, leaving Algoma to try to calm her son down.

"Just go," she'd said. "Come back later."

He wasn't sure she wanted him to return, but took her at her word. What else could he do?

With nowhere else to go, Simon found himself at Club Rebar, knowing that no one who saw him there would be sober enough to remember the next day. Going to the Club was like walking into a black hole; nothing truly escaped.

It was early evening by the time he'd arrived, however; the bar was packed. Over the clack of billiard balls and music blaring out of the tinny speakers of the jukebox he could barely hear his own thoughts. It was perfect. While he rarely drank, Simon found himself quickly spending the money he had left. He didn't look forward to having to ask Algoma for money to buy cigarettes the next day.

"You look like someone," the bartender said, as he poured Simon another beer.

"You've got that right," Simon said, leaning back on his stool. "I'm someone."

The bartender called him a smart ass and gave him a beer that was warm and mostly foam.

When they were growing up, Simon and Gaetan had often been mistaken for one another. It was only when they'd entered their twenties that they began to look different, Gaetan becoming broad and Simon growing even taller, leaner; however, there were still enough similarities to tie them together as brothers, something Simon resented. Tonight, he didn't want to be recognized as himself or mistaken for Gaetan. Neither was a good option.

Simon patted his back pocket for his pack of cigarettes, sure he could leave his stale-tasting draught beer behind untouched. As he was standing up to leave, Bay sat down on the stool beside him. Still dressed in her work uniform, brass name tag still pinned to her chest, she ordered a vodka and water.

"Should you be wearing your uniform here?" Simon asked. "Wouldn't you say that's inappropriate?"

Bay recoiled when she saw who it was. "Inappropriate? You should talk, fucking things up at my sister's house."

Of course Algoma had called her sisters, Simon thought. "They couldn't go on like that."

After he'd read all of Ferd's letters, he understood why the boy seemed to be holding it together while his parents hadn't. He wasn't. Ferd had fabricated a reality that suited his one hope and everyone had allowed him to believe it because it was easier—or some small part of them believed he was right.

"Why are you here anyway? He's gone," Simon said, referring to his brother. "You expecting him to show up just because you're here?"

Even in the dim lighting, Simon could see Bay turn red.

"Why don't you go back to Drummondville? No one wants you here."

Simon took a sip of his beer. "Maybe so."

The two drank in silence for a time. Bay kept her elbows tight to her sides, so she wouldn't touch Simon, but she didn't leave. She wouldn't be the one to give in.

"Have you heard from him?" Simon asked.

"From who?" Bay stalled.

"My brother."

"No."

"Sure," Simon said. He drained the rest of his beer and grimaced at the taste. "Maybe you want to stop fucking things up at your sister's house."

After Bay left, Simon caught the bartender staring at him again. "Is there a problem?" he asked. Even he was growing tired of the constant confrontations.

The bartender shook his head. "You just look like someone, is all."

"Not anyone you know," Simon said. He laid his money on the bar and stood up to leave.

The bartender's face lit up in recognition. "You're Gaetan's brother."

Simon shook his head. "Rimouski," he lied. "Here on a job."

It was time to go.

12:57 a.m. 19°C. Wind S, breezy.
A feather spinning on its string under the rearview mirror.

Bay flicked on her left turn signal and stepped on the gas. She quickly overtook the car she'd been trailing, but did not slow down once she'd passed it. She sailed along the highway, the other car disappearing behind her, its headlights reduced to a pin-prick in her rear-view mirror, then she was alone again. Leaning forward in the driver's seat, she looked up through the dusty windshield she'd been meaning to clean. A full moon hung high in the sky, illuminating the curve of every branch and stone in a pale blue light. She switched off the stereo and listened to the sound of the tires against the road. A monotonous roar.

Her exchange with Simon had left her numb. She'd forgotten how good he was at reading people, at knowing what was going on. Maybe he just listened more than everyone else, collecting details until they made a landscape in his mind, every peak and valley clear and precise. What would she do if he said something to Algoma? She would deny it.

Bay pressed the gas pedal down further, the car sailing along. Several times a year, she indulged in a fantasy. The idea of leaving. She visualized her suitcases packed and in the trunk, notice given to her work, and her house key pushed under the door after she'd locked it for the last time; however, that was as far as her mental planning went. She failed to account for her family, her twin. She could only manage to get herself out of Le Pin, even if only in her mind.

Others struggled as well. She'd seen it too often—when leaving meant cracking open another beer or filling every spare minute with mindless distractions. If someone didn't have the money or will to actually leave, he escaped inside, a slow and catastrophic implosion. And then there were the others, those like her sisters, who chose to remain because it was comfortable and familiar. Because their future children could go to the same school they'd gone to. Because they knew what kind of weather to expect each season. Because there was too much blood history tethering them to the town. Because they'd met someone and were trying to create that history.

Several weeks before, Bay had received a wedding invitation. One of her old boyfriends—the roofer—was getting married to a woman she knew. She'd immediately thrown the invitation away after reading it, but fished it out of the garbage the next day and checked off the attending box. She didn't know what she was doing going to the wedding, but some part of her wanted to watch the ritual, watch another person commit to staying in this town, as if the reason would be visible from the table at the back of the room reserved for those people who didn't know why they had been invited in the first place.

Driving along the darkened highway, Bay tried not to be conscious of the fact that she was driving north. North was not an escape from Le Pin; hundreds of kilometres later, the highway would eventually lead to a dead end and a spidering of gravel roads. However, if she went south, she might actually end up somewhere. An hour before, she'd left the last houses and gas station behind her as she'd driven out of town. She only ever felt free once she passed the No gas for 100 kilometres sign. Bay looked at her gas gauge. Full tank.

The highway scenery changed little as Bay drove: trees, road signs, and the occasional nod to civilization—a house or steel building. Moonlight glinted off the windows and parked cars. Evidence of the amateur races local teens indulged in was written across the road. Inky black tread marks and the occasional bent guardrail.

Bay slowed her speed and allowed her thoughts to drift off. She thought about the groceries she needed to pick up, a doctor's appointment, what the weather would be like tomorrow. She thought about Gaetan. His postcard. How it was too late to tell someone you'd made a mistake once they were married to someone else. Anything you felt didn't matter anymore. But Gaetan had opened the door, if only a crack. It was a revelation to her that he still felt something for her after she had left him. She remembered the way he'd held her days before she'd ended it. He'd smelled of cedar and sun.

A logging truck, high beams blazing, barrelled southward down the highway, creating a vacuum of air as it passed. Bay's small car shuddered violently and her mind was clear again. The needle on the gas gauge showed half a tank. It was time to turn around.

Up ahead, Bay saw a highway construction site, large orange-and-black pylons narrowing the road down to one lane. An assortment of heavy equipment was littered about the area. She eased off the gas pedal and guided her car in behind a bulldozer. Stalling the ride home, she parked and sat quietly in the car for a moment, listening to the ticking of the engine, before taking the keys out of the ignition.

Outside, Bay circled the bulldozer, which looked like a giant sleeping beast. She looked at her watch: 1:38 a.m. It was at least four hours until the first workers would arrive. She hiked up her skirt and scaled the side of the bulldozer, and finding the door unlocked, climbed into the cab and sat down. The driver's seat was more comfortable than she had imagined. She ran her fingers over the glass faces of the gauges, touched the top of each lever. Everything was cool and silent and there was the faint smell of diesel in the air. She flirted with the idea of leaving the hotel for a construction job. A sign holder. Two speeds: stop and slow. Everyone would obey her.

With the moon still bright and from her high perch, Bay could see across the road, the first rows of trees behind the fence that was meant to keep animals from crossing into what little traffic there was. Yet every year the local newspaper was filled with accident reports. Bent fenders, shattered windshields, amputated side-view mirrors. It felt like it was almost impossible to leave town without being marked by the effort. If you made it at all.

Bay froze when she saw another set of high beams coming down the road, this time too low to the ground to be another truck. She held her breath as she watched the car slow down to navigate the narrowed road. When it passed without stopping, she released her breath. When she could not longer see the car's brake lights anymore, she climbed out of the bulldozer and got back into her car. She switched on the radio and pointed the nose of her car south and started the drive home, grateful that she'd left the porch and hall lights on for herself. It was like someone was waiting for her.

Two empty bottles of wine bound for the garbage sat beside the door, and the sky began to lighten from black to deep blue. Morning. Bay swirled around the remaining wine in her glass before she downed it. She sat hunched over her laptop, as she did so many nights. She'd been scouring the internet for photos of the *Algobay*, her namesake ship, and was surprised by what she'd learned. She read that the ship was no longer docked in the Toronto Portlands, where it had been for years, but there was nothing on where it had gone. Through her web of searches she'd landed on someone's blog, a birder who briefly mentioned the "eyesore" was gone. She chewed one of her nails furiously.

The *Algobay* had been laid up in Toronto for a number of years. And now it was gone. Bay felt cheated, as if someone should have told her it had been moved. Or scrapped. She should have felt it.

Like her own reflection, Bay could picture every detail of the ship—which way it had faced, the degree of rust on its hull, how large it was in comparison to everything around it. Her name painted on the side in bright white block letters, beneath which read "Sault Ste. Marie."

The bird blogger had taken a picture of some cormorants bobbing in the place where the *Algobay* had been—ugly, oily-looking birds—however, even in the photograph, the space the ship had left behind seemed charged as if struck by lightning or haunted. Full of latent energy. Things had been left unfinished, but there was nothing Bay could do, no direction she could take from the missing ship, its absence a gap in her present.

She'd hoped that seeing a current photo of the *Algobay* would be therapeutic, that it would be her totem and tell her where she needed to go next, what she should do. So easy to find meaning in the tilt of its hull, the position of the small yellow crane on the deck, which way the flags reached, what luck would come to her if she correctly guessed the number of windows. It all mattered.

4:00 p.m. 23°C. No wind.
Neighbour's dachshund shitting on the grass again.

"No, I'm sure it's not my Oscar," Marie-Helene said, standing on the top step of her ladder. Her shoes—strappy leather sandals—made it nearly impossible for her to properly maintain her balance. She had made the same footwear mistake last year. Her husband had been out with a bad back, so she had taken it upon herself to trim the tops of the hedges. While trying to use pruning sheers to cut a thick branch, she'd lost her balance and tumbled off the ladder onto the flagstones below, the back of her head split wide open.

"My head is smiling," she'd said when her husband hobbled outside to see what had happened. It had taken eight staples to snap together the grin-like gash.

"It's just that I keep finding... surprises on my lawn," Algoma said. She hated confrontations.

"No, not Oscar." Marie-Helene continued snipping away at her hedges, some of the branches falling into Algoma's garden. "His are smaller."

Algoma shook her head. "Okay, fine."

To avoid further questioning, Marie-Helene quickly descended her ladder, so she was out of view. Algoma could hear her quietly ushering Oscar into the house, the patio door sliding shut behind them.

Algoma sighed and turned her attention back to her garden, which was in equal parts overgrown and barren. The garden had been neglected for months and it showed.

She silently praised the cedar hedges that hid the rot, weed, and tangle from onlookers, her neighbours who would relish the year that their gardens would outperform hers. She wondered if Marie-Helene had noticed. She'd seemed particularly happy today.

Every summer, neighbours dropped by unexpectedly to give Algoma plastic bags of vegetables from their gardens. Armloads of green tomatoes and hard little radishes. Under the guise of being "neighbourly" they used the opportunity to compare their gardens against hers and were instantly humbled by her brick-size beefsteak tomatoes, her perfectly symmetrical peppers. Algoma didn't let her neighbours offerings go to waste by tossing them into the garbage or to the birds; instead, she let the tomatoes ripen on her window sill until they blushed red and then sliced them for the tomato and bacon sandwiches she sometimes liked to eat for breakfast. Even if they were not good enough for her family, they were good enough for her.

She tugged at a vine that looked like a weed. It was difficult to tell the difference anymore. The vegetables, those that had survived, were hidden below half-rotted foliage. Even though she had ignored what she affectionately called her "dirt fridge" for months, it continued to produce, but what bravely grew had either eventually rotted into the ground or had been picked apart by animals, insects, or birds. The evidence was everywhere. Clumps of soft tomatoes that looked like melted Christmas ornaments. Green pepper plants honeycombed with holes. At first, she thought she had forgotten to plant another round of lettuce, but then found the nibbled-down remains wilted in the dirt. Hares. Snares crossed her mind, but she worried about catching a neighbour's cat or dog. The dachshund. She thought about snares again.

In some ways, Algoma was comforted that her garden had survived at all without her. The sun and rain had succeeded in raising her vegetables where she had failed. The world needed less of her than she thought. She raked her hands through the leaves and vines, pulling at the knots like a woman running her hands through hopelessly tangled hair.

With her knees protected by second-hand volleyball knee pads, Algoma knelt down on the dirt. Using a permanent marker, Leo had drawn a crude hoe and rake on each foam square, the tools crossed like swords. The drawings were now mostly obscured by several years worth of dirt and grass stains, but Algoma would not part with them. Happy to be busy and out of the house, she tossed rotten tomatoes over her shoulder onto a pile of compost behind her. She used her kitchen scissors to prune the vines back to expose clumps of small green tomatoes that looked like miniature apples and were just as hard. She wiped one off with her garden glove and popped it into her mouth. Crisp and sour.

With some work, parts of the garden could be salvaged. There would be less than in past years, but her family had shrunk as well. The child growing inside her wouldn't taste a crisp bean or pepper for several years. At least she would have all the radishes to herself now. A salt shaker in one hand, bowl in his lap, Gaetan used to eat radishes like popcorn whenever he watched television. Even when Algoma had tried to hide some for salads, he found them, salted them, and devoured them.

Overhead, birds sat on the power lines and chirped as Algoma worked. She sat back on the overgrown lawn and looked at the work that lay ahead of her. Her leather gardening gloves, sweat-stiffened, sat beside her like clenched fists holding nothing but salt and air. It was easier to be a good gardener in the fall—less maintenance—and it was easy to see which pumpkins and squash would thrive, which would cave into themselves under the pressure. Most of the work she did in the post-summer months was harvesting. The cold room in the basement would overflow with produce, most of it to eat and some of it to decorate the house with.

The first winter after Algoma had started her garden, Gaetan had asked her to take down the gourds from the window sills, the dried corn from the doors.

"It looks like I live in a goddamned witch doctor's house."

The decorations had remained until they softened. Their formerly hard bellies sagging and staining the sills.

In the winter, Algoma read seed catalogues like romance novels, full of blooms, shade coverage, and ideal circumstances. She thought almost entirely in zones, sunlight and rainfall. She was already thinking about what she would plant next year. Spring seemed far off, an impossible stretch of time away, but it would come and she would plant the garden again for another year. Each seed was like a rosary bead. Small miracles for her discipline. With gardening and religion, there were consequences for taking the easy path.

When the sun began to set, Algoma stood up, her knees cracking as she rose. She went into the shed and grabbed a wood chisel. When she returned to the garden, she sought out the still-green pumpkins. Using the chisel, just as her mother had years ago, she carved the names of her husband, son, parents, and sisters into the hard rinds. One name on each pumpkin. By fall, she would see which pumpkins had survived mole or mildew, which had grown fat and ripe, which had grown lop-sided, half rotted into the earth. She left one pumpkin blank for the unnamed baby inside her, a slow swelling tarot.

6:17 p.m. 23°C. No wind.
Jam stain on the table cloth.

Algoma was setting the dinner table for two when the police arrived. She had just put a bowl of sliced cucumbers from the garden on the table when she heard a knock at the door. A police car was parked at the end of her driveway. She wondered if she should make them a key.

It was Monday and Ferd was staying over at Steel's house. Simon was sleeping downstairs, still working off his hangover from the night before. When Algoma had found him sleeping on the sliding swing in the backyard, she'd regretted asking him to leave and invited him back in.

"Mrs. Beaudoin. It's the police. Please answer the door," a man's voice called out.

A police officer stood on the other side of the door, his hand cupped against the glass as he tried to look inside the house.

"One minute," Algoma said. She wiped her hands on a dish towel. Her gut told her that the visit was not about Ferdinand or Gaetan. Maybe one of the neighbourhood kids hadn't arrived home for dinner yet.

Just as the policeman was about to knock again, Algoma opened the door. "How can I help you?" She was polite, but not friendly.

"Mrs. Beaudoin?" the police officer asked.

Algoma nodded. She hadn't met this officer before, which surprised her. She thought she knew all of them by now.

"I'm Officer Dore and this is Officer Faucher," he said, pointing at the second officer standing to his right.

"How can I help you?" Algoma asked. "I have dinner in the oven." She motioned to the kitchen behind her.

"We've received information that Simon Beaudoin is residing here. Can you confirm if that's true."

"Simon?" Algoma asked. He'd barely left the house since he'd arrived. As if hearing her thoughts, Algoma heard Simon stirring on his mattress below, the coils creaking beneath his weight. He was up. She could almost feel him willing her to send the police away, to say that he wasn't here.

"It's just me and my son," she said. She felt a blush rise up her neck.

"And where is your son right now?" Officer Dore asked.

"At my sister's house."

The officer noted the table set for two in the kitchen behind her and made a sucking sound with his teeth. "I'm going to ask you again. Is Simon staying with you?"

"I'm right here," Simon said. He was standing at the bottom of the basement stairs, dressed only in a pair of jeans. "Just give me a minute to get my things."

"Simon," Algoma said, but he'd already walked away.

When he returned a moment later, he was fully dressed. He ascended the stairs to the side door landing where the two grim-faced officers stood.

"I'm Simon Beaudoin," he said. "I was wondering how long this was going to take you."

6:49 p.m. 22°C. Wind E, gusting.
Every door in the house thrown wide open.

"What are you doing, Mom?" Ferd kicked at a pile of his father's clothing that was strewn across the floor. In fact, there were piles of Gaetan's clothing all over the house. Every closet, drawer, and box had been emptied.

Algoma was seated on the bed in the guest bedroom, two of Gaetan's sport jackets draped over her arm.

"I'm making a dress."

"Can't you just buy one?"

Yesterday, Bay had left a message on Algoma's answering machine asking her to be her date at a wedding the following weekend. "I just can't bear to go alone," she'd said. While Algoma was sure that Bay could get a date if she'd wanted to, she'd called back and said yes. Her sister seemed different lately, distant. A night out would be good for both of them. Maybe she'd find out what was going on. Even Port had seen less of Bay lately, and Bay had always been someone who wanted to be seen, even if only by family members.

Lacking any formal wear that would fit over her pregnant belly, Algoma decided to make a dress. While not ready to destroy her own clothing yet, and still missing her own previously permanent date—her husband—she came up with the idea of making a dress out of his clothing. Even if he were to come back, she was sure he would not fault her a couple of destroyed jackets. It was probably to be expected.

The night before, while Ferd slept below, she'd been up

into the early hours sketching the dress she would make. Today, she was looking for the right fabric—something that was light, but had structure. Since no one piece of clothing of Gaetan's would accommodate her new girth, Algoma was looking for several pieces of like colour to build her dress from. In the end, she settled on three twill suit jackets, clothes Gaetan hadn't worn often, but that Algoma had on hand just in case they were ever invited to something nice.

Ferd picked up a white T-shirt from the floor. "Can I have this?"

"Sure," Algoma said, not looking at him. She was ripping out the lining of one of the jackets.

"If you're making a dress, then why do you need a pair of jogging pants?" he asked.

Algoma fingered the fabric on the grey jogging pants. They were well worn, and cut off at the knees. "I need the elastic."

Over the next week, Algoma spent most of her spare time at her sewing machine in the guest bedroom. From the living room, Ferd became accustomed to the hum of the machine, the needle going up and down, and his mother's soft swearing whenever she made a mistake, which was often. She liked to make clothes, but was not especially gifted at it. He made dinners for both of them—sandwiches and soup—and offered to clean up afterward. He did not want to break the spell of his mother's good mood. It'd been a week since Simon had left, and she'd been especially quiet since his departure. A new job, she'd said, on the other side of the country.

When Saturday finally came, Steel came over to the house early to watch Ferd while Algoma got ready. The guest bedroom was an explosion of knotted thread and cut-up fabric, and it was where she chose to get ready, dressing amid the scraps.

Bay pulled her car up in front of Algoma's house and punched the horn three times. After five minutes of waiting, she leaned on the horn with her elbow until she saw Algoma's hand in the window. Ten minutes later, Algoma emerged from the side door. Impatient, Bay tapped the top of her steering wheel while Algoma locked the door and put her key back into her purse. They were already late, which wouldn't be so bad if they hadn't decided to skip the actual wedding. "They'll never even notice that we're not there," Bay had suggested on the phone the night before and Algoma had agreed.

Algoma slowly walked toward the car, holding the wrapped wedding gift in front of her. Bay waited until the gift was safety tucked into the truck before asking her sister what the hell she was wearing. "I mean, where did you get the dress? The Shop? We can still swing by the mall if you want to change."

For once, Algoma was immune to her sister's tongue. She was proud of her dress, everything about it. "I made it," she said.

Bay sighed. "Of course you did. What kind of fabric is that anyway?"

"Jacket and jogging."

From the three jackets (each a different shade of brown) and the elastic band from the jogging pants, Algoma had sewed together a twill dress with a boat neck, short sleeves, and an empire waist that stayed in place because of the elastic band she'd built in.

"It looks like a man built that dress," Bay said as she sped through the streets.

"Thank you," Algoma said, and she meant it.

Well after the speeches and hours after most people had left for home, Algoma and Bay remained behind. There were still twenty people going strong in the rented hall. Even the bartender was joining in on the festivities, downing shots with the best man at the bar. Algoma recognized the best man as the officer who had taken Simon away from the house. She'd been right all along: there had been no girlfriend. The police had been looking for Simon in connection to a series of heavy machinery and vehicle thefts at construction sites in and around Drummondville. When Algoma asked how the police had known her brother-in-law was staying at her house, he'd said they'd received a tip and refused to say more. Despite the circumstances, she wasn't mad at Simon. Selfishly, she missed his company, the space he'd filled now empty again. She'd never had a brother before, never even considered the idea before he'd come along.

"I need another beer," Bay said, although she hadn't even finished the one she was drinking. "This one's warm."

"I'll get you one," Algoma said. "Just wait here."

At the bar, the officer was using his finger to stir his rye and cola.

"Hi," Algoma said.

It took a moment for the officer to recognize her. "Simon," he said quietly. A flicker of panic crossed his eyes, the collision of his personal and professional life. He tried to stand straighter, to look sober, but his head spun with the effort.

Algoma turned to the bartender. "One Molson and one ginger ale."

"I'm sorry about that," the officer said. "About him."

"Thank you," Algoma said, cradling the beer and her drink in her arms. She was about to walk away when she turned around. "Can I just ask you one thing?"

"Sure," the officer said, sounding unsure.

"Who told you Simon was staying at my house?"

He sighed, a defeated look on his face. "What does it matter?" he said, and walked away, leaving Algoma standing alone with her drinks.

As soon as Algoma returned to her table, Bay asked her who she'd been talking to.

When Algoma told her, Bay stood up and smoothed out the wrinkles in her dress.

"I owe that man a dance."

By the time that Algoma pulled the car into the driveway at her house, Bay was fast asleep in the back seat, her mouth open. Algoma had never seen Bay drunk before. She rarely let go of her control of any situation, let alone in public.

"Get up," she said. "We're home."

"Home?" Bay croaked from the back seat. She was sleeping on her side like a child.

"Come on. Get up and come inside unless you want to sleep out here. I have your keys. You're not driving home tonight."

Bay groaned and sat up. "Why did you let me drink that much?"

"There's Advil in the bathroom. Go take two."

While Algoma tried to be quiet when she walked into the house, Bay dropped her purse onto the floor and flipped her heels off into the corner where they banged against the wall.

"You can sleep in the guest room, if you want."

Algoma went into the kitchen and put in two slices of bread to toast. She was already hungry again. She wasn't used to staying up this late.

As Bay shuffled off in her nylons to the washroom, her

mascara smudged beneath her eyes, Algoma listened for Ferd. Nothing. He was asleep.

Once the toast popped up, Algoma slathered it with butter and sat down at the kitchen table. Her eyes adjusted to the dark and she saw Steel sit up on the couch.

"You home?" she asked and yawned.

"Bay, too. Why don't you just stay the night?"

"Mmm," Steel said and pulled her blanket up to her chin. She wasn't going anywhere. "Do you have bacon?"

"Yes, we have bacon. Goodnight, Steel."

"'Night."

Algoma went to the fridge and poured herself a glass of cold milk. It felt good to have a full house, even if most of them were sleeping. She walked to the bathroom and knocked on the door.

"You okay in there?" No answer. She tried again. "Bay, you good?"

"Come in."

Algoma opened the door and found her sister sitting cross-legged in front of the toilet. Her nylons tossed into the tub.

"I drank too much beer."

"I can see that."

"I'm sorry."

"For what?"

"I'm just sorry."

"You don't have to be." Algoma walked around her sister and sat on the edge of the tub. "Did you take the Advil?"

Bay nodded.

"Then why don't you just get changed and go to bed. I'll put out some pyjamas for you."

Bay pointed at the right sleeve on Algoma's dress. "Is

that from Gaetan's jacket, the one he wore to Christmas last year."

It was Algoma's turn to nod.

"Can you make me one? I mean, a dress?"

Algoma laughed. "You hate this dress and you'll still hate it in the morning. You really are drunk. Go to bed."

"I'm just going to stay here for a while," Bay said, leaning on the toilet seat. "Just in case."

Algoma told her she would put out some clothes for her in the guest bedroom. "See you in the morning."

It was almost 1:00 p.m. when Bay woke up. She walked into the kitchen and stretched. "What's for breakfast? I want coffee."

Algoma was doing dishes and Steel was watching television in the living room with Ferd.

"It's cold now, but you can microwave it," Algoma offered.

Bay yawned and opened the fridge. "I'm starving." She grabbed the plate of leftover bacon that Steel had cooked and sat at the table with it. "I meant what I said last night."

"What was that?"

"I want you to make me a dress."

"So you can laugh?"

"Just make me one, okay?"

"Okay," Algoma said. "But it will have to be after the baby."

"I can wait."

Neither Bay, Steel, nor Ferd left the house that day, the sisters staying over a second night to watch movies. An extended slumber party. After a couple of phone calls, Cen, Port, Lake, and Soo arrived with sleeping bags tucked under their arms, the house filled with the people Algoma knew she would never really lose.

"We should do this once a month," Lake said. She'd already pulled out her pocket calender from her purse as soon as she came through the door.

"You want to ritualize everything," Cen said. "Let it go. Sometimes once is enough. Plan and you're planning for disappointment."

Seeing the wounded look on her sister's face she playfully punched her in the arm. "Or once a month until we're dead and even after then, okay?"

Standing in the kitchen, Algoma winced at the comment.

"Oh shit," Cen stuttered. "Sorry, I meant—"

Algoma waved her off. "It's fine."

The evening became one of lower-middle-income extravagance. Plans were hatched and several women were sent out into town for supplies: wine, take-out, and movie rentals. Soon, they were settled into their old places on the floor—the same configuration they'd observed as kids. Cen and Steel by the window, Algoma, Port, and Lake with their backs to the couch, and Bay and Soo on their stomachs facing the television. The couch was empty. It was where their parents would have sat. Ferd sat in his father's old chair, legs draped over the arms.

Algoma looked around at her family, what was left of it. "Ready?"

3:21 p.m. -21°C. Wind E, light.
Snow like a never-ending blanket.

Everywhere Algoma turned, there was noise. The sound of family members quietly talking to one another, the creak and slam of the side door as it opened and closed again and again. Too many times, Algoma thought. Too much. The sirens were piercing. She didn't understand why they were still here. Hot red lights coloured everything. The emergency was over—over even before she realized it had begun.

Bags of chips—an impromptu dinner—were being ripped open, gutted, and poured into glass bowls. Bay walked around offering them to the people standing around in the kitchen and living room. Cen was in the kitchen making dip out of leftover sour cream. Algoma stared. Why don't you leave, she wanted to scream. The phone rang. Again. The sound grated against the inside of her skull. She was grateful when Gaetan picked it up and slammed the receiver back down. He ripped the cord out of the wall, walked into their bedroom, and slammed the door behind him. Someone was wearing heels on the wooden floorboards in the living room. Each step sounded like a gunshot. Outside, a dog barked. Its owner was likely standing at the curb in front of her house along with the others looking in, or trying to.

Even Algoma's own body was a grotesque symphony of unwanted noise. She swore she could hear each muscle sliding around beneath her skin like steaks in a plastic bag. Her knees popped like firecrackers when she tried to sit or stand, and she could not do either for any length of time. She rubbed her hands together, paper on paper. Her skirt sliding off her knees a waterfall of fabric. She tried to clear her mind using a technique she had learned years before. She had to focus on one object, every detail until everything else disappeared. Strawberries were her favourite. She pictured one, its contours, cleft chin tip. She counted each sharp brown seed and wondered how those small teeth did not tear your insides apart on the way down. Focus. The exact colour of the berry somewhere between a fire truck and a sunset over the river. How the sun reflected off the rippled water.

Water.

She couldn't escape it. Most of her body was made of it. Part of the town surrounded by it. Her oldest son had just drowned in it. Focus. She pictured the river as she had seen it a thousand times in her youth, but now Leopold was in it. Leo. Algoma imagined a bump in the river like a child hiding under the covers, the negligible amount of water that his small body would have displaced. Focus. Summer evenings, the river looked like blackberry juice, thick and dark. There were no natural beaches along the shore, only softball-sized stones, mud, and marsh. Algoma always wore her running shoes when she swam in the river, a barrier between her high-arched feet and the slick toupees of algae that covered every stump and stone.

The length of the river was bordered by trees, a mix of deciduous and coniferous. Coniferous. She liked that word, so much like carnivorous that as a child she had feared all pine and fir until she'd learned the true meaning.

Every year, a new person announced they would swim across the widest part of the river for a charity or cause.

Algoma did it once a year for no one, only to know that she had, and would continue to do it. She was a good swimmer—above average with enviable endurance for someone who was not particularly athletic. Focus. Further down the river, it thinned, became narrow. A shallow marsh complete with a neatly defined food chain: dragonfly, frog, snake, pike. Who was feasting on her son now? Or had he—his body—made it all the way to where the river widened again, where it became fast and furious and joined a larger river.

Focus.

Accidents were part of the river's history: a father drowning while trying to save his daughter who would later be rescued; a teenager who dove head first into submerged boulders; a drunk who forgot how to swim, or no longer cared.

Focus.

Gaetan came out of the bedroom and appeared behind her, placing two small white pills on the table in front of her. He swallowed the other two he had in his hand.

Stones from the river.

Algoma swallowed the pills with a long drink of water. Within minutes, her body was awash in inky river water that slowed everything down. Every movement exaggerated yet precise. Her heart thumped slower and slower until she wondered if she had to remember to make it beat. Around her, family, friends, and police buzzed themselves into a blur. The priest sat on the couch eating a butter tart off a dessert plate. There were empty paper cups everywhere like small burial stones around the house. The room was unbearably hot. Algoma clawed at her sweater, pulling the sweat-dampened wool over her head. Everyone else was too distracted by what they should do or say next to notice her peel off her camisole and nylons and drop them onto the floor. Her shoulders were slick with sweat. Half-dressed, her bare feet tapped out the seconds.

When Ferd came out of his room, she motioned him to her lap. "Come here," she said.

He hadn't sat in her lap in years, but quickly climbed up into her comforting arms. His eyes were unfocused and pooling. Gaetan stood behind them, his hands gripping her shoulders, making bloodless impressions in her already pale skin. His head above hers and hers above Ferd's. A totem pole of grief.

It was difficult to grieve when there was no body. It was not just the closure of being able to see the body, to trust what the authorities had already told you: that your loved one is dead. It was the practicalities. Should I buy a casket? Who do I have to call? Do you need a grave stone to mark the grave if the grave is empty? What should the inscription read?

Wish you were here.

Algoma tried to concentrate on the service instead. She was at least sure of that, what needed to be done. There needed to be a proper service, if not for her, for everyone else.

The first item: a photo. She needed a photo of Leo to have enlarged, so that it could be posted at the front of the church on an easel like they had done for the young private who had died overseas. The soldier had stepped onto an IED and his remains, what could be collected, had been shipped back to Canada—first to Trenton, then Toronto, then home. An impossibly long trip for the family. Algoma had attended the service. Several hundred weeping faces, only some she recognized. They had kept the casket closed while the priest spoke of service, acceptance and deliverance. Algoma still had the funeral card folded in her wallet.

She went into her bedroom and pulled out two family photo albums from the top shelf in her closet. Both albums had been sale purchases. She had immediately made herself like the tacky album covers because she was saving a dollar off each. The first cover was a Vaselined-lense shot of a fawn sitting in a field of dandelions. The second was of a young woman kneeling down at the base of a tree, her hands pressed together in prayer, her dewy face in perfect relaxation. Algoma sat on the floor and flipped through the thick pages of the album. The protective plastic covering on each sheet crackled under her touch. It didn't take long for her to realize that there were no appropriate photos. Famously camera shy, Leo was always half out of the frame or had one hand obscuring his face in the last second before the flash popped. The only photos where he was in frame were when he was fishing or hunting. Leo and a wide variety of dead animals. Speckled trout, hares, partridge, pike, and pickerel. Algoma traced a finger along the edge of a photo of Ferd. He was leaning against the family car with his arms crossed over his narrow chest. He had the cool air of a twenty-five-year-old stuck in a miniature body. His face partially obscured by shadow and turned so the side of his neck where Leo's birthmark would have been wasn't visible. It was perfect. She carefully pulled back the plastic covering and peeled the photo off the page.

Who would know?

Ferd stared at a photo of his own face at the front of the church. Unsettled, he shifted in his seat, but said nothing. While he was sure someone had made a mistake, he didn't want to upset his mother by pointing it out. The entire service, he thought, was ridiculous. All the effort and incense for someone who wasn't dead. He'd woken up that morning convinced his brother was alive—he could feel it. Or more accurately, he couldn't feel Leo's absence. They would feel ridiculous when Leo came home. He stifled a laugh.

"We're gathered here today by loss," the priest said. He paused deeply between sentences so each one seemed more profound. "But we've always been together."

"Beloved son," Ferd read off a blue ribbon that stretched across the centre of an impossibly large wreath of white carnations. White carnations were his mother's favourite flower, not his brother's. Leo had loved Orange Hawkweed, a bright orange and yellow flower that grew alongside gravel roads and in meadows. The prickly stems that said don't pick. In his mother's next life, he hoped she'd come back and choose a different flower. Something harder to find. She made it too easy for people to show their love—even he knew that. Too cheap. A twelve-for-ten-dollar bouquet.

Anemone.

He would try to remember to tell her after the service that her favourite flowers should be anemones. His teacher had received them on her birthday last year and made the entire class repeat after her. Anemone.

Ferd untucked his dress shirt and unbuttoned the bottom button, his way of reminding himself that he had something to remember. He fidgeted in his seat and absently flipped through the pages of the battered hymn book while the priest droned on about mourning, God's open arms, eternal happiness, whatever. Ferd thought that the priest in his long robes, threaded with gold, looked like a magician as he waved his hands over the child-sized white casket.

"I have to bury something," Ferd had heard his mother argue with his father two days before.

It was like burying an empty time capsule. Nothing for future explorers and archaeologists to find hundreds of years from now when they unearthed the casket. Ferd laughed. He wished he could see their faces when they popped open the lid and found nothing at all. Maybe some dried out flowers, faded silk.

A blonde altar boy with rosacea swung the incense ball.

"Abracadabra," Ferd said. "Poof, he's gone." He clapped his hands together and immediately felt the sharp jab of his mother's elbow in his ribs and his father's eyes on him.

"Have you no respect for your brother?" Gaetan hissed.

Ferd realized that his parent's expectations were no longer split in half between him and his brother, that everything he did or did not do would be magnified. He was an only child by default, at least for now. He looked around at the other mourners seated in the church and tried to pick out the other only children. Tabitha. Jean-Marie. David. Lise. There weren't many. The service droned on as family members took turns speaking about Leo's love of nature: "So vibrant, so full of life." Ferd rolled his eyes. They needed a thesaurus instead of a bible. Already he could picture making fun of the service with Leo when he returned. He'd have to remember to tell him that Aunt Danielle called him "a boy who had succeeded in being a part of the nature he loved so much." It was like Leo had been turned to mud or a log. Ferd undid another button on the shirt his mother had carefully ironed the night before.

"You don't even have to mist the shirt," he'd tried to joke. She had been crying so hard that her tears had spilled onto the ironing board.

"Go to your room," she'd said. "Just go to your room and get into bed. You don't even know what you're saying."

Ferd wondered if there was a different category for only children who were only children because their siblings had died. Listening in on his parents' card games when they had friends over, he felt he'd learned all he needed to know about life and death. From his bedroom, he could hear everything: cards slapped down, pots of quarters won, the fridge door being opened and shut. Tongues loosened with wine and beer, personal histories spilling out. He learned that not all babies lived through childbirth. Or some did, but with problems that would take them within the first year. There existed caskets even smaller than Leo's. Everything did not always go as planned. Old age was a privilege, not a right.

Those nights standing at his bedroom door Ferd had wondered if the parents told their next child, the one that lived, that they were not the first. Not the only. A permanent replacement. He liked knowing that he had entered the world with a friend. His parents, through no conscious effort of their own, had ensured that he would never be lonely. At least in the beginning.

"In the name of the father, the son and the holy spirit, amen," the priest finished. He walked down among the pews holding people's hands, handing them tissues that he pulled out from the voluminous folds of his hassock. He held Ferd's hands especially tight.

"Yes, yes, he's with the holy son now."

Son. Algoma looked at her remaining son with confusion. Was he smiling? He sat there, legs splayed open, feet dangling, shirt partially unbuttoned, staring blankly at the front of the church.

"You're in shock," she whispered, but his eyes did not meet hers. He was somewhere else entirely.

1:48 p.m. 25°C. No wind.
Attempt to cook an egg on a parked car: failure.

"Leo!"

A lanky redhead stood in the middle of the street, her dirty hands cupped around her mouth. She yelled again: "I'm only going to give you one more chance, Leo. It's your turn."

The hairs on the back of Ferd's neck stood up. Though he'd told the girl his name was Leo, he kept forgetting to respond when she spoke to him. He didn't know why he had given her his brother's name, but he liked the way it sounded when she said it. As if Leo would turn the corner and show up at any second.

"Just give me a minute, will you?" Ferd finished writing a note to his brother, which he slipped down the sewer before running over to the girl.

"What were you doing over there?" Beth asked.

"Nothing," Ferd said.

Beth's mouth twitched with suspicion, but she didn't pursue further questioning. "Whatever."

Even though Beth and Ferd were the same age, Beth was taller, which gave her ultimate authority. She was balancing on a tar-filled crack in the road, her sun-burnt toes dug deep into the black bubble gum.

"It's your turn," she repeated, exasperated. "Here." Her face was tight and serious. She stepped off the crack slowly and carefully, as if removing herself from a landmine. A light breeze ruffled her long curly hair, which was threaded with bits of twigs and leaves. An afternoon of roughhousing with the boys.

The crack in the street reached from one side to the other. Ferd took off his running shoes and socks and took Beth's place in the tar. The warm tar felt oddly familiar—like flesh—as it closed around his toes. The mid-afternoon sun bore down on his head. He thought he could smell burnt hair.

The crack was central to the game the kids had been playing all afternoon. At all times, someone had to have their toes pushed into the tar to keep the street together. If the crack was abandoned, the street would split apart and suck in everything around it. The fate of the world rested on the shoulders of six kids from Le Pin. The tar lodged under their toenails would be there for days.

"Don't move, Leo," Beth commanded breathlessly as she hopped by on one foot. "We're counting on you." She thumped her chest with a fist to emphasize her point.

Ferd wondered how long he would have to stand there; that particular rule of the game had not been established. He had already been standing in the tar twice as long as Beth had. None of the other kids strayed close enough for him to ask. They flew about like sparrows, flitting and chirping rules they made up as they went along.

"You can't touch his arm with your hands, only your feet."
"No shadows!"
"Three handfuls of grass for one stone."
"You have to roll over first."
"Rip the leaf in four."
"Jump ten times, shadow-stepper!"

That morning, Ferd had biked to the south side of town where the kids went to a different school. A parallel universe of latchkeys and Popsicles. He had trolled the tree-lined streets for unfamiliar faces. On a slow roll, he had passed mailboxes with last names he didn't recognize; a shirtless man polishing his car, the driver's door left open, stereo blaring AC/DC; a lawnmower abandoned on a half-cut lawn, the orange extension cord snaking into the open garage; an elderly woman in thick black support hose sweeping her already clean sidewalk. Most of the front lawns were empty. Bursts of laughter and shrieks tinkled from backyards. Ferd could smell the barbecued meat and he could almost taste the tall glasses of lemonade he imagined accompanied it.

After a stop at a corner convenience store, he had encountered a pack of kids on 12th Avenue. They had just been released from microwaved pizza lunches on Corel plates and juice boxes sucked dry into hourglass shapes. They had sprinted full tilt from their homes, inmates released from life sentences. Wild-eyed, they had come to halt around his bike. He was immediately, wordlessly, absorbed into their afternoon.

The last summer that Leo had been alive, he and Ferd had gone into the woods every day and never encountered another kid, let alone a pack. Every night, they prepared backpacks full of everything they thought they could possibly need: granola bars, matches, comic books, snare wire. With their mother's approval, they left the house in the morning and didn't return until the street lights flickered on, their bags emptied and filled again with forest fare.

"Now you have to sing the birthday song backwards," yelled Tracey, the smallest girl of the group. Her nose was flat and round like a crushed blueberry and she was missing both of her front teeth.

Toe-deep in tar, Ferd began to feel dizzy from the heat, but he didn't dare move. Beth's eyes were always on him, and he could tell that she was someone who wouldn't take mutiny with grace. He licked his parched lips, squared his shoulders, and stuffed his hands into his pockets. He could do it. He dug his toes in deeper. They were depending on Leo.

The game had changed. Ferd watched from the street, his T-shirt slick with sweat, the back of his neck hot to touch.

"You're the bear and you're the boy," instructed Beth.

Ben and Michel walked to the nearest lawn and lay down on the freshly mowed grass. Michel made breaststroke motions while Ben dog paddled in place behind him. Even from the street, Ferd could hear Michel's heavy breaths, Ben's grunts and growls.

"Swim faster," Beth yelled. "He's going to get you! He's going to tear you apart with his teeth." Michel screamed when Ben grabbed onto his ankle and dragged him closer.

It hit Ferd. They were reenacting what they had heard about Leo. He stepped off the crack. The world fell apart, everything sucked into his anger. "You're wrong," he hissed. "It's all wrong."

Ben stopped air swimming. He was sweating. "What are you talking about?"

"It's all wrong." Ferd's ears and neck were bright red, but he couldn't find the right words.

"You're ruining everything," Beth shrieked, her previous calm shattered.

"Leo was chasing the bear," Ferd said. "The bear wasn't chasing him."

The kids looked at Ferd like he was a ghost. The two boys stood up. For the first time that day, Beth's voice sounded unsure: "What did you say?"

Ferd pumped his legs as fast as he could, blasting past stop signs, weaving in between cars, coming close to hitting people crossing the street. He stopped for nothing. With each block he peddled through, he shed a small piece of Leo. By the time he arrived home he was entirely himself—Ferdinand. He threw down his bike at the end of the driveway and stood there. His mother was standing in the living room talking on the phone. She didn't see him. He could see the half-moon silhouette of her pregnant belly and it soothed him. His breathing slowed. Soon, he could stop living for two.

10:21 a.m. 33°C. No wind.
Large purple bruise spreading around the IV needle.

"Name."
"Gaetan."
"Last Name."
"Beaudoin."
"Date of birth."
"What happened?"
"Primary physician?"
"Where am I?"
"Emergency contact?"
"Who?"
"Emergency contact?" the nurse repeated.

Gaetan's mind drew a blank. There was no one he could call. And even if he did, he didn't know what he would tell them. He looked at the nurse who sat patiently beside him as she waited for him to figure out his situation. Who was important. She tapped her clean white runner against his bed like a metronome.

"You were beaten," she offered. "You're lucky to be alive." Her hair was the same colour as Algoma's.

"So—" Gaetan started.

"So, we fixed you," the nurse said. "The police still want to talk to you. I'll call them and let them know you're conscious now."

Gaetan reached up and felt a turban of gauze wrapped around his head.

"Quite a gash," the nurse said. "You'll feel that one for a couple of weeks."

Gaetan looked down at the rest of his body, noting every bruise and bandage and the cast on his left arm. He lifted up his right hand and looked at the IV line. "What happened?" he asked.

The nurse put down her clipboard. "You were robbed and beaten, hon. Simple as that."

When Gaetan tried to remove the IV line from his hand, the nurse slapped his leg. "No," she barked. She picked up her clipboard and wrote something down. "You'll need to stay for another day or so. Do you have someone to watch you when you go home? Someone to help you out?"

Gaetan thought about his apartment. He hadn't vacuumed since he'd moved in. Had he picked up the mail yesterday? There were dirty dishes piled in the sink and he was out of toilet paper. "Yes," he said.

The nurse nodded. "Do you want me to call them for you? What's the number?"

"No. I'll use the phone here," Gaetan lied. "I'd just like some privacy. Is that alright?"

The nurse nodded and looked at her watch. "I'll be back later so we can fill this out, okay?"

"Sure," he said. As soon as she left, he shut his eyes. His last memory was of eating in a restaurant in Chinatown, how the bell rang every time someone went in or out.

A phone rang. Startled, Gaetan bolted up in his bed, his heart pounding. His panic lessened when he realized the phone wasn't for him. It was for one of the other patients in his room. His breathing slowed back to normal. While he dreaded the idea of his phone ringing, in a way, he desperately hoped it would.

A nurse walked into the room with a tray of food. Gaetan didn't even wait for her to look his way: "Is the phone working? My phone, I mean."

She put down the tray on the table beside him and removed the lid: poached white fish, lukewarm canned peas, overcooked instant rice, a covered bowl of cherry Jell-O, and a plastic mug of tea.

"Can you check for me?" he asked. "Please?"

The nurse picked up the receiver and tapped the receiver button repeatedly. "You've got dial tone. It's good. You expecting someone?"

Gaetan said no, pushed his lunch tray as far away as he could, and turned toward the wall. Had no one intuited his injuries, or felt that something was wrong? Maybe his ties to his friends and family were thinner than he had already thought. Maybe they had already forgotten him and moved on. He ignored the fact that he had been the one who had left.

Gaetan tried to picture Algoma in bed with another man, strange hands on her naked breasts; someone else picking up his son from school. He half expected to see his wife and their two sons walk in at any moment. One son, he corrected himself. One son. He always pictured Algoma in the last thing he had seen her wearing: a pair of jeans, a floral dress layered over top, and a black headband she'd made out of the bottom of an old T-shirt.

"Wear your hair down more," he had asked so many times. "It looks more feminine." He realized now he wasn't a good man, but it didn't matter anymore.

He desperately wanted a drink, something strong, but there were only IV bags, it seemed, for miles and miles.

Later on in the afternoon, the nurse returned with a vase

of tiger lilies. "I thought your corner of the world could use some colouring up," she said.

For the first time since he'd been there, Gaetan noticed that the nurse had a thin scar on her upper lip that extended to her left nostril. He came close to asking her about it, but instead said: "I don't need a dead man's flowers." The lilies were slightly wilted, the water dingy. He knew she'd taken them from another patient's room, another patient who didn't need them anymore.

"Fine," she said. She picked up the vase again and turned on her rubber-soled shoe with a squeak and started for the exit. "Asshole," she said just loud enough so he could hear it, which he did.

Gaetan turned back to his view: a thin belt of grey morning sky over top of the west wing of the hospital, hundreds of windows, endless rows of pigeons. He pressed his hand to his head. It still hurt to touch. He concentrated on his body, the other injuries, to see if he could feel each one, but the pain blurred, it was everywhere.

Two new patients had been wheeled into his room the previous day to replace the two who had left. The older one, a woman in her eighties, slept in the bed directly across from his. She was using her yellow housecoat as an improvised blanket to shield her frail body from the hospital's fierce air conditioning. Her hospital-issued blanket was on the floor; she didn't have the strength to retrieve it. Gaetan watched the thin wisps of her white hair dance every time someone walked in or out of the room, a soft coral.

The bed beside the old woman had been assigned to someone half her age who was sleeping on her back, blanket pulled up to her sharp chin. She was so still Gaetan wondered if she was dead. She hadn't moved in hours. His hand hovered over the button he used to call the nurses' station, but he pulled his hand back when he noticed her uneaten food. Yes, he thought, I would eat the cold dinner of a dead woman. Waste not, want not. The patient mumbled in her sleep and turned over on her side.

Gaetan sighed. He'd had enough. He wanted real food and to go back to his apartment. Once there was a lull in the hallway traffic, he quietly pulled the privacy curtain around his bed and put on the clothes he had arrived in. His jeans were cold and damp against his skin, his shirt wrinkled. He picked at an unidentifiable stain on his sleeve. Blood, he guessed. It would never come out. He reached into his pocket for his wallet and then recalled the nurse had said he'd been robbed. As he left the room, he scooped up the old woman's blanket and draped it over her as he had once done for his sons.

The hallway was empty except for abandoned wheelchairs and overflowing laundry carts, but he could hear women talking at the nurses' station. Laughter. He walked in the opposite direction toward the stairwell. Holding his broken arm still, it took him nearly half an hour to hobble down seven flights of stairs. By the time he reached the bottom, he was sure he'd ripped the stitches in his left leg. He kept checking his jeans for bloodstains. He'd have to remember to pick up detergent on the way home.

Once he arrived on the landing of the main floor, Gaetan tried to stand straighter, to square his shoulders so that he would look like a visitor, not a patient. He stared blankly at the community bulletin board while he tried to compose himself. There were dozens of coloured posters pinned to the cork: bake sales and walks for several kinds of diseases, a missing wallet, a litter of kittens free to a good home and a second litter of kittens available for five dollars a piece, a patient on the fifth floor was trying to sell a tuxedo. Gaetan felt dizzy. He turned and stood with his back against the board, the push pins digging into his shoulder blades. He was incredibly thirsty. An orderly wheeled a very pregnant girl down the hall. She couldn't have been more than sixteen. The girl waved at Gaetan like she was on a parade float. He waved back.

Once the orderly and the girl had turned the corner, Gaetan ripped off his blue plastic hospital bracelet and tucked it into his pocket. He stepped into the gift shop, which used to be an old cloak room. They hadn't even bothered to remove the brass hooks that lined the walls. Every inch of the room was filled with things to distract: cheap novels, magazines, crosswords, yarn, every kind of gum.

Gaetan stared at the stand-up glass cooler that was filled with tightly bundled bouquets. Small white "Get Well" cards were wedged into the leaves like kites in trees. If he shut his eyes, it smelled like a funeral home. For Gaetan, walking past a cooler of gift shop flowers, a florist, or even the old Chinese woman, who walked through the bar every Saturday to sell single roses wrapped in cellophane, was like having a black cat cross your path, or walking over someone's grave. It was bad luck. It smelled of injury, of funeral, of apology.

He dug into his pocket for money and was surprised to find a folded twenty-dollar bill. Apparently, the thieves had been amateurs. The elderly cashier, who looked like she could have been a patient, or soon would be, put a hand over the cotton-soft bill he put on the counter even before he'd said what he wanted.

"A book of stamps," he said.

She nodded and smiled, her thin white lips pulling back

to reveal an oversized set of dentures.

Outside the hospital, six nurses stood in the middle of the painted perimeter of where they were allowed to smoke. The ashtray stand was overflowing with stubbed cigarettes and garbage. The nurses were trying to get in a quick smoke before their next shift started. They sucked back on their filters as if they were trying to pull their next breath in through the eye of a needle. Gaetan walked over and leaned up against the clear Plexiglas of the partial enclosure. It felt like a bus stop or a penalty box. The nurses didn't acknowledge him, the gently panting patient, until he spoke.

"Any one of you got a pen?" he asked. "Please?" He peeled a stamp from the packet and affixed it to the back of his hospital bracelet. There were no postcards of the hospital, so it would have to do.

One of the nurses, an older woman with a faded green rose-and-dagger tattoo on her forearm, took a final drag and tossed her cigarette onto the ground. "Sure. You don't mind red, do you?"

The other nurses stopped to watch the exchange. They didn't like patients in their space. Gaetan smiled and accepted the pen and wrote an address on the back of his bracelet.

2:08 p.m. 24°C. Wind SE, breezy.
Class mascot belly up in the aquarium.

When Ferd saw his Aunt Bay through the window of his classroom door, his heart thudded like a tire gone flat on the highway. He prayed the door wouldn't open. Our father, who art in heaven, hallowed be thy don't open the door.

"Mom's dead," he whispered into his open math textbook and then immediately pinched himself for thinking that at least he wouldn't have to do his geometry homework.

For months, he'd had a recurring dream. In it, he held a black egg speckled with white dots. The egg would begin to crack and he would watch the pressure cracks snake through the shell. By the end, he would be left with a fistful of broken shell that cut his palms and streaming blood he could not staunch. The rest of the dream would be spent searching through the blood and shell for the hatchling he could never find.

Bay tapped the window with her manicured index finger and waved at him. She was smiling. Ferd relaxed a little and hoped his mother had only hit her head again. Maybe she had broken something. An arm or a leg. He crossed his fingers and his toes for good measure and whispered the prayer a second time. At least he would be able to write on the cast. He thought about which marker he would use and what he would say.

Bay opened the door and spoke with Ferd's teacher who looked back over her shoulder at him and nodded. His stomach was knotted, his mouth dry. After Bay was finished talking, Ms. Prevost put down her piece of chalk and motioned toward the door.

"Go now, Ferd," she encouraged. "Go with your Aunt."

"Now," Bay said.

As he put his books away, his teacher called out to remind him not to forget his homework.

Ferd smiled. If his mother was dead, his teacher wouldn't be asking him to do his homework. For the first time ever, he happily put his textbooks into his backpack.

Illegally parked in a drop-off zone across from the hospital, Bay and Ferd ran across the street. Bay's thick braid slapped against her back as she ran unfazed by the swerving cars and hurled insults.

"Nice thing to teach your kid," a driver yelled from the open window of his rusting Reliant.

Bay responded with her middle finger. She turned to Ferd once they reached the sidewalk, "C'mon, kiddo, your mom's gonna pop."

The waiting room was small, but it had a vending machine and a television, which was enough to keep Ferd occupied for at least an hour. After he had flipped through the channels a dozen times, he asked Bay for quarters.

"There's nothing on," he whined. "I'm bored and hungry."

She gave in and a few minutes later, he needed more change.

"I pressed the wrong buttons," he explained holding up two packages of black licorice.

"I'll take those," Bay said and plucked the packages out of his hands. "My blood pressure is too low anyway." Bay knew the medicinal and caloric value of everything.

Two by two, Algoma's sisters began to show up in the waiting room. It quickly became apparent that the small room had not been designed with families the size of the Belangers in mind. Port, wearing pink and yellow checked pyjama bottoms and a black hoodie was the last to show up to complete the set. They instantly fell into old alliances, teasing and chastising one another for decades-old mistakes.

"Mr. Bernard used to hit on everyone."

"Especially you, hot stuff."

"Might've been those short skirts."

"Shut up."

"Remember when you cut Lisa D'Alosio's pony tail?"

"Snip, snip."

"She wanted short hair."

"All I remember is Mrs. D'Alosio pounding on Mom's front window while holding up Lisa's chopped pony tail. I thought someone had knifed a horse."

"Someone did."

They all laughed.

Algoma had been away from home when her water broke. Instead of doing the laundry, which desperately needed to be done, towels and T-shirts overflowing onto the floor, she'd decided to spend what little money she had left on a matinee. She knew it was Lake's day off. While she wanted to be around people, she didn't want to be around people she knew. She wanted to have the comfort of company, but not the obligation to talk.

Seated with a bucket of popcorn coated in extra butter and salt, Algoma settled into her seat. Her water broke as soon as the curtains went up. The liquid pooled on the tacky floor beneath her seat, drowned the M&Ms someone had dropped. The teenager seated beside her was horrified to find the hem of his jeans soaking up the spill.

"Oh gross, lady," he said as he stumbled toward the aisle. He ran to the washroom without asking her if she needed help.

Algoma turned to the woman to her right. "Would you please get someone to help me to my car?" She was smiling.

Two panicked employees escorted Algoma out of the theatre and into the parking lot. She refused their offer to call an ambulance, insisting she could drive herself. "I prefer it," she told the shortest of the two who had turned ashen at the sight of her wet skirt. "It's not an emergency. I'm just having a baby." Algoma wanted to be in complete control of this birth. She would not allow anyone, with the exception of the doctor, to have access to her baby. It would be all hers.

Algoma had known for months that her suspicions had been correct, that she was carrying a girl, but had refrained from correcting Ferd's defiant statements that it would be a boy—that it would be Leo. She was grateful for his calm moments, when he took over, entertaining her and the unborn child with stories the way Gaetan had. She felt that once her new child arrived, everything would be set right, that Ferd would understand.

Once at the hospital, just after her contractions started, Algoma made one phone call to Steel knowing that one call to her would be enough to let everyone know what was going on. Within minutes of arriving in the emergency room, she was being wheeled to a delivery room. While the doctor and nurse assessed her progress, Algoma kept a watchful eye on the door, hoping to see Gaetan walk through it. With the arrival of each sister, she was both happy and saddened. She slid in and out of pain and refused the constant company of any one of her sisters, instead relying on one of the nurses to guide her through the birth. She didn't want Gaetan to show up and feel replaced.

Ferd slipped out of the waiting room while his aunts rehashed the details of another gruesome childhood scandal. Something involving a crowbar and a rabbit. He walked down the hall until he reached the glass that separated visitors from the newborns. The glass was already heavily fingerprinted, and he added his to the mix. Fourteen. He tried to read the tiny name tags on the clear plastic bassinets: BOISVERT (girl). BEAUMONT (girl). GRAVEL (boy). He looked at one of the empty bassinets and pictured Leo's angry red newborn face, his tight fists waving in the air.

BEAUDOIN (boy). Leo.

Ferd continued down the hallway, passing a number of delivery rooms on his way. He stole glances into the rooms with open doors. Inside each was the same configuration, but with different faces. A pained mother lying on the white hospital bed. A panicked father standing close by, or at the window. An efficient nurse taking care of the details without a degree of misplaced emotion.

When he happened upon the last room, his mother's, he stood outside the door and peered in. Algoma was alone with a coaching nurse who sat at her bedside. Her hair, tangled and matted with sweat, was ghastly against the bleached white hospital sheets. Ferd longed to see his mother surrounded by bright colours and warmth. If he had some of his allowance money, which was tucked beneath the carpet in the basement, he would have bought her a bouquet of the orange and red flowers he had seen in the hospital's gift shop. Something for her to look at.

In between contractions, Algoma caught sight of Ferd at the door. She smiled and motioned for him to come in. "Come here."

The nurse turned her head and addressed Ferd sternly: "Wash your hands."

Ferd washed his hands in the bathroom and then launched onto this mother, hugging her as if she might drift away like a birthday balloon if he didn't hold on tight.

"How much longer?" he asked. "Can you hurry it up?" He looked hopeful.

Algoma looked at her son, "Could be an hour, could be a day."

Ferd frowned. "But you've already been here for forever."

As she was about to reply, her mouth open, Algoma was overcome by a contraction. The nurse tersely insisted Ferd go back to the waiting room.

"We'll tell you when it's over," she said. "Alright?"

Ferd walked back to the waiting room and kicked one of the chairs.

"There you are," said Port. "Let's get you some dinner."

Together, Ferd and Port managed to kill twenty minutes trying to figure out how to use the ancient vending machine in the hospital cafeteria. The cafeteria had closed at 4:00 p.m., so they had to rely on the rotary machine for their dinner. Ferd marvelled at selections of food behind the glass: lunch meat sandwiches, little plastic bowls of soupy coleslaw, an assortment of chips, sweaty tablets of cheese and stale crackers on Styrofoam plates, containers of chocolate milk, and single-serving cereal boxes. After a lot of thought, he settled on a ham and cheese sandwich and a small container of chocolate milk.

"Can we get something for Leo, too?" he asked. "He should be here soon."

Port stared at him. She pulled out a handful of quarters and snapped her gum. "You want some chips, too?"

By early morning, Algoma had still not given birth to her third child. Exhausted, she vowed to pledge allegiance to whatever higher power could make it happen faster. Some of her sisters were still in the waiting room, while others had gone home for a few hours. Ferd was one of the few who were left. Algoma had encouraged him to go home with one of her sisters, so that he could sleep and eat, but he'd refused and she didn't have the strength to fight him. Despite the nurses' efforts to keep him out, he stood there, arms heavy at his sides, a mustard stain on his shirt collar.

Delirious with pain, her judgment skewed by drugs, Algoma looked at Ferd's face with a dreamy expression and called out, "Leo."

Ferd's eyes grew wide. Leo had returned, just as he had prophesied.

"Yes," he said. "Yes."

Algoma smiled, put her head back into her pillow and shut her eyes.

"Yes."

*3:03 p.m. 18°C. Wind unknown.
Recycled air. Dull roar of a thousand parts.*

Gaetan stared down at the dense land of northern Ontario below. The mottled forest was punctuated by kettle lakes and winding rivers that looked like mercury when the sun hit them. From this altitude, the clear-cut lands looked inverted, like islands rising above the trees. He could see where the workers had tried to hide the damage, leaving up thin ribs of trees along the roads. The appearance of undisturbed land. And behind the scrub, logging trucks hauled away lumber, like organ thieves emptying a body.

Gaetan fell asleep and when he woke up the plane was over the prairies. From a distance everything looked like something else. An ox bow river was a great looping signature. The ragged edges of dry river bed looked like an old woman's pursed mouth. Square patchwork fields were replaced by circular ones—endless pie charts of wheat and soybean.

He pulled the in-flight magazine out from the pouch in front of him, its edges dog-eared, greasy thumbprints on the cover. He flipped through the pages until he found the menu and spent a great deal of time assessing each option, giving more thought to what he was going to eat than to where he was going, or what he was going to do when he got there. That morning, he had left the hospital and gone to his apartment to pack a suitcase. He'd called and left a message for the building's caretaker, that she could keep or toss whatever was in the apartment. He left a second message at the bar saying he wouldn't be in for his next shift or any other shift.

"I'm sorry," he'd said into the receiver, but he wasn't. He'd requested that his last cheque be sent to Algoma and recited her address, providing no explanation about who she was. "Just make sure she gets it."

It was getting easier and easier to leave things now that he had practice. The thought of Algoma and Ferd filled him with a warm nostalgia, as if they were his ancestors or characters in a novel he'd read.

Gaetan tapped the menu with his finger. Pizza. He would have the chicken and feta pizza for dinner. And a beer. Domestic. He turned his head toward the window and was lulled back to sleep by the murmuring conversation of the passengers around him. The next time he woke, it was to the white blindness of complete cloud cover. A milky sea lapping up against his portal window. His hand prickled as feeling returned to it.

"Can I get you anything from the menu?"

Surprised, Gaetan jumped in his seat.

"I'm sorry," the stewardess apologized. "Would you like something to eat or drink?" She motioned toward the food cart and smiled, but her eyes were flat and expressionless. She looked tucked into her tight polyester uniform and seemed to resent his inability to make a decision. "I can come back, if you want."

After the stewardess rolled on, Gaetan ate his cold pizza and lukewarm beer in silence. He looked outside. At first he thought he was looking at two layers of clouds, one much lower than the other, yet as his eyes refocused, he saw there was only one layer of clouds. The second lower layer of white was snow—they were flying over the Rocky

Mountains. The black ridges of the mountains looked sharp enough to cut air.

Instinctively, other passengers started to move around and put away their belongings. They were almost there. Gaetan took a bite of his pizza and allowed himself to imagine the plane crashing into the mountains, the wreckage and fire that no one would see. The plane trembled and the seat belt light blinked on. He tried to think of something else.

There were no mountains back home, only one large hill that everyone called "The Mountain." Gaetan had never had the heart to remind people that The Mountain was a reclaimed land fill. Even people who had lived in town for eighty years or more couldn't remember a time before The Mountain was there, a backdrop to their lives. It had grown with them and was part of them. A single man-made path wound round the hill, going all the way to the top where teenagers went to drink at night. The "summit" was always littered with cigarette butts, broken glass, and the occasional half-burnt log from a late-night bonfire.

The captain announced over the intercom that they would begin their descent shortly: "The weather in Vancouver is sunny. Twenty-two degrees. Welcome and enjoy your stay. Please ensure that you take all of your belongings with you. Thank you for flying with us. We hope to see you again." The nose of the plane dipped down like a nod of approval, or recognition of the inevitable.

As the plane finally circled around in preparation for landing, Gaetan sat up straight and looked out the window. A view of the calm ocean gave way to the dark mud flats along the shore. He clutched his arm rests and hoped for a smooth landing. For the first time since he'd left, he felt the cool empty space on his ring finger as keenly as if the ring were still there.

The wheels touched ground and the plane bounded and screeched before moving into a slow parade-float roll. Even before the seat belt light was turned off, passengers flipped open their cell phones and started dialling the people who were likely waiting for them on the other side of the arrivals gate. He pictured the expectant faces on the other side of the glass, some holding flowers, others the keys to the cars that would drive them home.

The plane seemed to taxi forever along the tarmac, choosing new paths to a familiar destination. Impatient to arrive, passengers began to move around in their seats. They shifted their weights, looked at their watches, checked the zippers on their carry-on luggage. They looked at their seats to make sure they hadn't forgotten anything—a book, toys, earphones. They patted down their pockets, flipped open wallets to stare at their ID, their own faces floating beneath the plastic.

Inside the terminal, the luggage carousel jolted to life. Gaetan stood at the edge and carefully looked at each suitcase that passed in front of him. His suitcase was the seventh to show up, but he refrained from picking it up, instead watching it spin around in slow lazy circles along with the others. Each suitcase, except for his, had some kind of personal identifier to set it apart from the others: red scarves, twine, or string; children's stickers stuck to the wheels; Mayan designs painted with Wite-Out; freehand needlepoint. Gaetan looked at his suitcase. It was uniformly black with no special markings, nothing to tether it to him or him to it, so he felt no regret when he left it behind.

5:14 p.m. 22°C. Wind NW, strong.
Waves like loose hair across the river.

A girl.

As soon as the delivery room door opened, Ferd lunged toward the opening, escaping the many octopus arms of his aunts who reached out to grab him. He ran down the hall and past the bank of elevators. At the end of the hallway, he reached the stairwell and took two steps down at a time, nearly keeling over with each leap, his legs not long enough to match his commitment.

On the landing for the third floor, he paused. There was a man standing in the corner. A patient dressed only in a pale blue hospital gown and paper slippers. Ferd could see the angry tip of a healing heart surgery scar peek over the collar of the gown. In one hand, the patient held up his IV bag, and in the other hand, a cigarette. The man pointed at Ferd with his half-smoked cigarette: "Shhh…"

Ferd backed up slowly and continued down the stairs.

On the main floor, he raced through the maze of obstacle-filled hallways until he found an exit that wasn't locked or wouldn't set off an emergency alarm. He burst outside, nearly bowling over a woman on crutches, and ran across the main visitors' parking lot.

"Where are your manners?" she yelled out as he ran away, shaking her crutch at him.

When Ferd reached the other side of the parking lot, he slowed down to see if anyone was following him. There was no one, only row on row of empty parked cars glinting in the sunlight. He waited another minute, half expecting, half hoping, one of his aunts, or even his mother, would come out.

A girl.

His uncle had been right. Ferd turned away from the hospital and ran, his thin arms pumping up and down as he blasted through parks and over hot asphalt. He ran until he could taste blood at the back of his throat, a hot metallic tang. His lungs burned like twin hot air balloons taking him further and further away from everything.

The day was bright and the sun was a high white orb in the sky, the air as clean and clear as liquid glass. Everything shimmered. Everything looked sharp. When he reached the centre of town, the streets and sidewalks were overflowing with people. A street fair. All around him, the burnt-sugar smell of cotton candy and the bright blinking lights of the poorly constructed rides. There was even a frog ring toss. His favourite. Throw a ring around a plastic frog and win a stuffed animal.

"Try your luck, kid. Three rings for a dollar," the barker yelled. "You feeling lucky?"

Ferd looked at the man's ill-fitting clothing, his yellow fingernails and thinning hair, and ran. He pushed his way through the sweaty bodies, using his elbows like paddles to dig into fleshy hips and stomachs.

The river.

That his mother could betray him this way was treason. She was no longer welcome in his country, his world. The girl—his sister—was not family. She was a butcher bird who had murdered for the nest, usurped his brother's place.

Ferd cut through a familiar alley until he reached the trail he was looking for: a shortcut that led to the bridge. By the time he reached the first wooden slat of the walkway, his legs gave out beneath him. He stumbled, falling hard on his hands, slivers of wood threaded through his palms. He picked himself up and looked in both directions. No train. The rails were unbroken rays of steel that shot out in two directions. Ferd put his hands on the rails. They were cool and still. Despite the good weather, there was no one on the bridge. They were all in town at the fair, buying tickets, eating corn dogs, being spun dizzy on cheap rides.

What was his mother doing now? Had she already named the girl? She'd probably already forgotten about him. It was probably what she'd wanted all along: a new family.

Ferd was half-way across the bridge when he noticed something in the water below. He stopped. A small island appeared to be making slow progress across the widest part of the river. He leaned over the railing and looked down.

A black bear.

His already thin chest deflated. He tried to regain his breath, but it was gone. Even from the bridge, Ferd thought he could hear the splashes of water as the animal's legs punched the surface with each stroke.

The railing was all that separated him from the animal below. Awkwardly, he clambered over the top rung. The hot metal had the names of a hundred teenagers carved into the layers of paint. An ephemeral memorial.

Stefanie and Leesa BFF.

Roger was here '94.

Mary Lou Rulz.

Once over the railing, Ferd stood on the thin rusting lip of the bridge. His narrow body arched out like a bow as he steadied himself.

He looked down.

The black mass was directly beneath him now. It looked like a planet slowly escaping an undesirable orbit one huff at a time.

Ferd closed his eyes and tried to picture Leo, but all he could picture was a reflection of his own face as he saw it every morning in the bathroom mirror. Despite the sun, his hands were cold and his body chilled. The wind had picked up. The tail of his too-large white T-shirt—his father's—waved like a surrender flag.

He released one hand from the railing, flakes of multicoloured paint sticking to his palm, and then the other, leaving behind an audience of teenage autographs, knife-carved professions of undying love and friendship, for his ride below.

*5:30 p.m. 21°C. Wind NW, strong.
Clean windows like frozen puddles.*

A small bell tinkled as Josie pushed the door to the toy store open. On entry, she was offered two options—the left aisle or the right—and both were equally terrifying. To the left: pastel lions, giraffes, and bears piled three deep on glass shelves; the animals' thick glass eyes sparkled under the round light fixtures that hung from the ceiling like disembodied pregnant bellies. To her right: dozens of glassy stalactites, high-end baby bottles, their pink and yellow rubber nipples erect and pointing toward the ceiling. All of it so new. Objects with no stories or history.

"Get in and get out," Josie whispered to herself. Her hands hovered nervously at her sides, her fingers twitching.

"Can I help you?" the shop girl asked, her voice high-pitched like a child's.

Startled, Josie uttered a small yelp and flushed in embarrassment. The girl had appeared out of nowhere. Her dark brown hair was pulled up into a high ponytail that bounced every time she spoke. Trampoline hair. She couldn't have been more than seventeen, Josie thought. What did she know about babies? "No, I'm fine," Josie stuttered. "I'm just going to take a look."

She veered toward the stuffed animals, her elbow taking out a half dozen in one shot. "Oh Christ, I'm sorry," she apologized and rushed to pick them up. The shop girl bent down and picked up a stuffed bear and cooed into its dead eyes:

"Dere you go Sergeant Brown. All beddar." She propped him up on a pile of folded afghans. "Don't you look tough!"

Determined to get out of the store as quickly as possible, Josie took a deep breath and stuck her hand into a mountain of stuffed animals and pulled out whatever she grabbed first: a pony. It had a white spot of fur in the shape of a heart on its narrow forehead. Its tag read: My name is Sammie. I'm yours. Love me and take care of me. Josie tucked Sammie under her arm and quickly scooped up a half dozen baby bottles, a yellow receiving blanket with pink trim, and a small sun hat that she could picture Algoma wearing if it were adult-sized.

At the counter, the shop girl, her cheeks perpetually flushed, her face radiating obscene joy, gushed over the pony.

"She's my favourite," she said. "Makes me wish I had someone to give it to."

Josie could swear the girl's eyes were beginning to well up. "Can you wrap all of it up? Fast?"

In the parking lot, Josie loaded the brightly wrapped packages into the passenger seat of her truck and used the seat belt to secure them in place. Seated in the driver's seat she sighed. "In and out. In and out." She turned the key in the ignition and drove toward the hospital.

5:50 p.m. 21°C. Wind NW, strong.
Housefly crawling through the rip in the screen door.

Algoma had given birth. A girl. Bay listened as her sister happily described the newborn over the phone, the child's tight and angry face, her impossibly small nails.

"She's good luck, I know it."

"You should really name her after me, you know," Bay said. "I could show her the ropes." Algoma's laugh stung. It was the laugh of someone who hadn't even considered the idea for a second. Bay tried a different approach. "How's Ferd doing with all of this?"

Silence on the other end of the line.

"He ran out," Algoma said. "But he'll be fine. He'll come back soon. Steel's out looking for him." She didn't sound sure.

"I'm sure he's fine," Bay said. "I'll come see you tomorrow."

Algoma said she was getting out in a couple of hours. "I just want to go home."

"I'll see you soon," Bay said and hung up the phone. She turned off the ringer. Joy was exhausting.

Early evening light spilled in through the windows of Bay's house. There was no need to turn on a light. She went into her study and sat down at her desk. She picked up the hospital bracelet that was sitting beside her computer and tried to wrap it around her wrist. The ends had been destroyed when it had been ripped off, so that it wouldn't stay on.

While Bay did not believe in good luck, she believed in bad luck. Superstitious, she thought it a mistake to keep a hospital bracelet, yet she'd held onto this one after it had come in the mail the week before. She wondered what the mail carrier had thought when she'd delivered it. Port had kept both bracelets she'd "earned" in recent years from the two concussions she'd had: one from skiing, the other from one too many drinks at a house party paired with an unforgiving oak window sill. Despite Bay's constant insistence that Port throw them away, she kept them. They were souvenirs from a trip where she had been able to forget the bad details.

"A collection only grows," Bay had warned her sister.

Port had rolled her eyes.

Bay ran a finger over the laser-printed details on the plastic bracelet: G. Beaudoin. There was also some sort of hospital identification number. She turned her computer on and searched for hospitals in Toronto and called every one she could find. Most of the operators were reluctant, bound by privacy laws, they said, and were unable to tell her anything. Finally, someone let slip that, yes, they'd had a patient by that name, and yes, he had been discharged, but the operator had stopped short of telling her why he had been hospitalized in the first place.

"Are you his wife?" the operator asked.

The line crackled. Bay stalled.

"Hello. I said, Ma'am, are you his wife?"

Bay pressed the receiver button to end the call, but continued to hold the earpiece tightly in her hand. She listened to the dull hum of the dial tone, as if it would reveal some mystery to her. If Gaetan had been discharged, he had to be okay. She examined the bracelet further to see if it would give her a sign, but there was nothing. What she did know, however, was that the bracelet did not belong to her.

Using a Sharpie, she blacked out her address. For good measure, she used a ballpoint pen to scribble circles over top, confusing the impressions so that it was unreadable, untraceable. Knowing that she had a few hours before Algoma was released from the hospital, she took the bracelet and got into her car.

On arriving on Algoma's street, Bay did a slow roll-by to ensure no one was house sitting, but the driveway was empty, the curtains drawn. Even from a distance, she could see that the property was in disrepair: the grass overgrown, broken tree branches on the lawn, the asphalt at the end of the driveway crumbling like old bread. How much longer could her sister hold it all together when everything was falling apart so quickly?

Bay parked her car several houses down. It took her ten minutes before she convinced herself to get out of the car and ten more to cross the short distance to her sister's home. The wooden slats of the front porch creaked as she walked over to the mailbox. She dropped the hospital bracelet into it and tried to close the lid, but it was jammed and refused to move. Using both hands, she tried to force the lid shut. A bolt snapped and the lid slammed down.

"Fucking hell," she choked and sucked on her sliced palm.

Two thick streams of syrupy blood ran down her forearm, collecting in the soft bend of her elbow. Patches of the limestone-coloured silk blouse she wore turned dark red, almost black. She held her hand in front of her and looked at the messy flap of skin, the growing blood stains on her shirt. Her shoulders grew limp, her mouth slack. She was tired.

Bay stripped off her blouse and wrapped it around her wounded hand. Dressed in her skirt and bra, she sat down on the porch in plain view of the neighbourhood. She leaned her shoulder against one of the support beams and let her legs dangle above the marigolds as she waited for her sister to return home.

7:18 p.m. 19°C. Wind NW, strong.
Running shoe caught between two rocks down river.

His cheek pressed into cool, wet dirt, Ferd's eyes fluttered open. A curious grackle walked back and forth in front of his face, its pale yellow eyes staring back at him. The bird's feathers were iridescent, oil on black asphalt. It was the closest Ferd had ever been to a live grackle. If he reached out, he could probably touch its sharp, black beak, its long tail. When he sat up, the bird let out a noise like a rusty hinge and flew into the pine trees that lined the riverbank.

Ferd looked around. To the West, the sun was almost behind the trees, and to the East, he could see the train bridge. From where he sat, the bridge's iron truss looked unfinished, a house awaiting walls. A beginning instead of an ending. And down by the water, he saw it. What he'd lunged after so hungrily was caught in limbo in the waves several feet from shore. A large, black garbage bag. Amorphous, the empty bag took new shape with each wave.

In that moment, Ferd knew that Leo was not coming back. He never had been. Cold and wet, his body aching, Ferd stood up and walked barefoot along the riverbank. He stripped off his wet T-shirt and tossed it into the water. The grackle flew down from the trees and landed behind Ferd, following him as he looked for the opening in the woods that would allow him to find his mother and sister.

8:32 p.m. 18°C. Wind NW.
Yellow light from the hallway cutting
into the darkened hospital room.

A lifetime of waiting was over. In her daughter's face, Algoma saw a glimpse of her own. What her mother could not give her, what no one could provide, she had created. The baby's weight against her chest felt like an anchor.

She lifted her head to acknowledge the nurse who had quietly entered the room.

"Your ride is here," the nurse said. "Let's get you ready. It's time to go home."

Algoma could hear Steel and Ferd talking in the hallway.

The nurse carefully lifted the baby from her chest. "I'll get this one ready if you can take care of yourself."

Algoma sat up and slowly swung her bare legs over the side of the bed. She remained still for a moment, listening to the sounds of the hospital. The hum of wheelchairs, the soft snores of the new mother in the bed beside hers, the sound of her family's voices in the hallway. The laughter. When the nurse took the baby out of the room, Algoma lay back down on the bed and closed her eyes. One more minute, she thought. She imagined the roads she would drive down to take her daughter home, every stop and turn. She saw each of her sisters' homes, the plot where her parents were buried, The Shop. Her small planet. Drifting off, the road turned into a river—glossy and black as a crow's wing—and on it, a freighter moving slowly from port to port. A ship bound for better things.

ACKNOWLEDGEMENTS

Thank you to Stephanie Domet for her editorial insight and to Nic Boshart, Megan Fildes, Robbie MacGregor, Julia Horel-O'Brien, Chloe Vice, and everyone at Invisible Publishing for incredible enthusiasm, hard work, and vision.

For invaluable advice, for guidance: Samantha Haywood.

For lending her skills to the manuscript early on: Becky Toyne.

For conversation, for research, for sharing your knowledge: Eugenia Catroppa, Ben Gibson, Kelvin Kong, Andy Willick, and Julie Wilson.

For friendship unfailing, for couches, for listening, for meals and take-out, for late-night walks, for everything, always: Stacey May Fowles, Chris Gramlich, Shawn Levis, Stefanie Stevanovich, and Natalie Zina Walschots.

For energy, for love, for feedback at every stage, for BBQ, for fishing in the little green boat, for 5:00 a.m. walks into woods and swamp: My parents, Debbie and Réal Couture.

For a lifetime of stories, for good company, for endless games of cards and Western movies: Joseph Couture and Simone Belanger, Rudy Couture, Liette Couture and Richard Trudeau, Guy Couture and Giselle Perron, and Garnet and Kathy Deneau.

For influence that will never be forgotten: Dr. John Ditsky.

For the boy from Algoma District, for being my anchor for the past twelve years, for always being there. I'll miss you always: David Gold.

For reading and re-reading every word several times, for thoughtful notes and late-night correspondence, for generous encouragement, for friendship I'm lucky to have: Carolyn Black.

INVISIBLE PUBLISHING is committed to working with writers who might not ordinarily be published and distributed commercially. We work exclusively with emerging and under-published authors to produce entertaining, affordable books.

We believe that books are meant to be enjoyed by everyone and that sharing our stories is important. In an effort to ensure that books never become a luxury, we do all that we can to make our books more accessible.

We are collectively organized and our production processes are transparent. At Invisible, publishers and authors recognize a commitment to one another, and to the development of communities which can sustain and encourage storytellers.

If you'd like to know more please get in touch.
info@invisiblepublishing.com

Invisible Publishing
Halifax & Toronto